The Familiar Encounter

Jessica Strong

The Familiar Encounter

Copyright © 2012 Jessica Strong

All rights reserved.

ISBN 979-869-142-3543

To those that told me to publish the book anyway.

I

Amy and the Grasping of Birdsong

 Amy looked down at the palms of her hands, scratched and bloodied, numb to the feeling of pain. It was the shock, or the adrenaline. She could feel her heart beating throughout her entire body. The thought of escaping made her stop running and freeze as the image of her family misunderstanding what she had become, invaded her mind. Could she return to her perfect life, knowing she was far from the ideal girl everyone saw her as before? Staring at the blood now dripping from her hands, she imagined fighting so hard to return, only to be cast out. She was so far away from what she used to be, sure to become someone the tight-knit community of Hanfield would be wary of and keep at arm's length forever. The town loved to propel rumours, and the truth would be like sweet poison to their ears.

 She felt as though she no longer belonged anywhere. Amy hadn't heard crowds of locals come by searching for her in a long while. They had given up and left her for dead. Amy couldn't make up her mind whether it had been a year or a few months, lost amidst a forest that went on for miles. The sun seemed to always look the same, shining through the thick canopy of trees, leaving Amy no reference for time.

Some mornings when she awoke and thought about how many days it had been, it felt like they had all rolled into one. Often Amy would lie on her bed thinking of these things, head resting on some rags and still wearing the clothes she went missing in, dirty and ripped from living in the forest all that time. Back at base, Amy had a fleece for the colder nights, which she had thought of as a surprising kindness from the creatures that were holding her captive. But right now, Amy was feeling completely alone, in the middle of a small clearing with no idea what to do, and with the sound of footsteps rapidly closing in on her.

Amy weighed up the total heartbreak she may have to face back home, or the utter torment she would surely go through if she was caught. The options were not good. If it weren't for those creatures in the woods she told herself, she would try to adapt and remain in the forest, laying low for a time and building up her confidence, before heading in search of another city where she could begin her life again. She would sometimes escape to this daydream to pass the time. But now she was confused and disorientated, as the hurried steps approaching her position became louder, and that menacing feeling of what would happen if they caught up, sunk in. The instinct inside her to keep fighting strengthened her, as she advanced towards what would likely become another battle, but she had to put that to the back of her mind and keep moving to get anywhere but here. Amy couldn't face the thought of those things coming after her and laying their hands on her flesh. Their rough skin felt like jagged sandpaper, and despite being very human-like, she had observed and concluded that they were not, in fact, human; far from it. They wore dirty clothes that hung limply from their stumpy frames. Their lumbering, ape-like, bodies were consistently slouched over, and they had sharp, pointed teeth and black, empty eyes.

The cold, dark night had taken hold of the evening. Despite moving carefully but swiftly, the steps she could hear following her path over the dry leaves, were getting louder and quicker. She could hear the occasional snorts they made while breathing, and their clumsy bodies trudged, one foot in front of the other. She knew it would only be a matter of time before they caught up. Feeling as though she were being hunted by these monsters, she needed to think of a plan. Amy could not get caught out. She had been here many times, attempting to escape, but they had always caught her and maltreated her back to their base. Each time was entirely soul-destroying, but she had never managed to get this far before!

I could pick up the pace and keep running; keep focused on running until I see street lights, they won't follow me into the light – but I've never seen them tire, I don't know how far away the town is, if I continue on they will catch me...

I could sprint to get way ahead until I tire. I could climb one of these trees...pick an easy tree to get a foothold and go for it. But my hands are in bits, and I've seen them climb before. If they see me, I'll have nowhere to go...

There had to be something she could do to get away. Panicking, she looked around for ideas, and noticing an especially darker area thick with moss and shrubbery, she began running over to it.

I could hide behind some thick cover, the forest floor is made up of dried leaves and mud, I've seen how prey rub their skin with this, and it helps them camouflage. They would pass on by, and I could hide out for a while, that's my only chance here.

She knew she may not be faster than them now, or stronger. Still, they were not bright, and she could outsmart them, hiding in amongst the trees. If she played this out, they might pass her by. Feeling as though her heart would beat from her chest, she quickly positioned herself behind some thicker areas of shrubbery, grabbed a handful of the moss, leaves, and mud, and rubbed it on her exposed arms and chest. It wasn't ideal by any means. Still, she prayed it was enough to camouflage her further existence in these woods.

Her long, once brightly coloured auburn hair had been muddied over the time she had been living in these woods like an animal. She felt a loss of humanity. The food offered up to her that she'd initially refused, now didn't seem so bad. Amy thought it seemed so simple to make camp and settle in the wild, but this could have been down to the survival mode that had gradually taken hold of her once 'high maintenance' personality. Or she now just preferred the simple life away from civilisation. Whatever it was, her priorities had changed.

She could hear them getting closer and closer, those menacing footsteps drawing in. Telling herself to relax, take control of her breathing and lower her heart rate, by telling herself that it wasn't real, and that she was back in her old bedroom in her cotton pyjamas. Those were the evenings she had taken for granted before this happened; the dance routines she would be so frustrated to learn, the sports she would compete in and the friends that gave her some of the best days.

Her life seemed so simple and high; the problems she had back then were nothing compared to the weight she now felt on her shoulders. She missed her broad group of friends and her family – even her sister. Everything had changed with this nightmare she had been sucked into. The person she was now, fighting so hard to return, was not the person that had left many weeks ago. The secrets she had learned about this town were darker than she even first thought, further than anything she could have imagined; the sort of secrets these forest dwellers did not want returned to the town of Hanfield.

As her pursuers drew to a close she could see their creepy figures hobbling past, their movements jerked and jostled through the trees, and the very image of it from her safe space in the moss made her shiver with revulsion. In all the time she had spent missing, she had never once heard them speak. Moans and grunts seemed to be enough for them to understand one another. The rags they used for clothing would hang from their pink, irritated skin, their jaws hanging open in a zombie-like fashion.

Having got to know them as well as one person may become familiar with a monkey, Amy could see they had an agenda. A singular thought lurked behind their small black eyes; to keep her in line, and to use brute strength if required. She had never come this close to escaping before, and it worried her what they may do if they did, in fact, catch her this time. She would have to work to gain their trust all over again, and Amy would be locked away for even longer than before. That might drive her crazy, or she would finally prove more trouble than she was worth and be killed.

It was there among the bushes she stayed. Still and quiet for what seemed like forever, feeling as though every scenario was rushing through her mind at lightning speed. To try to calm her mind, she would focus on the dew beginning to drip from the leaves, and the beetle walking up her mud-covered leg, on its way somewhere for shelter or food. Amy wanted to be able to close her eyes and quiet her mind, but the fear wouldn't let her. Thoughts about her friends and family came rushing back like a big wave of anxiety, washing over her curled-up body. She couldn't shake the feeling of what they all might think, *a fall from grace*. She would have to hide her secrets, but how to pretend the last few days, months, *(year?)* hadn't happened.

With thoughts shooting through her head, Amy noticed her hands had begun shaking again. *How long have they been doing that?* She worried the quiet tremors would be heard within the foliage. Focusing in on her hands, telling herself to stop shaking didn't help. But what most likely saved her was the morning mist softening the dry leaves and twigs. She turned her attention back to the beetle, which was now perched on the top of her knee.

Amy was crouched over, but still on the tips of her feet, ready to set off sprinting if she needed to. Listening as best she could to the sound of those creatures fading off into the distance, hearing them getting further away. It comforted her to know they were leaving the area, and they became harder to hear until she could no longer detect anything other than the wind through the trees every so often. Amy couldn't feel the cold from the breeze, but as more of her body began to shake, she knew it was time to start moving again; to start getting through the forest and back to her home in Hanfield. She remained hidden while setting up the courage and motivation to emerge.

It was common knowledge to Amy even before she vanished that the Hanfield woods had remained only partly explored. It was always viewed as an old wife's tale that townspeople would walk through the forest never to be seen again. No one questioned the history of the woods, but it had now occurred to Amy that if these creatures could live undetected all this time, what else could be lurking around each dark corner? She couldn't remember how she had got so deep into the forest. Amy had been so set on escaping the clutches of those hobbling monsters that she hadn't thought so far ahead as to which direction her home was in.

Noticing the small beetle still settled on her leg, she wished her life could be as simple. Taking her index finger, she saw the once manicured nail was now misshapen, overgrown and was black with dirt wedged beneath it. Amy no longer cared however, and placing it on her leg beside the insect, she watched as it manoeuvred onto her finger, crawling up to her hand. She smiled and noted how it didn't see her as a threat. Staring at the beetle as it prepared to show its wings and fly off, she sighed and thought how simple her life would be if she could fly away, but then, not knowing where she now belonged, she only knew her home was the only real option she had left.

Beyond the noise of the beetle's wings as it hovered upwards and onto a large, deep green leaf above her head, she could hear the branches moving in the wind and the faint call of a blackbird in the distance. No grunts from strange oaf-like figures or the footsteps of any other being. The blackbird calling remained, periodically emitting a long, shrill squeal which echoed between the giant trees. Not knowing where to go once she had risen from her hiding place; she made the decision to follow the musical sound of this blackbird. It had been a strange place for her, and Amy's gut told her to follow any signs home, the blackbird being as good a sign as any.

Moving the clusters of leaves above her head, taking special care not to disturb the beetle, as this was the new friend she had hidden with keeping her company. She began to rise from her tiny safe place and out to the woods, paying attention to sweep off the dried mud from her skin and clothes as she did so. But, upon exposing herself, she looked upwards to find a horrifying sight. A hobbling beast stood before her, ten feet or so, away, eyes widened and staring right at her, with no facial expression. Both parties startled to a pause, before the disjointed mouth of the monster let out a blood-curdling grunt ahead of throwing its entire body weight into a lunging, terrorising dive in Amy's direction.

II
Danas' Heartbeats

Hanfield was a close community that embodied all the makings of a vibrant town. Covered in lush greenery, large parks, and pretty tree-lined streets, it was full of residents who took pride in making their gardens more beautiful than the last. The main square was made up of Hanfield High School, a collection of convenience stores and the village hall. Most of the townspeople lived within the centre without any issue of overcrowding. It was one of those places where non-residents would get an eerie feeling passing through, and like a lot of small areas, Hanfield had its share of locals who shot suspicious glances rather than welcoming smiles. A stranger walking into the pub would send the more sociable town's members into a buzzing gossip.

The town itself had a long history of distributing Hanfield apples to the rest of the country, "It's what put the area on the map" some locals would always say. Much of the outskirts had been taken up for miles with orchards, and bordered by wild forests, and while children would enjoy running through the apple trees, they would be wary of the tales told through history warning not to wander too far from civilisation. Legends of witches and cannibals that are inherent of a small town scarred in the memories of its people. Mothers would tell their children not to stray from the orchards, a rule they always heeded.

Although the inhabitants were quaint and generally got on with the simple life at Hanfield, a tragedy had now occurred, shaking the community to its core. A schoolgirl had gone missing without a trace. Amy was very well known in the town, and this had sent shock waves through everyone's homes. Something terrible had happened on their doorstep. Some pointed fingers while others simply held their children that much tighter before bed.

It had been ten weeks since Amy Ferhulse had gone missing, and although there were posters of the red-headed girl with the perfect smile in every window and on every lamppost, the atmosphere was stale, and new signs she could still be alive had long since gone cold. Rumours circulated, as they often do in these small communities, and there had been quiet whisperings that her successful parents had something to do with her disappearance, but it was hearsay with no evidence to back it up.

Amy's father, Richard, worked as an accountant for the council, he was one of the Mayor's right-hand men having worked his way up the financial ladder. Her mother Dana worked enthusiastically as a performance arts teacher at the school. She awoke every morning with the sole purpose of staying positive for Amy. There was no question she was still alive. It was merely a case of not giving up hope that her daughter would return to her one day.

Dana's optimistic attitude at this point, fed the rumours of people feeling uneasy and suspicious of her. Still, for now, she was left to continue tirelessly helping the police with their enquiries, handing out the posters she had designed, and organising the evening search parties. She could not stand the thought of being away from the family home for too long in case her daughter returned to her. But unable to turn her back on the students that needed her, she would hold her dance coaching from home, welcoming the small semblance of normality. Coaching Amy from an early age to dance and compete had given them an especially close bond.

However, this setup allowed people to speculate further. Dana let them. She was the type of woman who wouldn't succumb to influence; a strong, dedicated mother who had gone down in Hanfield history, making the town well known for the dance competitions her teams had won over the years. A well-respected asset to the community. "You don't get that sort of group success without being focused and committed to each task, no matter what!" She would tell her daughters, having been scrupulously organised her whole life. She was a firm believer in pursuing your dreams, something she aimed to instil within all her students.

Preparing for another 'stay at home' training session with the dance troupe, she began to change from her typical glam, but casual, everyday outfit and into her activewear leggings. Looking in the large mirror standing on the plush cream carpet, she took in her appearance. Her routine now, whenever she caught a mirror was to look back at her reflection and smile. Things were rough, but she needed to keep reminding herself to stay positive. Being a performing arts teacher, she could hold that smiling façade, and still project positivity, without feeling remotely happy. The only thing worse than feeling her fears, would be communicating them to her team. Dana's competitive nature was ever-present as they were coming up to the annual Summer Sling Tournaments, an event where dance teams all around the area would battle it out. Missing the lead performer, Amy, the team was feeling lost.

Dana began grooming, paying attention to the same auburn hair she shared with her daughter. She enjoyed dressing for every occasion and always looked well turned out. She shopped enthusiastically, and retail 'therapy' was especially true when it came to Dana. She now had a wide variety of 'search party' outfits; practical cargo trousers and waterproof boots for trailing through the longer grass and marshes. You couldn't blame people for talking. Despite her daughter being missing she always looked fabulous. But it was the only way she knew how to cope; to continue with her life as best she could. There had always been a certain level of jealousy from other women within Hanfield, and envious comments were something she had become used to over the years. Still, aside from getting Amy back, her primary focus remained with The Hanfield Heartbeats.

The students began arriving at the Ferhulse household. The group was made up of twelve girls, all hand-picked by various figures within the performing arts department, and all embodied the spirit of Hanfield High. Most of the girls just happened to be the popular students at the school. The general qualifications to be a Hanfield Heartbeat seemingly consisted of simply being tall, slim, and beautiful, though qualities that Dana would always look for were energy and stage presence. If a student had those two magical ingredients, she would endeavour to get them to try out for the team. The members were required to attend every practice outside of school hours, while keeping up with their studies.

Usually, the first one to arrive at each practice was Monica, who was dropped off on this occasion by her new boyfriend. She was tall and fashionable with long, glossy hair. Despite always being able to 'turn on the smile' while dancing, generally, she always looked stony faced; her green eyes gleaming gently against her dark skin. Only having joined Hanfield High recently she was reasonably quiet but always listened carefully to what people said... or didn't say. She spoke bluntly to most, and only opened up to a few.

The Hanfield Heartbeats' unofficial spokesperson was Hannah, who ran the three miles to the Ferhulse household as an impressive warm-up ahead of the two-hour coaching session. She was athletic, self-assured, and gorgeous. Hannah seemed to be the face of Amy's disappearance alongside Dana, speaking publicly, and leading events to heighten the awareness. At school, she was held in high regard, and many of the girls in the lower forms looked up to her. They found her inspirational due to all the fundraising, appeals and school spirit she exuded, while also subtly demonstrating that you don't need any real talent to be successful, just bags of confidence, and unstoppable drive. Arriving to practise, she took her hair scrunchy out to reveal long honey blonde hair which curled at the ends perfectly and bounced as she walked as if fresh from a shampoo advert, rather than finishing up a jog. Being Amy's best friend, they were in all the sports teams together as well as into dancing. Naturally, Hannah would feel something was missing when she would turn up to practise, but without Amy's presence, she had felt elevated. With no one else around to take the spotlight in the weeks since Amy's disappearance, Hannah had gone through a rainbow of emotions; from feeling sad and coming to terms with the fact that Amy might never return, to hoping she never did.

A great perk of working from home was that Dana had her fabulous kitchen to provide light bites. Something not available at the sports hall or dance studio where they usually trained. She noticed the girls were beginning to arrive as if by routine. She had to pinch herself that it had been ten weeks now since the team had started using her home to train in. Pouring out orange juice, she watched them running up and down the steps in the back garden to warm up.

One of the few boys in the team offered to help her take the refreshments out to the garden table. It was Scott, an outgoing sort, broad and tall looking but with a heart of gold. Dana couldn't believe her luck when he relocated to Hanfield as he had similar proportions to Danny – another member of the Hanfield Heartbeats. As a coach, this made her excited as she could now work on creating the perfect pyramid with the two of them at the base.

"Thank you so much, Scott, you're too kind!" she exclaimed.

He exhibited the tell-tale signs she had come to notice over the last few weeks, of someone that didn't quite know how to act around her. She was getting pretty used to painting on a manufactured smile for the people around the town, but sympathetic looks made her feel uncomfortable. To her, it was unnecessary.

Scott carried out the tiny sandwiches and the orange juice to the garden for the group. He thought that Dana must have so much time on her hands to have gone to the trouble. He often looked at her, imagining the pain she must be feeling and found it a little concerning that she was still doing so much. Since his family's decision to move to Hanfield, Scott had noticed strange things happening around him, but right now he couldn't get his head around why Dana was spending so much time with the team whilst Amy was still missing.

He had arrived at the table outside and was about to put the food items down when a tiny, brightly dressed girl came bounding towards him. Scott flinched, struggling to balance the food in his hands and prepare himself for an Izzy cuddle. He quickly balanced the jug of orange he was so close to tipping all over himself when Izzy suddenly slowed to a stop. Standing on her tiptoes, she gave Scott a sharp peck on the nose.

Scott rolled his eyes at her "Calm down, Iz!"

Ignoring the slight frustration in Scott's voice, she exclaimed "Hey! I've not seen you all day! Ready to get sweaty?" Izzy was now star jumping on the spot in her neon blue hooded sweatshirt.

Izzy Briggs had approached Scott on his first day at Hanfield High and shown him around, and he liked her energy and positivity toward just about anything. They had been inseparable ever since. Izzy had been a comfort for Scott as he started out at the school, and eventually, they morphed into an item. He'd never had a girlfriend before, but he liked her company and the way she made him feel. She was popular at school but not in a way that made her conceited. Everyone loved her and saw her as a good friend, someone to come to in a time of trouble. Izzy had a caring way about her, and when she first spotted Scott wandering the empty halls of the school looking confused, she couldn't resist trying to help him. She always put a lot of energy into her school life and activities, but sometimes it got a little much for Scott.

"Put that stuff down and join me in a warm-up, guy!" she said, not breaking the rhythm of her star jumps.

Scott found himself always having to calm Izzy down, which would inadvertently make him feel like a killjoy some of the time. He had to keep reminding himself to have more patience with her, and not take their relationship for granted. He was aware that their personalities didn't quite match, as he was usually somewhat laid back while Izzy was the total opposite. When opposites attract, the by-product could often end in disaster.

"Okay is everyone here? One, two, three, four..." Dana came out with her stereo in one hand, and pointed with the other, counting heads. "So we're missing Natalie? We'll get started, and she can catch up."

As a dancing coach, Dana was hard but fair. She commanded the respect of the team and the students around Hanfield High and was one of those teachers that rounded the school off, becoming everyone's favourite. She could laugh and joke but wouldn't stand for any backchat or disruption in her classes. Dedicated to dancing, it had been her entire life. The success of the team was her most significant professional accomplishment, but not everyone appreciate how hard she worked. Still, each training session had been carefully thought out. She would think about what she wanted to get from each class and each student, and she would plan it in a way that would keep it fun.

"Today we're going to brush up on the entire routine. Some reminders from last time... Hannah you need to smile more... Danny, I need sharper lines in your pushes... Michelle don't change a thing, you are killing it!" The training session would usually last around two hours, but so close to competition time the whole team was up for staying as late as it took. It was common to be working on the same routine all evening.

"Okay guys you know the drill. Let's begin our usual warm-up and then on to stretches swiftly, so we can iron out this routine a couple of times!" The team adopted their usual warm-up stances and began; they had this down to a fine art.

Dana noticed some women walking past the house, pointing and whispering. She knew people thought her behaviour was strange. Not giving it a second thought she kept the goal of winning yet another trophy in the forefront of her mind, and she knew this was what Amy would have wanted after all...

III
The Gasps

The day began the same as any other. Richard Ferhulse woke up and proceeded to get ready for work. His main priority was to make it through the day without having to talk about his daughter's disappearance. Like his wife, it was strange to some that he seemed to have mentally disconnected himself from the situation, but this was the result of his sheer denial mixed with unwavering hope. Richard liked to think of himself as the backbone of the family. As far as he was concerned there was no right or wrong way to deal with a missing child, but he was sure he was coping just fine.

It had been nine weeks since Amy's disappearance, and he was regularly haunted with images of her expression before she ran away from him. It seemed likely to Richard that he was the last person to see Amy. He recalled this during his dull morning routine while the torturous memory of their last encounter whirled around in his head. Looking back, Richard remembered how he'd come home from work that day. He hadn't been alone as he'd been having an affair. In an extraordinary coincidence, Amy had skipped her singing lesson. Something must have been troubling her he thought, as she loved her singing lessons. Richard sat at the breakfast bar in the kitchen, as he did every morning before he left for work, his brain replaying that fateful moment Amy had discovered him before walking back out the door, over and over, like a broken record.

Spooning his Weetabix around the bowl, Richard remembered pouring wine for the attractive brunette that afternoon. As karma caught up with him, the front door to the house swung open and the gasp Amy let out had chilled him to the spot. He dropped the spoon and shook his head in an attempt to sweep the memory away. It was not a memory he needed right now, as he had important meetings today, and he needed to stay sharp.

Having lived in Hanfield his whole life as an only child to a working-class family, he kept his head down and embarked upon as many work ventures as possible. Richard had realised from an early age that he wanted to be successful. During that time, he had networked with some of the town's leading apple farmers and distributors. Being able to switch his charms on and off had made it easy for him to gain favourable opinion, as Dana knew only too well. It was a skill he had consciously developed over time, and this advantage became a catalyst in working his way up from a young PA in the town's council office to head accountant for the Mayor. Never on the front line publicly, but a big deal behind the scenes in the running of the town – precisely the way he liked it.

Opening his briefcase using the secret key code, he double-checked all his paperwork quickly. As Richard fingered through the various figures and graphs of that month's quota he frowned and decided at the last moment he would run to his study. In the pale green room stood a large bookcase filled with several hardbacks and photo albums. In the centre of the room a large desk was piled high with papers, stationery, and a slimline desktop computer. This office was where Richard spent most of his time whilst at home, occupied with drafting his most significant presentations and meeting plans; a place where he was rarely bothered by anyone. Somewhere he could find peace in his work and his thoughts. He was a secretive man when it came to his career and kept all but one drawer of his desk locked. He fished in his back pocket for the ring of keys which allowed him access to the Mayor's office, his home, his car and this curious desk full of secrets.

He unlocked the bottom drawer of the deep wooden desk and removed a black file marked;

HIGHLY CONFIDENTIAL 12-04-2019

Ensuring he locked his desk drawer, he made his way back to his briefcase with the file in hand, placing it carefully within a hidden seam in the lining. Looking over at the half-eaten bowl of Weetabix he suddenly poured the rest into the kitchen bin. He had a sickly feeling in his gut, anxious with the memory of Amy's 'gasp' playing on repeat in his head.

Quietly walking through the master bedroom of the four-bedroom home to brush his teeth in the ensuite before leaving for work, he noticed Dana had begun to stir. It was usually 50/50 each morning as to whether she would wake before he left. Being a workaholic Richard liked to be in the office by at least 7 am to get a head start on the day and devise an action plan.

Dana continued to stir. Richard regarded himself in the bathroom mirror, toothbrush in hand, admiring the sharp haircut to his now greying hair before staring back into his own eyes. To him, they appeared empty and sad where they had once been filled with joy. A movement reflected behind him drew his attention, and through the space of the open door, he caught sight of the duvet being flung about as Dana turned uncomfortably. Grimacing slightly, he switched his electric toothbrush on knowing full well an argument was imminent.

She hadn't slept properly for the last few nights, and these days there always seemed to be something wrong. Despite being understanding, Richard couldn't help but feel resentful. He needed to stay strong alongside his wife, but she seemed to blow so hot and cold; so happy on the outside, but behind the scenes would snap and argue with Richard. He didn't think she was coping well at all; he thought she was taking it out on him, maybe they were both taking it out on each other.

Dana was still huffing and sighing, moving about on the bed in a bid to get comfortable.

"You know, you may as well get up and start the day with me!" Richard said with a hint of playfulness in his voice.

"You do this on purpose! You take pleasure in waking me!" she exclaimed from their super king-sized bed. The duvet appeared so fluffy when he looked over that he could barely make out Dana's small frame within it. "I know she's going to return soon and when she does, she will find her mother exhausted, and I'll tell her it was you." Everything seemed to come back to Amy.

As Richard opened his mouth to respond Dana nagged "I'm exhausted just living with you, you don't see me getting up and heading on over to work!"

"Oh, Dana stop this." he snapped at her. The veneer of happiness she presented in public would drain from her face when it was just the two of them, and he felt she would take out everything on him. He was beginning to grow tired of it.

Despite both believing wholeheartedly that Amy would return, his thoughts were beginning to waver, with his position becoming increasingly self-protecting as the weeks had progressed. He liked to tell himself that his overly dramatic daughter had a friend in some other city or country and had left. Selfishly, he had to keep telling himself this as he had done everything he could with the connections he had to find her. He wouldn't tell anyone else what she walked in on that day, but he was sure she was punishing him. Initially, he needed to get to her and speak to her about what she saw – or what she thought she saw - upon charging home to find him with Victoria Rhompski, a Russian work colleague. The 'gasp' would continue to play in his head today... he just knew it would be one of those days.

Looking down at Dana, she was asleep again. With her eyes shut Richard noticed her long eyelashes. Having successfully got that dig toward him off her chest, it seemed she was settling in for a morning of snoozing. He leaned into her and kissed her gently on her head, a small gesture to say he was glad she settled and wasn't pursuing an argument as she usually did these days.

During Richard's commute to work, at every roundabout, junction and along the dual carriageway, he saw the posters and signs; the shining innocence of his daughter staring back at him. It was Amy's school prefect photo which the family had framed and hung proudly on the wall above the stairs, surrounded by various other pictures of her achievements. With her red hair, her big, bright green eyes, and a slight smile on her face, it was a photo he had so treasured at the time it was taken. But he now loathed it. So many times, he had stared back at Amy in this picture and wondered genuinely, 'Where *are* you?'

Richard noticed some of the posters were beginning to look worn, the ink from the bold 'MISSING' along the top had blurred, as it ran in the rain. Holding a button on his steering wheel a soothing automated voice kicked in "Good Morning Mr. Ferhulse, would you like to create a memo?"

"Remind me on my way home to get those damn posters replaced."

"Done! I will remind you on your way home to 'get those damn posters replaced'" the voice repeated. Richard let out a rare, genuine chuckle at this. It was sad, but the voice seemed to be the only thing in his personal life that would listen to him.

Arriving at the large, modern building with glass façade construction, and wide staircases to every entrance, he drove smoothly into the assigned parking space marked with his initials.

The only workers at the office at this time of the morning were the part-time receptionist Stephanie, who was just getting set up, the post boy sorting through that morning's mail before heading on to school, various staff that hadn't quite been on track for deadlines and who were arriving early to type hurriedly at their desks, and the cleaners. Richard liked the atmosphere of the building this early in the morning. In a couple of hours, the place would become so loud and busy with visitors, phones ringing off the hook, and his co-workers rushing around, usually in the direction of the nearest photocopier.

Each morning, upon seeing him, Stephanie would jump up from her seat. "Good Morning Mr. Ferhulse, would you like a coffee?" This wasn't in her job description, but he had taken to asking frequently enough that now she would just offer.

"I'll be in my office, if you could bring it through it would be a big help!" he would always reply with a wink, and she smiled back at him, flushing red. Mr. Ferhulse was a regular topic of conversation with her friends as the 'sexy older man'.

Starting up his computer a wad of emails came through and right on queue Chris, the mail boy, brought through a handful of letters addressed to him. He was a bit of a joker, but since Amy's disappearance he had seemed to be all out of jokes with Richard.

The Familiar Encounter

"I sure hope you're holding up well, Sir. We are all praying for Amy's safe return at school." Richard couldn't even bring himself to look up from his computer screen let alone respond to the boy. He instinctively signalled to Chris to put the letters down on his desk. Richard directed any resentment he felt about the gravity of his situation, towards those that showed the most concern, rejecting their attention.

That was the thing about Richard: he could be the most pleasant person to some, but with others he simply couldn't be bothered. Not that he was unnecessarily nasty, but he just had an air about him that gave people the impression he thought he was better than they were, somewhat overly confident. He was too busy, and in the back of his mind, he knew he had higher responsibilities than most. With his success over the years his ego was now more prominent than ever.

He continued to work his way through his most essential emails, before updating his presentation off the back of various figures that had come in for that day. By the time 9:30 am rolled around, Richard was more than prepared for that month's presentation of the financial action plan. This was something with which he was well-rehearsed, and the way he had taken to presenting was like a fish to water, or more like a 'weatherman' to a green screen since that seemed to be the setup in the presentation room.

As the Mayor walked in with his two advisors, they were able to chat casually, as they had a relationship more akin to friendship than colleagues. To everyone else it was as if they gelled seamlessly, discussing sports teams results and the new Audi that had been released, not close friends but they had known each other for many years, and had the secrets to boot.

"I noticed Rich, and I'm curious – that suit you're wearing, it wouldn't happen to be Jeorgana Calipsi now would it?" The Mayor had a powerful, rich voice that filled a room. He stood well over six feet tall, and with his ample belly, he was definitely a prominent presence in overall size and personality.

"You have a fantastic eye, sir! Jeorg is a personal friend of mine." Richard had many Jeorgana Calipsi suits gifted to him, as he and the designer went way back. In his youth, when Richard worked in the orchards, they had both made a pact one night when their hands were raw from the 'twist and pull' of apple picking. They'd both had enough, and they agreed they'd become wealthy and successful one day. Richard had received the promise of elegant suits from his friend, made from the most marvellous fabrics – wool, linen, and silk.

The Mayor raised his eyebrows, impressed with their matching tastes in tailoring, by which point everyone had arrived and was seated in the long meeting room. Around twenty of the primary department supervisors within the council and Mayor's offices attended this meeting. These were the key players who ran the town of Hanfield.

Richard proceeded with taking control of the meeting as he usually did. No matter the overall feeling in the room regarding the finances that month, Richard's aura, and energy would save him. It always ended in planning a dinner or a golf trip with the highest 'rollers' of Hanfield. Richard was behaving as his usual self, so it helped everyone who saw him day to day, to forget the tragic circumstances that surrounded him. This was the way he liked it to be. In his field he knew not to show weakness, as he had witnessed so many times before. It was a cutthroat dynamic, and if he couldn't carry out his responsibilities to the highest effect, someone else would soon come along who could.

Later on in the day, he went back to sit at his desk. Behind the glass wall encasing his office, separating him from the rest of the financial department, he would sit and stare out at the accountants and financial analysts, watching them hunched over their monitors like robots. He got up to make his way to the copy machine walking past his personal assistant, whom he could have directed, but he often needed to stretch his legs. Richard walked with a steady gait, towards the little room that housed the copy machine. Hoping to avoid some of his more tedious colleagues asking him questions, he increased his pace. Casually avoiding eye contact while passing rows of desks full of co-workers looking up at him expressionless, open-mouthed, and lost. 'Computer zombies', he thought. Turning a sharp left to the little room, he jumped and was horrified for a moment. He was confronted with a large, dark figure, a mound of a person. He heard a sudden intake of breath, a gasp which startled him further.

"Oops! I wasn't expecting anyone to walk right in, I was in my own little world!" Sheila said as she walked past him, leaving him alone with the photocopier. She was one of the administrators and a nervous, shy woman, deemed by Richard to be 'gargantuan' due to her physique, and another colleague he found intolerably dull.

As he stood there, alone, he inhaled deeply for a moment; not because of the encounter, but because the 'gasp' that had left Sheila's lips, sounded precisely like the voice of his daughter, and her unnerving inhalation of shock. Something was going on in his head today; those last moments with his daughter were taunting him more and more.

"Get yourself together!" Richard said to himself, still alone in the copy room. He needed to shake off these thoughts and get on with his work. The overwhelming feeling of anxiety meant he had to concentrate that little bit harder on everything, and as the weeks had passed by, it seemed to come and go with increasing frequency.

He had been looking forward to finishing up and later, dragging his feet up to bed. With the help from a couple of sleeping tablets the day would be finished in no time. He would receive a brief respite from being the father of a lost child. His days seemed to roll by on repeat; the constant battle of trying to remain somewhat sane and keep up with productivity, sometimes seemed an impossible task. The moments the dreaded memories and thoughts went away, felt like pure bliss to him now, but it would soon pass as fleeting moments do, to be replaced with guilt for the relief those brief intervals brought him.

It was later in the evening now. Richard was no stranger to an 8 pm finish from a day's work. He preferred to get everything wrapped up neatly, which wasn't an uncommon practise within the office. A few of his colleagues would work well into the night on occasion, the sector within which they had all chosen to pursue a career, demanded time. Picking up his polished, black briefcase he took some of the notes made in that day's meeting. They had finished putting money into a public fund to create a large park for the locals. Still, space was scarce within the town and this would require encroaching on parts of the orchards, meaning some of the beloved trees would need to be cut down. Skimming through the minutes he shook his head...

'Good luck with that one...' he thought to himself as he arranged everything neatly in his case. He was suddenly reminded of something, and Richard pulled apart a hidden seam in the case to reveal the file marked 'HIGHLY CONFIDENTIAL 04-2019'.

Having checked to see it was still safely in place, he was content to close up and turn off his office lights.

Richard looked forward to the nights becoming darker again as the days were moving towards the end of summer. Driving home in the dark calmed him. It was a great way to empty his mind of the day's work before getting back. This evening he decided to listen to the radio which was playing a live version of Have You Ever Seen the Rain by Creedence Clearwater Revival. He listened to the lyrics and found them soothing as he made his usual route home, as if on autopilot. The smooth roads were often quiet in the evenings at this time of year, and they relaxed him perfectly. But the tranquillity was about to be interrupted.

"Mr. Ferhulse, you have a reminder set for this evening; get these damn posters replaced!" The classy, female voice quoted his frustration from earlier that day, and just like that, soothing radio or not, Amy was back in the forefront of his mind. The fatigued look on Richard's face said it all, and maybe this was karma's way of telling him to try harder.

IV
Hanfield Heartthrob

An alarm clock began to sound in a bedroom decorated with white and blue wallpaper; built-in wardrobes containing a basketball kit and Hanfield High's coloured PE kit, untidily hanging from between the half-open doors. Scott awoke with a groan, turned over to snooze and noticed half a dozen texts from Izzy. Smiling to himself, he thought *'she's such a morning person'*. Squinting at his brightly lit phone trying to focus on what her piled-up messages said, he gave up. Stuffing the phone under his pillow, he proceeded to roll back around and go back to sleep, attempting to avoid wasting the eight precious minutes left on his snooze.

Scott had a beaten-up looking bicycle which he rushed to school on each morning, his floppy blonde hair being blown about in the wind as he listened to his favourite playlist. He idolised a crowd of indie guitarists, and their music put him in the right mood for a day at school. He proceeded to pedal faster down the winding country road leading to the main square. Unconcerned about traffic, he would sing the lyrics out loud. He was easy going with the world at his feet. Even six months after moving to Hanfield, Scott was still taken aback by the view from this road. With fresh air breezing past on this fine summer's day and the miles of trees beyond, the town looked spectacular to him.

Izzy was already waiting for him by the gates when he rode up, he could spot her from a distance away. Her dress sense was unique in that she would wear such vivid colours that didn't necessarily go together. Izzy always looked so naturally fresh-faced. She had slightly frizzy, brown hair, that was bobbed to her shoulders with a blunt fringe. For school, she always wore the same red Converse with rainbow style laces, loving anything that had a rainbow theme. She had a rainbow keyring hanging off her backpack, and a rainbow stationery set.

"How is your day looking?" Izzy was straight in with the questions before Scott could even dismount from his bike.

"My day is looking fine thanks... The usual! How's it going?" Scott was as chilled as Izzy was excitable.

"My messages! Did you get them?! Maybe there's something up with my phone..." She continued to mutter to herself, looking down at her mobile in puzzlement as they walked into school together.

"My bad!" Scott reassured Izzy. She was wearing her hair in a French braid today as she always did for school, and he quietly admired the frizzy baby hairs poking out.

"Well? Are we volunteering for 'Help a Hand' together this year? It really is a lovely cause!" Scott hadn't read her messages, but he knew what she was talking about. The 'Help a Hand' foundation focused on fundraising for the local retirement home. He could think of many other things he would rather be doing, but he didn't want to disappoint Izzy as she felt so passionately about it.

"Erm, I mean... yeah sure... when do we start?" The half-heartedness was apparent in Scott's voice, yet Izzy was so excited that she didn't notice.

"Brill! I'll meet you in the English classroom at lunchtime..." her voice trailing off as she skipped away, towards another corridor, en route to her first lesson, while he continued towards his Psychology class.

Scott wasn't the smartest student, but neither was he bottom of the class. Easily distracted, he daydreamed about basketball, and fast-paced snippets of the latest game he had played, bounced around his head. The shouting from outside, the noise of rubber trainers squeaking along the floor, and also how football practise had been so much fun recently, playing out until late in the summer sun, and how he couldn't wait for his first driving lesson next week. The directions in which his mind would wander were limitless. Snapping out of his reverie and realising everyone else in the classroom had their heads down writing, he looked toward his open book. Ignoring scribbles and doodles on the pages from lessons before, he picked up a pen and began making notes, attempting to understand what Dr. Showfield was explaining.

"Is it okay to hold back your emotions? What does that mean to you?" She spoke openly to the class.

"It's subject to personality, to environment, to what emotions that person may be feeling..." one student stated, and Dr. Showfield nodded encouragingly, leaving the floor open for someone else to give their take.

"Its personal choice." another said.

"Why would you want to hide your everyday emotions, though? Hiding something?" Chantelle asked curiously, with a half-grin on her face. Chantelle always had something to say about everything, or at least it seemed that way.

"You know, it depends on who you meet. Generally, human behaviour demonstrates that people will behave differently with different people. It may not be a bad thing, but sometimes that means holding back emotions too", Dr. Showfield explained. "Each individual experiences a different connection with different people, it's something that occurs at a subconscious level. Some people 'click' immediately and enter a 'comfort zone', while with others, the connection can take a little bit longer."

This thought had grabbed Scott's attention for a little while before he drifted off into another daydream. Had he behaved differently towards different people in his life? The first person that came to mind wasn't Izzy, and how they had clicked upon meeting. Instead, his thoughts went to Amy Ferhulse. She appeared in his mind, and he found himself thinking back to the first time they had met. It wasn't at school or through the few friends they had in common, but at the local supermarket. It was a Saturday. He remembered this because he was still wearing his football kit after that morning's game. He had stopped in on his way home and was waiting in line to pay for a single can of cola and a chocolate bar. Looking out of the enormous windows in front of the checkout, he had seen that the weather was changing, and the sky had turned from blue to dark grey, as it started to rain heavily. The droplets hitting the aluminium roof of the store, echoed throughout the building, and it was at that moment, his ears pricked up as he heard Amy speak for the first time.

"Is that the secret diet of Hanfield new pro footballer?" she asked jovially from behind him in the queue, as Scott hadn't long started at Hanfield High.

Scott turned around and saw a red-haired girl, with perfect, porcelain skin and a wide grin on her face. He recognised her from school as one of the 'untouchable' popular girls, almost a local celebrity amongst her teenage peers. In an instant he felt a sinking feeling, as if she had broken his heart already.

"That was supposed to be a joke..." Amy said, her grin slowly disappearing with the now, awkward encounter. Her comment made Scott realise he had been expressionless and mute, awestruck that a girl like Amy even knew who he was. Holding his Mars Bar and cola, he forced himself to respond; his forehead becoming sweatier by the second.

"Ha! ...it's a rigorous diet... a big secret, so you can't be telling anyone our tricks!" Scott said, trying his best to speak confidently over the noise of the rain, and detract from his red face. To his surprise it worked, and she laughed.

Amy's laugh was music to his ears. He felt a warm glow and a flutter of butterflies in the pit of his stomach. It was the sort of feeling you get when you're on the edge of a cliff looking down at the beauty and danger beneath. Scott smiled back at her, making eye contact, and there, in the loud supermarket, darkened by the stormy skies, Scott knew Amy wasn't just anyone: she was unique.

Snapping back to reality from thoughts he hadn't visited for weeks, Scott stared aimlessly out of the classroom window. He had lost track of time, and Dr. Showfield was wrapping up the lesson for the day. He had been so engaged in his own thoughts he hadn't realised that the sunny sky from earlier had now turned ominously dark, threatening a sudden thunderstorm. He was still relatively new to Hanfield and the storms that occurred randomly, were taking some getting used to.

Lunchtime was upon Hanfield High, and the various student cliques were manoeuvering around each other, with most huddling in the cafeteria, hiding from the pending storm. Scott's main circle of friends were the 'lads' of the school, and if messing about during class, having a competitive, athletic streak, and being able to speak to girls without feeling utterly awkward were a boy's character traits and skills, then they were usually welcomed as part of this crowd. Their routine of going to loiter outside the PE hall was a given since they spent so much time there anyway, even if the weather was horrific. Frankie, a short, smart-mouthed guy who, despite being in the top year of school, was as baby faced as a much younger boy.

"How's it going with your dancing?" Scott knew Frankie was goading him, as he had been the butt of every joke since they found out he was involved with the dance team, but Scott answered him anyway.

"It's ace! Mrs. Ferhulse is making us loads of food at the moment, and it's fun to be outside while the weather is so good." Being teased didn't bother him one bit.

"Oh yeah dude, that's totally weird she has practise at her house. Does she ever talk about Amy?" Justin asked as they walked along the tarmac outside, with the clouds beginning to show a hint of a blue sky once more.

"It's all crazy suspicious!" Frankie said "Their daughter goes missing off the face of the Earth, and my mum said her dad hasn't taken a day off work! Something funny there!"

"Yeah, I guess so... I dunno..." Scott had his own doubts in the back of his mind, though he didn't want to get into it. It was all anyone seemed to have talked about for weeks on end.

"Where is your little lapdog today?" Frankie asked. It had been recently noted that Scott often wasn't seen without Izzy by his side. The guys would poke fun at either his dancing or Izzy, but today they were throwing both grenades at him.

Scott stopped as the rest of his friends walked on for a second. "Oh, crap! Got to go!" He had remembered the meeting for 'Help a Hand'. He ran back the way he had come towards the English classroom, leaving his friends, now sniggering in the distance behind him. Giving up yet more of his spare time for something Izzy had put in place, rather than being with his friends, didn't seem like the best idea right now, but *'I can't back out of charity work'*, he argued resentfully with himself.

"Hey babe, sorry I got caught up. I hope I'm not too late!" he said barging into the classroom, and briefly kissing Izzy. Her body language lit up as she saw him and, just like that, Scott had been forgiven for running behind.

"You're here now!" Izzy only seemed to have one gear, and that was pure enthusiasm, not unlike a puppy. "I'll continue if you want to take a seat Scotty..."

Her grin faded as she went back to address the rest of the class. "So where was I? ...the elderly people over at Cliff Edge Care Home are in real need of some company. I thought we could get in groups to help out, with one set going on a Tuesday and another on a Thursday after school. They just need some companionship; they don't have a social life like you or me."

Around eight students were listening to her pitch the idea, none of whom Scott knew, but had recognized as being part of the 'geek clique'. "I just know they would super appreciate the effort, and hey, old people can be quite funny!" Izzy laughed at herself while the majority of the volunteers sat there blank-faced, as if they were only there in the first place to avoid going out in the rain.

Scott was so proud of Izzy. She was so caring and talented. She must have asked lots of people to join the charity group, as he couldn't imagine any of the guys he knew ever being a part of it. Hanging out after school at the care home didn't seem like the greatest way to spend his time, but then, his grandmother always had the most entertaining stories.

Just after Izzy had made her presentation, a representative of the home, in a simple blue uniform stood up, and began chatting to the class about the logistics. He could feel his mind wandering off again, but a squeeze of the hand from Izzy, who was now sitting next to him, brought him back into the room. She turned to smile at him, making her nose crinkle. She was so delighted he was taking part.

After lunch, Scott walked towards his next class, Chemistry. His lab partner for the last few weeks had been Danny, and knowing him already from Hanfield Heartbeats, they caught up over the Bunsen burner while the lesson was getting started.

Danny had a deep chuckle that could be infectious, and they always had a great laugh together. To top it off, he made the perfect lab partner as he knew what he was doing, and he didn't seem to mind Scott copying from him, as long as he received advice on girls in return.

"I think Hannah has started to notice me more now that I've been killing it in practise." He whispered to Scott while Mr. Malick, the teacher, informed the class about equations.

"Yeah definitely mate, I've seen her look over at you a couple of times... ask her out! Go for it!" Scott said, despite not having a clue about girls himself. He knew Danny only valued his advice because he had a girlfriend, but that had happened naturally. There had been no special tricks or games.

"Do you think?" Danny's excited whispers were sharply interrupted by Mr. Malick.

"Danny, please don't tell me you already know about atom classification?" Mr. Malick snapped sarcastically, "because if so, you can come up here and teach us all about it... it'll give me a break!"

"Erm, no Sir, I'm, I'm not too fami -familiar." Danny stuttered nervously. Scott wondered if something as small as that set off his stutter. If so, he had a long way to go before asking someone like Hannah out, which would probably be for the best, as he'd noticed Hannah always referred to Danny as 'Denny', despite having attended school with him her whole life.

"So, please turn to page 156 and observe that lovely atom diagram." Mr. Malick continued on with the lesson and Danny didn't dare speak up again.

Scott's mind wandered. He had plans to meet friends over at the Fade Away Diner after school. It was an accessible hangout location for the majority of the teens from Hanfield High, and usually the place any after school drama would transpire. It was always bustling in the evenings and at the weekends, frequented by a variety of cliques from Hanfield. The diner was managed by an older lady named Pauline. She had lived in Hanfield all her life, and like every career restaurateur, she was effervescently enthusiastic about food, creating some signature ice cream sundaes for different days of the week. She was rarely away from the premises, as the waiting staff were usually young students from the school.

As the school day ended, the wide corridors of Hanfield High became crammed with teens and children excitedly rushing about to catch their bus home or grab their lift.

Scott jumped on his bike and sped off. Rusted paint from the bike's frame flaked away as he struggled to pedal up the steep hill towards his friends, waiting at the after-school hangout. The diner boasted a pool table, TV and a jukebox, all in a fifties American style. The diner had a red and blue colour scheme with red leather booths being the most coveted seating areas.

Scott joined his friends over by the pool table. They could often be found here, although no games were ever played.

"Did you catch up with your tiny girlfriend earlier 'Scotty'?" Frankie mocked Scott, pronouncing his name in a high pitched, impersonation of Izzy.

"I did, it was great – you should try it, Franks!" Scott joked back. He was always able to shake off Frankie's comments. "You guys will think it's lame, but I'm getting involved with that care home volunteering." Scott added.

"Oh, this just gets worse! Don't be that guy!" Frankie said, his voice laboured and disappointed, as though Scott had done something outrageous.

"I think it'll be kinda cool, you know, like you'll get to listen to their stories from the olden days." Michael joined in, who was as easy going as they came, if not a little simple sometimes.

"My thoughts exactly..." but before Scott could go on, he was suddenly distracted by someone entering the diner. She had dyed, jet black hair, wearing black wet-look jeans accompanied by a purple lace-up top. Her pale skin contrasted with her dark outfit and hair in a way that was beautiful; her heavy eyeliner enhancing her big, blue eyes. But Scott was distracted because she was, unmistakably, Amy's twin sister, Bella.

The boys noticed Scott's gaze drift to the door behind them; they each turned around to stare too. Bella wouldn't usually go to the diner, but she carried a pile of 'Missing' posters over her arm. She began to give them out with a sallow look on her face, and the whole atmosphere of the diner completely shifted. Bella acted as a reminder to everyone that a classmate was still missing.

"Oh man, that's all you need to bring the mood down in here, a 'goth' looking for her dead sister... someone should tell her it was her parents that did it." Frankie muttered.

"Really? Seriously not the time Franks!" Rory rolled his eyes in outrage.

The Familiar Encounter

It was all background noise to Scott. He stood there unable to take his eyes from Bella. The resemblance was uncanny, as if Amy had changed her hair and dress and she was now in the diner with him. So many features were the same and yet, the mannerisms were so different.

"I've not seen her for ages. I hadn't even known they were sisters until some 'chick' in French class told me", Frankie continued.

"Yeah, can't say I've ever spoken to her. It must be awful for her the... whole thing" Scott murmured, masking his real thoughts in front of his friends.

They all became quiet as she reached them, holding out a black and white poster displaying the photo of Amy along with the headline 'Last seen outside Glendale's Orchard at 4pm...'. The posters had been located all around the school, for the last two months. As Scott offered his hand to take the poster, he made eye contact with Bella. Her blue eyes stared back at him for a second. Still, it felt like longer to Scott, as if time slowed. In that instant, her expressionless face could have been Amy's. Bella, unaware of Scott's profound reaction, turned toward another group of people and continued handing out the posters. Scott didn't know Amy well but Bella's presence only highlighted Amy's absence, and the reality was painful; more painful than he expected.

V
Hannah Henry's Garden of Personalities

"Vapid!" The nail technician blasted at Hannah.

She sat in the nail salon. Looking down her nose at her manicure, stretching her arm out, frowning at her cuticles, then bringing her hand right up to her face for a closer inspection.

"No, they're still not right!" She said. Hannah didn't care enough to realise, but the salon loathed her monthly appointments. She was a hard client to please, the sort of client a lot of the girls working there were frightened to treat despite being only sixteen. She would shout and humiliate them.

Hannah had been called vapid in the past, but as far as she was concerned, those that had anything negative to say towards her were jealous. In her eyes, she knew how to look good, and that didn't make her a bad person. Being confident had always come naturally to her since she was a child. Her mother had sent her to performing arts and dance classes after school from a young age.

Hannah saw herself as a guide for other students at the school. She was an inspiration and felt everyone should treat her as such. Sometimes she would come across as rude or arrogant, but it was hard to keep up appearances. It was in these moments Hannah felt a twinge of sadness, as she didn't have her understanding, best friend around anymore.

People would only see Hannah for being naturally gifted, but, in reality, maintaining high grades, keeping on top of sport teams, and improving her singing, as well as staying socially relevant, would sometimes feel like spinning plates. Amy had some of the similar issues. It was overwhelming, and she just got it.

During the first week of her disappearance, Hannah felt strongly about getting her back. She would work with the police, providing information on Amy's favourite hangouts and usual school routine. She would sit in tears in the police station wondering why this would have happened to her friend, racking her brain for clues as to where she could be. Hannah began organising search parties, while also writing articles for the local paper to keep Amy's disappearance relevant when the weeks started to roll by, even speaking out in public about why everyone needed to keep searching.

But with the community starting to look up to her, being noticed that little bit more around school, and replacing Amy as the lead in the Hanfield Heartbeats, for once, she was beginning to enjoy the attention. Someone had called her a 'graceful prodigy of Hanfield' recently, and that never would have happened if Amy were still here, the voice in her head would tell her. She would get to speak in most school assemblies, and as the weeks without Amy passed, the more rewarding it became.

Hannah was now filling an Amy sized space, and as time passed by, she felt less upset about her friend going missing and instead, began thinking that Amy had done her a favour by vanishing. She couldn't help herself. Although she was always popular (mainly because people were scared of her), and no one would deny her talent, she came in second to Amy. But now she was 'Number one', and it felt good.

She had become greedy with the attention of it all. Still, she wasn't stupid, and despite knowing the worst thing that could happen to her would be Amy's return, she was conscious that she needed to keep up appearances. To do this, Hannah continued to spend much of her time fixing the posters to the lamp posts and shop windows. She maintained an appropriately melancholy expression at church when they would speak about Amy, and she made certain her newspaper articles expressed the sadness and longing of a best friend.

People thought of her as Amy's less friendly counterpart, but when Amy disappeared, the stigma had melted away and she became an angelic figure. Yet, if anyone had felt inspired enough to strike up a conversation with her directly, they would have discovered the meaner side. But now, two months on, Hannah's real personality was falling back into place.

"Ew. Why are you wasting my time? Go away!" she would snap, rudely dismissing those that weren't on her level', while glaring through her Dior sunglasses, a really complicated coffee order - mainly foam. - in her hand. Being insensitive was a die-hard trait of hers, and the nail technician was right, she was vapid.

The Hanfield Heartbeats girls were her closest friends. They followed her and went along with whatever she liked, even with her ideas for the style of the troupe. Skilled at getting what she wanted from people, and being young and beautiful she had minimal experience with the word 'no'. This only bolstered her attitude.

The latest project she had recently taken upon herself to introduce to the school was a choir that would create and perform a song 'For Amy'. As always there was a hidden agenda, and in this case, everyone would get to hear Hannah's fantastic singing voice. When she saw the 'Amy drama' had hit national headlines, she had to do something to get her voice out. Right now, she headed home from the salon to practise, her school bag still on her shoulder.

Hannah's house was modest in size, but with a beautiful, floral garden, and ivy creeping up the walls and taking over the windows. It enthralled passers-by and had bursts of colour all around the perfect lawn. The stones of the little wall and pathway looked old and asymmetric, while the ivy travelling up the walls would sometimes bloom with pretty white flowers that attracted a host of butterflies. She swung the front door shut on the sunlight of the day. Hannah's house was full of deep wood furniture and dark shadows. The downstairs had a very thin, threadbare carpet, and furniture straight from the seventies that overflowed through the hallway and living room. Dumping her bag on the floor for her mother, she hopped up the stairs towards her room to begin her attempt at perfecting the high notes.

Her mother was a keen gardener and very concerned with nature. As a spiritual person, she found being in the garden calming and a great way to get in touch with her inner self, while encouraging life around her. Hannah's mother loved collecting old trinkets and rocks, pressing flowers, and keeping jars of various herbs. Hannah's least favourite item on the living room bookcase was a deer skull. Her mother would speak about how deer in the woods would come to her in dreams and talk to her, and the skull was a good omen to keep evil out of the home. Hannah used to have nightmares about the skull when she was younger, but now she considered it dumb.

As she began practising her solo for the school choir, she was distracted. There were loud bangs and groans coming from outside her window. She tried to ignore it, but increasing in volume, it was putting her off. She would begin her solo perfectly, then the moans and groans coming from outside would start again, interrupting her concentration. Knowing exactly what was getting in the way of her practice, she grabbed her music sheets, crushing them in her hands dramatically and threw them down onto her bed. She stormed towards the window and shouted:

"Stop being a freak for five minutes so I can practise!"

In her dark robe, cross-legged on the lawn at the back of the house, sat Hannah's mother. Burning incense cubes which gave off thick smoke twirling into the air she continued to meditate. Surrounded by beautiful flowers which petered off into dense shrubbery as it melded into the side of the vast Hanfield forest. She usually contemplated each day, and she swore people would visit her during meditations, appearing as smoky spirits to speak to her. She would tell people they provided her with a different perspective on any complicated situation, or to sometimes warn her about things happening in the future. She would call them her visions, and in return, the locals would say she 'wasn't all there'.

Hannah hated her mother acting on these 'messages'. She would dismiss her mother's 'sight' during meditation as being 'drugged up on incense fumes', and if they were ever in public together, she would whisper, "Don't speak to me, don't look at me."

As Hannah's mother kept humming and groaning deep in a trans-meditative state, unaffected by Hannahs objections, Hannah could feel her cheeks burning with annoyance.

"I'm trying to practise my singing here you know, like an actual important talent I have to work at!" She shouted down from the window.

Her mother paid no attention.

"Argh! I hate you!" Hannah spun round to face her bedroom again and flopped onto the bed in frustration. Whether it was prompted momentarily by hormones, anger, or something more sinister, Hannah emitted a long, drawn-out, high pitched scream.

She wanted to get out of the house she shared with her mother. The older she got, the more embarrassed she became of her interests, and she found it disturbing that her mother could completely detach when in meditation mode. Hannah would plot ways of getting her mother sectioned and taken away. She would envisage men coming to drag her off, her mother's fingers digging into the stones along the garden pathway in protest, before throwing her into the back of a van. Hannah fantasised about this for a while and cackled uncontrollably, the tears that streamed down her face from screaming, still visible on her cheeks. She would have her home to herself and flourish without the inconvenience of her mother's insanity dragging her down.

Hannah lay on her bed, violently scribbling down her frustrations in her diary. Fantasising that this song would get her discovered would be the proverbial cherry on top of overtaking Amy's once-promising future. She was seething at the prospect that her mother might get in the way of her dream. She was so sick of living in other people's shadows all her life. She didn't have the natural talent Amy had, despite what people might think, but she worked so hard. It always seemed to have come easily to Amy. Still, as far as Hannah cared, she didn't deserve it. She now realised it had been exhausting watching her friend be perfect at everything. Her fingers pressed the pen to paper hard as she kept writing down her feelings, until it was all off her chest.

To drown out the wailing noise her mother was making outside, she turned her radio on in a huff, and began undressing. Stripped down to her underwear, she walked over to the large mirror which almost covered the entirety of her wall. Draping her locks over one shoulder, she examined her back. Her bra strap squeezed tightly around flaky, raw skin. Taking the cream from her dresser, she used the mirror to apply a pea-sized amount to one of the many pustulating ulcers. The remnants of that morning's application were crusty and white. As she picked off the Tippex- like substance, the abscess burst, oozing black, tar-like contents. Losing her temper, she hurled her fist into the mirror, causing it to break and shatter. *Britney Spears - Toxic* played in the background. Breathing heavily, she stared down at her intact hand. Although she had always been hot-headed, she was losing her temper increasingly of late, and her aggression was escalating; the dent she left in the salon wall earlier, the telegraph pole she had kicked a chunk out of last week, the filing cabinet drawer she had pulled off its metal hinges with ease when at school earlier... the countless punching of inanimate objects, yet she was never marked.

Later that evening there was a light knock on her bedroom door. Hannah was still furious, but she was very good at holding on to her anger.

"Can I come in?" A voice enquired timidly while the door was slowly pushed open regardless. Hannah's mother revealed herself walking over to the foot of the pink frilly bed.

She looked up to her mother standing over her. With her mother's short dark, modest dress and soft features, they were polar opposites.

"Practising for the choir solo is of actual importance... talking to the forest Mother? It needs to stop, they are insane made-up fantasies you have..." Hannah said.

"Something is happening you mark my words, the energy coming from the trees... things have begun to cause a ripple effect." her mother replied.

"Everyone thinks you're crazy, talking all this rubbish all the time, I'm glad you never leave the house. You are standing in the way of my dreams Mother, you always have, and I'm not letting anyone do this to me anymore. My destiny is on the stage with everyone looking up at me. Not sitting here trying to understand your fantasies!" Hannah looked at her mother with disgust and pity.

As she looked into her mother's eyes, and the tears resting on her lashes, she felt nothing except the hope that the message had gone through. Hannah turned her back dismissively to keep writing in her diary. Her mother took a glance over her shoulder before walking out of the room, noticing the pages were full scribbles and strange shapes. But Hannah continued to wonder whether her honesty had burst the bubble that her mother had for her alternate world.

The following afternoon, during dance class she approached her glamorous coach, Dana. Sharing ideas she had for the fast approaching competition, she found Dana to be positive and receptive to her propositions. She really seemed to appreciate and respect Hannah's talents and contributions to the group. Hannah believed Dana's appreciation had grown for her even more so, now her daughter had gone missing. She would welcome Hannah with an embrace, a way of giving and receiving comfort as they were both in turmoil. They had seemed to bond over Amy's disappearance, and it didn't take much for Hannah to wish her mother was more like Dana. She was so supportive and charismatic, not a reclusive weirdo like Mother.

Bella was all that remained. Rarely noticing her around school, Hannah would sometimes see her looking out from the top window of the house, down onto them practising in her garden, never reacting, only watching the entire time. Amy had never spoken about her, and to Hannah, Bella didn't appear to fully appreciate how great a mother Dana was. Always being so embarrassed by her own mother, Hannah resented Bella's seeming apathy. *How is it fair, how different her life would be if her mother was more like Dana, she thought.*

Never allowing it to fully consume her, she concentrated on the appearance she was projecting to those around her. Her whole image was based on her being the upset best friend, the heartbroken artiste, and she needed to keep up with the charade. Sometimes the paranoia that came with pretending to be something she wasn't, was a heavy burden to bear on her own, but she had to continue telling herself she was strong enough. Careful and self-aware, she rarely allowed her real agenda to leak out from beyond the mask. Something evil was growing inside her. The seed of opportunity her best friend had left behind wasn't transforming into a beautiful sunflower as everyone thought, but a horrible poisonous weed; a weed whose growth she had initially encouraged within herself, but that now was taking control.

VI
Misty Night

Izzy skipped along with her camera, taking photos of the trees as the sun was beginning to go down. The sky had warm summer tones running through a deep blue; baby pink and peach bled into each other, creating a dramatic yet calming view. Perfect for her photography project.

The apple orchards were an area in Hanfield which was open to the public. It was calming for Izzy who liked the way the apple trees had been planted in rows parallel to each other. It had created the effect of a maze with a couple of memorial benches dotted around. This underrated area was somewhere the residents could get away from town, read a book and munch on an apple.

Scott was at football training this evening. She always hated being apart from him, but she'd planned to meet him afterwards to show him her photographs. She contorted into different positions in order to take them from interesting angles, hopefully contrasting the red and green of the apples on the trees, against the perfect backdrop of the sunset. She would go to meet him in an hour or so, surprising him when he finished training.

When they first met Scott had just started at Hanfield High. Izzy noticed him roaming the corridors looking lost, and she took him under her wing. But even when he had established himself in the school, making friends with the sports lads, he always made time to catch up with her. Their midweek routine would be to walk home via the coffee shop from dance class and chat for hours. Soon enough, she started developing feelings for him. Not only because he was conventionally good looking, but she noticed the cute way he would laugh and pay special attention to her if she'd had a bad day. A love began to flourish between them, and it wasn't long before they were an item. Watching the sunset, it evoked the same feelings she felt for Scott, pure and beautiful. Before long she had made it to the end of the orchard, meeting tall, cross-hatched fencing that separated her from the forest beyond. The fencing was old now, and there were gaps all along it where kids had created access points so they could play out in the woods. For a moment she thought she saw something move out there; something from the corner of her eye, grey and moving toward her. She stared into the dark forest and could swear she saw the shape of a man's face staring back at her, still and unflinching. She believed people could see whatever they wanted if they looked long and hard enough into the trees. There were so many shapes and shadows, causing the mind to play tricks. Unlike some of her friends, the forest didn't spark any curiosity in Izzy. Turning around to head back, she was happy to remain in the orchard, and in any case, the sunset had finished its colourful display, and it was beginning to get darker.

    Izzy would always feel even giddier when she knew she was going to be seeing Scott, and she loved to surprise him. Her life was perfect now that she had the guy of her dreams. Walking up to the football ground she could hear the noise of the football being kicked about, and the shouting between competitive boys. The game hadn't finished yet, so she took her phone out of her backpack and opened up her 'selfie' camera to check on her hair, using her free hand to run her fingers through it like a makeshift hairbrush. She sensed someone behind her. She dropped her phone and turned around in shock, but it was a trick of the streetlights. She walked right up to the side of the pitch and, clutching her camera, she caught the end of the training session before the whistle sounded. One of his teammates tapped Scott on the shoulder and pointed in her direction, and he turned and gave her a little wave. She began waving enthusiastically with both hands, the camera wedged between her legs. Overwhelmed with happiness, she appreciated all the little things of her day, her heart full to the brim. Being able to spend this evening, walking hand in hand together, enjoying the warm summer night, was priceless to her.

Finished up for the day he began jogging over, giving her a quick kiss on the lips "Hey Iz! I wasn't expecting to see you tonight! You love surprising me!"

"A nice surprise I hope!" Izzy laughed. Not waiting for an answer, she turned the camera on. "Look at the photos I took this evening! Look, look, look! The sky was extra pretty by the orchards, that way. I might even get some of these printed – what do you think Scotty?" She said enthusiastically, hardly holding the camera still enough for Scott to even focus in on the photos he was trying to see within the tiny preview screen.

Scott was used to Izzy getting overly excited about the smallest things, but this is what he loved about her. He gently took the camera from her hands and started to scroll through the images, as she explained each one. He slowly walked along the pavement in his muddy football kit, still covered in sweat. He looked at a couple of the photos and passed the camera back to Izzy, "Don't you get up to some adventures!" he said. Izzy knew Scott wasn't ever quite as enthusiastic about these things as she. "Those photos are so pretty... like you". Scott smiled at her, his compliment making her chest fill with fluttering butterflies, causing her to smile brightly, and even though it wasn't the feedback she was after she didn't care.

"Wow! Thank you so much." She said, still getting used to reacting to his compliments. They still seemed to make her feel a shyness she didn't know she had. "So how are you feeling about our first go at volunteering together? I am super-duper excited!" she asked, changing the subject as they walked along the quiet street.

She knew Scott would become enthusiastic about volunteering once she showed him how rewarding it could be. She loved helping people and getting involved in her community.

"Oh, the Coffee Hub is shut! I hadn't even realised how late it was getting!" Izzy noted. Scott looked over and continued to walk along. "I assumed we were heading for Fade Away anyways, I need me some carbs after all that running about!" Scott put his arm around Izzy, holding her close for a moment as they walked, before taking her hand in his again.

Often, if it had been a warm day, a mist began to rise at this time of the evening. The streets in Hanfield were wide and clean, with each house almost a copy of the last, but with slightly unique features. They walked past Hannah Henry's house. It had always given Izzy the creeps for some reason. It was set back slightly compared to the others on this row, all on its own. The ivy covered the majority of the speckled black and grey house, and it looked even scarier to her at night, with the mist having enveloped it. But there was something else that led Izzy to feel the way she did, an unusual feeling. Maybe it was the way the roof peaked high in the shape of a witch's hat, or the way the windows were always black. She thought the world of Hannah, having known each other their whole lives, but the house was so, soulless. When Monica had first started with the Hanfield Heartbeats, Hannah had invited Izzy over for apple pie, along with Amy and Monica, to welcome her into the group, but Izzy couldn't accept the invitation, the house unnerved her that much.

And as they walked past the Henry house, Izzy stared at it, still unable to quite put her finger on what it was that disturbed her so much about it. Noticing her glaring as they walked by, Scott took hold of her hand a little more tightly and they continued to chat about their volunteering. He made her feel safe when she was with him.

The mist was getting thicker as they walked, and through it, they could see the shadow of a figure on a bike rapidly coming towards them. Within seconds it zoomed past the couple. Scott reacted quickly, jumping out the way so that the bike would miss him. Izzy just managed to catch sight of the person on the bike, and she couldn't mistake that fair skin, red lips and black hair... It was Bella Ferhulse.

"Woah, she had really picked up speed! Are you okay?" Izzy asked.

"Yeah..." Scott responded "she looked kinda upset. I wonder where she was heading at this time and in such a hurry. I guess she has a lot going on."

For a moment Izzy was puzzled. She didn't realise Scott knew who Bella was. Hardly anyone spoke to her at school, as she had always been a bit of a Jane Doe. Still, he obviously knew her as

Amy's sister, as word travels fast. "Perhaps she's late to meet a friend!" Izzy said.

Izzy had Maths with Bella. She was perceived as a loner in school and had always avoided being involved in any school activity. It was always the minimum of effort with her, and she had never bothered making friends. Bella appeared unapproachable, the opposite to her sister Amy who got involved in everything and had for as long as Izzy could remember. That's just how it had been with those sisters. It would certainly be right to say that up until Amy's disappearance, most people didn't even realise they were sisters.

Despite vocalising the most favourable reason for Bella's night time bike ride, deep down, Izzy did wonder where she was actually going. There was nothing back in that direction except the empty football pitch... and the forest. It may have been because of the thick mist but Bella didn't seem to notice their presence on the pavement at all, as if she were preoccupied and focused on something else rather than avoiding pedestrians. But what could Izzy do about this right now? Perhaps Bella needed to get out of the house for some fresh air. It was probably so depressing in the Ferhulse household right now. She told herself that it was one of her business, she should stay out of it. Still hand in hand with Scott, she cuddled his arm for a moment, feeling thankful for all that she had.

Arriving at the Diner, Izzy's mind switched from Bella, to deciding which milkshake she would order. There were always people at Fade Away that would happily have Izzy sit with them, but tonight she thought sitting with Scott at a separate table would be better, keeping him all to herself. There was just the issue that Betty had seen the two of them walking in. Betty was known as a bit of a trouble maker. She was Izzy's partner in Drama class, and with a smile on her chubby face, was beginning to get up from her table, leaving the huge stack of pancakes that were in front of her. Betty was the 'busy body' of the school, and she always wanted to catch everyone's secrets. In drama class, Izzy would have to try to evade some of the awkwardly personal questions Betty would ask, without seeming too rude. Izzy was about the only one friendly enough to partner up with Betty, and she was about to pay the price.

Walking over towards the couple, she wore a red and white summer dress, which was old fashioned and out of style, like something your grandmother would wear. As she was on the larger side, her body would almost seem to move in slow motion, bobbing from side to side. her curly blonde pigtails being the only thing moving in real-time as the ringlets bounced quickly up and down.

Izzy sighed, an internal eye roll. Being the nicest girl at school, even she knew the smile on Betty's face would bring bad news. She smiled back at her and gave a half-hearted wave all the same, as she walked over.

"Betty! What's up!" Izzy said, getting up to give her a hug. She hugged everyone.

"Well, well, what do we have here, are we on a date?" Betty said slyly as Izzy looked expectantly over at Scott. "You know what Scott..." Betty moved her attention over to him, "I was sure I didn't think Izzy was your type! I remember myself and the girls commenting that Amy would have been more your type. Shame she's 'poof' gone without a trace!" Betty was like a dog with a bone when it came to any 'Amy drama' she might be able to get her hands on. There were a few girls like that at school but Betty was one of the worst.

Receiving no response from Scott, she looked at Izzy for a reaction, whose face had noticeably dropped at the comment. "Anyway, Scott I can see you have made Izzy oh so happy which is great stuff. Toodles!" Feeling content that she had stung the happy couple, she returned to her pancakes.

The thought of Scott being interested in anyone else made Izzy's heart hurt. She sometimes obsessed over the idea that Scott was out of her league. She knew Scott had been seen around Hanfield chatting to Amy, but she didn't know people thought of them as a potential couple. She realised the worry must have shown on her face when Scott reached out and grabbed her hand resting on the table.

"Hey, don't even listen to that Betty for one second, let me get that milkshake ordered!" He got up and walked to the other side of the diner to get the waitress' attention. Izzy told herself people were not used to seeing a connection such as they had. She had never felt this way about anyone and knew Scott could feel the chemistry between them too. Although Izzy liked to think the best of people as a general rule, she knew that girls like Betty would be jealous of what

The Familiar Encounter

she had in Scott, as he was so strikingly handsome. But they'd been dating for ages, so how could people not see it?

She grabbed one of the cheap napkins from the dispenser and started folding it anxiously, all different ways. Izzy thought she should move the relationship forward more quickly. She didn't like that girls were still referring to the connection between him and Amy, months into their relationship. Scott walked back over to the table with her banana milkshake. He set it down next to her and began drinking from the straw in his glass of icy cola.

"Ha, sweet... where did you get that?" Scott asked.

Izzy was now fidgeting with an origami cat made from various paper napkins. "Oh, this?" Discarding it to the side of the table, she continued. "Can I ask you something? It's rather important."

Scott opened his mouth slightly to let the straw in his mouth fall out, his expression becoming serious. "Sure Iz!"

"Would you join my family this weekend for dinner? My parents would love to meet you!" It was the only logical next step she could think of. She had gathered from watching rom-com films that this was a big deal for guys, and she felt nervous having asked.

Scott's eyebrows raised and he began to stutter. "Oh! We're at the 'meet the parents' stage already?" He noticed Izzy looked as though she might burst out crying. "But yeah... of course, I would love to have dinner with your family! Next Friday? After the Summer Sling? I have football this weekend."

Izzy felt a sudden wave of relief. Wow, that would have been embarrassing if he had said no. The weight of Betty's comments had been lifted from her shoulders. As she listened to Scott talking about meeting her parents, and describing the film 'Meet the Parents', she watched his perfect face. While he was speaking and taking sips of his coke, his burger arrived. Before the waitress had time to put the plate down, he used his fingers to pick up some chips and stuff them in his mouth. Some of the ketchup dribbled down onto his football top. It was then it had dawned on Izzy. Will they even like him? What would they have to say about him? Will they approve? She had thought they would see what she saw in him right away, but as she watched him trying to get the trail of cola and red sauce off his white football top using the end of his somewhat muddy fingers, she had a slight fear. They may not see him in the same light.

VII
Monica's New Beginning

Moving quickly through the trees, dodging branches barefoot. The ground is thick with fallen leaves. It's daytime, but you'd only know it from the very few rays of sunshine filtering through the dense canopy. Running from what, or to where, she didn't know, but it was exhausting. Scaling the steep bank, she came to a sudden halt, toppling backwards at the sight of an unusual figure, like no man or animal she had ever set eyes on before. As her head hit the forest floor, she awoke suddenly, opened her eyes and gasped, her pyjamas were cold and glued to her skin with sweat.

This was a recurring nightmare for Monica, and she would be left puzzled, wondering what it meant, if anything. Sometimes small details would change. Sometimes she was sure she was running away from something, a large animal, scaly and fast. Other times it was nighttime, or she would be running through her empty school, trying desperately to find somewhere to hide. It always ended the same way, with her encountering a tall humanoid, painfully thin with translucent, grey skin. It would frighten her so much that she would wake in a flash before the dream could progress. She instinctively looked at the time over on her phone - 4 am - plenty of time to get some more sleep in before school. It was a long day ahead with back to back classes followed by dance practise.

The Familiar Encounter

The Summer Sling competition was just around the corner. The dance troupe was missing its main body in Amy. She was someone that had been dancing her whole life and knew the routine backwards, so there had been a shuffling of positions within the group. Hannah Henry had now made front and centre. Monica, being quite an observant person, had noticed that Hannah seemed far too excited about replacing Amy as the lead in the routines. Noticing little clues over time about Hannah, she saw that on first appearance, she seemed friendly and fun, but she had also observed how Hannah had behaved when she thought it was of no consequence. She had decided that Hannah was not a genuine person, the things she said and the way she spoke didn't portray her true feelings. Monica was sure of it.

There was now news that Hannah was producing a choir performance, with her lead solo being a tribute to Amy. The way everyone spoke about Hannah annoyed Monica. It was as though everyone else was blind, and only she could see what Hannah was really up to. The news was being announced during the school assembly, and as everyone began taking their seats, Monica sat on her own, selecting a seat reasonably far back. Being in the Hanfield Heartbeats meant she was automatically in the top tier of the school, and she had plenty of friends. But she was an introvert at heart, and sometimes didn't enjoy all the extra attention. Contentedly sat on her own waiting for the assembly to start, she played around with a bit of thread hanging from the denim skirt she had teamed with thick black tights and boots, and considered her dream. *What could I be running away from with such desperation, something dark, with scales and mounds of hair? It's nothing I've ever set eyes on before, but then I've never had time to get a good look at it.*

"Hey, girl! What's up?" Hannah asked, greeting Monica in her superficial, spirited voice as she sat down next to her, breaking Hannah's train of thought. "Y'know what's happening this morning?" Hannah knew the secret was already out, and she didn't pause long enough for Monica to even pretend to hazard a guess. "The new choir I'm organising will be announced, it's all happening for me! Isn't it super exciting?"

"I heard. I think it's so kind-hearted of you to make it about Amy. I'm sure her parents will appreciate it, everyone is missing her so much." Monica cleverly responded in a way to bring Hannah back to earth. She couldn't believe this was Amy's so-called 'best friend' who was speaking with such happiness in her voice. Carefully gauging Hannah's reaction, she observed as her face ever so subtly dropped, and her shoulders slumped; her body language speaking volumes for a moment.

"It's fantastic isn't it, all that I've accomplished. But don't beat yourself up Monnie, everyone is doing their best." Hannah said, her ego too big for Monica's careful reminder to fully penetrate.

The headmaster moved out onto the centre of the stage and began the usual weekly assembly by congratulating various students on their achievements that week. His voice always sounded dull and monotonous, as if reading from the phonebook.

"Toby Lim in form two won First Place in Miss Bradley's spelling bee. Well done!" Everyone began clapping.

"Frankie Davidson in form four won 'Man of the Match' in the game against Calie High." The clapping continued. "A huge 'Well Done' to Frankie."

"Finally, Hannah Henry of form five will be closing this year's Summer Sling with her song for Amy Ferhulse. I know Amy's disappearance has hit the community hard, and we are very proud to have someone like Hannah working to make this year's Summer Sling an exceptional one." Everyone in the hall clapped harder this time, along with gasps of appreciation. Monica looked around; some teachers even appeared emotional at the dedication Hannah had put in. She's fooled everyone, but she does not fool me.

Monica wasn't the jealous type, but she was a good judge of character and suspected that Hannah was undoubtedly seeking personal gain in playing to her missing friend's memory. It didn't sit well with Monica but to come out and accuse someone of such an awful act, wouldn't go down well without proof. She knew she had to hold back and review Hannah's actions silently. Everyone praised her as an angel, but Monica would not be surprised if Hannah were complicit in the disappearance of Amy in the first place. She had sensed Hannah's envy toward her during dance training, months ago.

"Hey babe, you free later?"

Walking through to class she received a text from her boyfriend, Rick. Although she was carefully reserved, she had been swept away in a romance with him. Rick worked at the local supermarket as a manager and would often drive her around in his Ford Shelby Truck. It was nice for her to spend time with someone not caught up with all the drama of Hanfield High, and he was someone she would often confide in. Beginning to respond to the text she noticed the time, and that she was running late for Maths.

Walking to the back of the class, she took the only remaining seat next to Bella Ferhulse. She quickly pulled out a book but struggled to find her favourite pen in her backpack. The class had begun, and she felt awkward, hoping the teacher wouldn't say anything about her late arrival. Bella was staring at her as though she was looking right through her. It wasn't helping, this girl always made her feel on edge.

"You should run away from here," Bella said softly to Monica, not breaking her gaze.

"What did you say?" Monica paused in horror from the pen search.

"I saaaid, it's not like you to be late!... Jeez, no need to look so shocked! I do sometimes talk y' know!" Bella huffed back to pay attention to the class while casually throwing a pen in Monica's general direction. It bounced off her shoulder and landed on the floor.

Urgh, what? I need more sleep, she thought. She rubbed her eyes.

On her way out of class, she caught up with Izzy, who was bobbing along with a skip in her step, which was pretty usual for Izzy, so pure and so utterly uninterested in any negativity. Izzy was Monica's best friend at Hanfield High. She was one of those people whose happy energy seemed contagious. But Monica was still distracted by her weird encounter with Bella.

"You seem troubled!" Izzy said.

"Yeah, I didn't sleep great last night. I keep having this weird nightmare." Monica explained as they walked through the school's beige corridors.

"Oh, I get those sometimes! You should try listening to whale noises! Although that's not exactly helping my sleep as of late. I need to level up to some beach wave sounds instead!"

"You're getting them too?" Monica asked.

"I think I just have a lot on my mind Mon. I'm thinking of asking Scott round to meet the parents, though I'm not sure. I'll surprise him after football later and see, I suppose I'm worrying that..." Abruptly, Izzy jumped up, easily distracted as always. "Oh, hey Miss!" she called, as she saw Dana Ferhulse walking in the distance, despite the corridors being crowded with students. Still, she couldn't miss her characteristically long auburn hair. "Mrs. Ferhulse! Hey!" Izzy waved her arm.

Spotting them, Dana stopped and smiled. "Hello Monica, Izzy. I'm just on my way to the headmaster's office. Looks like I should be coming back to school soon."

"That's brilliant news, we have missed you!" Izzy said excitedly.

"Really?" Monica's first reaction was concern. She couldn't understand how Amy's parents were so collected about Amy's disappearance. She remembered how distraught they were initially, but over the last few weeks, they seemed to have come to terms with it and moved on.

"Yeah, I cannot stand sitting in that house for much longer – you girls and the team have helped a lot by getting me through some of the darker days. But I'll just be coming back part-time for now. Keep it a secret and I'll see you girls after school tomorrow for practise!" Dana quickly said with a wink. "We need to work on perfecting every move, to blow everyone else out of the water!" She seemed as spirited as she once had been, before the disappearance of her daughter, and she walked confidently past the girls.

"Oh that's great that she's coming back!" Izzy said without any suspicion in her voice.

"Yeah... brilliant news, getting back to normality again." Monica said slowly, her thoughts about the situation trailing off into confusion.

When it came to the disappearance of Amy Ferhulse, Monica didn't know what to think. The majority of the sentiment in town was that she had taken a late afternoon walk in the forest and had become lost. Like many of the old stories told, it was something that used to happen all too often. But then over the last few weeks, there had been whisperings about Amy's parents; how they seemed less affected by the loss of their daughter in such a short amount of time. With the way gossip spreads in Hanfield, some people believed Amy's mother and father of having something to do with their daughter going missing.

Monica often thought back to that day at the very beginning of summer; the last day she ever saw Amy. She remembered bumping into her in the girl's toilets and making small talk. Amy was an intimidating character to most in the school, but for all the right reasons, because she was so talented and so strikingly beautiful. Monica remembered reaching for the soap dispenser and washing her hands, as Amy talked about dance rehearsals that morning while applying lip gloss in the mirror. She had a natural way about her that was so carefree, yet classy.

"I've thought that the triple kick near the end needs to be sharpened up, but it has potential." She didn't make eye contact with Monica, and she was busy dabbing her lips now with tissue. "...what do you think Mon?"

That was the final encounter with her friend, and though she seemed fine, Monica couldn't help but wonder if something had been off. There was nothing wrong with our triple kick, Monica remembered. Was Amy deflecting? Whenever she recollected like this, she felt guilty: *why didn't I chat more, I should have noticed something wasn't right*. The truth was the majority of people wouldn't have seen any signs in Amy from that conversation, but Monica prided herself on being able to judge people effectively. She could see things in people that others couldn't, so why didn't she catch this? Even now, it was almost three months later, and she always thought about what happened to her?

It was lunchtime in Hanfield High, but Monica only had time for a quick slice of toast before she went running. This was a regular activity for her when competitions were looming. It usually helped with her anxiety, but lately, it wasn't as successful. Her mind was full of too many questions, and she didn't have a single answer. The grass was still wet from the morning dew, and as she began her jog around the cross-country field, she was pleased the ground was still firm. Most didn't venture this far at lunchtime, and she relished having this big open space all to herself. It was quiet and calming despite the distant yelling of school children. The air was fresh, and as she got up to pace her breathing quickened. Following the outline of the field, she began dipping down to the lower areas at the far end, the school buildings disappearing from sight. She thought about Dana Ferhulse's return to work. She couldn't get it out of her head.

The end of the field marked the beginning of Hanfield forest. The trees in the foreground that she was running past and and the thick woodland beyond, had such darkness and depth. "What's out there?" she asked herself. She jogged parallel to the treeline, which seemed to clear at one point, and jogging past she didn't take her eyes off them. It was a better view than the empty field ahead. But in the clearing, something abruptly caught her eye. She saw a man in the trees, walking quickly with a wide grin on his face. For a moment he stared directly at her before disappearing behind more trees. She jumped back from the treeline and landed on her back. She peered into the woods, squinting her eyes to see into the shadows, as she caught her breath. Her eyes were scanning the trees as if studying lines from a book, but she couldn't see a hint of anyone out there. She looked around behind her, still aware of the distant noise of her fellow students at lunch, but there was no one nearby. She was seeing things; her mind must have been playing tricks. It was a trick of the light. She stood up, and got herself together, and continued her run. Although she wouldn't let herself believe what she saw, the menacing smile on the man's face gave her goosebumps. It may have been a shadow, but it was a creepy figure, all the same. It felt as if he was following her. She ran the next kilometre of the course in her best time so far, with the hairs on the back of her neck stood on end at the thought of the smiling man lurking nearby.

She changed and rushed along to prepare for her next class, Psychology, her favourite with Dr. Banner, who was the sort of teacher that made the subject interesting for her. Dr. Banner was older, had no sense of style. Her thick reading glasses, usually pushed up to sit on the top of her mousey brown hair, would magnify her eyes to look huge whenever she used them. She spoke so wisely that it was clear to a lot of the students she was very knowledgeable. The concept of being able to study human thoughts and behaviours was something Monica eventually wanted to do as a career. Thus, she had sought to build a great relationship with Dr. Banner. She was hoping to arrive early to this lesson as she usually did to pick her brains, something Monica could tell her teacher found amusing, but she enjoyed having a student so keen to learn her subject, nonetheless. She hurried along, power walking towards the classroom on the upper floor of the school, with a question on her mind already.

"Hi Ms," she said, walking in and taking a seat at one of the front row desks.

Dr. Banner looked up from her desk and smiled.

"I was just thinking how would one observe denial or guilt, they're both closely connected are they not?" Monica didn't have much time and needed answers, so she dove right in.

Dr. Banner, her red pen hovering over test papers, laughed, "Good afternoon Monica." She stood up and started filing the documents away with her back to her. "Denial is a coping mechanism for extreme types of stress. True denial that is - would be a subject who is unable to grasp the reality of such a situation and would behave as if it really had not occurred." She paused and looked around at Monica.

"Okay, so one might try and pass off guilt as denial perhaps?" Monica dug for the answers she needed.

"I suppose, in some cases – just like someone who has been accused of a crime will act, as if their mind is unsound, to receive leniency on a sentence." Dr. Banner continued to file away the graded tests. "There are some psychologists that will swear that everyone has a 'tell', whether it be fidgeting or being unable to make eye contact, or even something much less noticeable. It could be anything, something the subject would not be aware of."

"So that's the only way to tell the difference?" Monica asked.

"The human brain is so complex many there are many but, conversely, very few ways to tell if ultimately a person is experiencing guilt or traumatic denial." Banner paused a moment with a pensive look on her face as she often did when discussing stimulating topics with her students. "The brain really is a fascinating thing. So difficult to understand sometimes, you would have to spend years studying the subtle movements of a person to be able to give a definitive answer."

Monica slumped off the desk. This was not the sort of answer she was looking for. She felt none the wiser, and her classmates were now beginning to arrive. "Okay thanks Dr." she said, dejectedly.

"...and Monica, I do hope these are rhetorical questions rather than about anyone in particular." Banner alluded that she suspected her interest in Amy's parents.

"No one particular in mind, Ms!" Monica realised she had asked enough and proceeded to organise herself ahead of the lesson.

Monica wasn't the only person wondering why Amy's parents had bounced back so quickly. Still, for every one person stating that there was something fishy going on, there would be a whole host of people disgusted at the thought of these parents being accused of any wrongdoing.

With her hands under the desk, she finally responded to Rick's text, to say that she would indeed want to see him after school today.

VIII
Half of Bella

    Today marked twelve weeks since Bella had heard that her sister had gone missing. She sat at the bus stop scratching the dark blue nail varnish from her thumb. Thinking about how, just a few weeks ago, she wasn't the least bit worried about her. Never having known a feeling like it, her mind would always send her back to the evening she found out, when her mother came bursting through her bedroom door that night.

    "Where is your sister? She never misses a singing lesson!" Dana would keep asking her daughter.

    Bella remembered back to how her mother's voice was trembling with sheer panic, but she could tell she was trying to remain calm and keep it together.

    "Hey' teenage girl misses singing lesson!' Better call the police!" Bella dismissed her mother. As far as she was concerned, there was no cause for concern here, and at the time she was too busy to care either way.

    "Something is seriously wrong Isabella, and I will be calling the police!" Her mother snapped, turning away from the doorway and letting it slam behind her.

    At the time, Bella was sitting cross-legged on her bedroom floor: dark laminate wood with a circular, purple carpet in the centre of it, on which she would often curl up to study, her school books sprawled out around her. She was avidly reading a book she had found in the library earlier that day. It was thick and heavy; and it had an old-fashioned binding, decorated with detailed swirls and embossed symbols. She was attracted to gothic styles and artistry, much to her parents' disappointment, the walls were black apart from a dark purple feature wall that matched her purple bedding and rug. She had got away with it as Amy had been allowed to paint her walls pink. Bella had numerous posters of various rock bands, and her desk was consistently piled high with fantasy books and stories. Her preference was to stay in and get lost in a book, over socialising.

Listening to her mother walk along the landing and downstairs, she laughed to herself. It was amusing to her at the time, as she assumed that her mother was dramatically overreacting as always. The thought crossed her mind that her mother wouldn't react this way if it were her that hadn't come home one day. She didn't have much of a relationship with her sister, and, as they were twins, it was always a running joke within the family that they were opposites under the same roof. Unlike Amy, Bella would always do her own thing and keep to herself. She didn't like being the centre of attention as her sister did and preferred to sit in her room most evenings. She had a couple of friends at school but was far from the socialite Amy was.

She could now hear her mother in the kitchen below her bedroom. Bella remembered not quite being able to make out what her mother was saying but presumed that she was now on the phone to the police. The high pitched murmurs of the pointless panic in her voice grated on Bella, as she grabbed her phone connecting it to the speakers all around her bedroom so she could listen to one of her favourite bands, and drown out the distraction.

Fast forward to now and here was Bella, sitting alone at the bus stop, having gone through every emotion possible over the disappearance. She had felt anger towards her sister, for deciding to do something silly or run away. She felt resentment that Amy had left her alone with their unstable parents. Back then, she was convinced that this was undoubtedly Amy's doing, that she had run away on purpose. At the time Bella saw her as overdramatic and attention-seeking, so it had always been clear to her that Amy would have taken it upon herself to run away.

As the weeks passed with no sign of Amy, the anger and the resentment had begun to fade away, leaving Bella with a sense of loss. Right now, she was way past thinking Amy had gone off her own accord. She had now lost someone who had been by her side right from birth. As she was beginning to grieve this loss, she started to think, what if Amy hadn't taken it upon herself to disappear, what if someone had taken her?

This idea had been haunting her for a couple of days now. She couldn't help it. She was convinced. When she thought of all the people that would have the motive to carry this out, it seemed to be a gateway into utter paranoia. Amy was so well known in Hanfield as being the 'it' girl. She had everything, and with that comes jealousy which then, so easily becomes motive. There were many people Bella had in mind. She had made a list of names in her notebook, the same notebook she would usually use to jot down her feelings and her poems. She had an incredible imagination. Being an introvert, she used various journals and her writing as an escape, rarely concerned as to who came across them and read them. She didn't care for anyone's approval, or their opinion, whether it be good or bad. It allowed her to feel free.

But now the deep red notebook, dog eared and damaged, was being kept by her side at all times. She couldn't risk anyone getting hold of this book. She was now in a world where she didn't know who she could trust. She found herself seeing people differently, paying attention to everyone's subtle movements and actions. Her usual behaviour was to sit and watch, and she was almost entirely off the grid anyway, so no-one was aware of her analysis of them;,noting everything down in her book, like a detective or a secret spy.

Most of the community didn't even know she belonged to the Ferhulse family at all, let alone that she was Amy's twin. Sometimes she would overhear locals talking about Amy, about her parents having murdered or abused her. They would continue gossiping like this in front of Bella not knowing who she was. Sometimes she felt a desire to correct these strangers, whether in the shops, on the bus, or in class. She would feel the temptation, but she held back. She would later tell herself it was an advantage for her to remain invisible to most.

Their opinions didn't matter anyway, Bella knew her sister was still alive. She was never close to Amy, but they could always feel each other. Knowing her sister was out there somewhere, her thoughts on the disappearance had shifted from it being due to Amy's attention driven personality, to instead, being down to someone in her home town knowing exactly what had happened to her and where she was. Bella was now determined enough to find out what had happened that day. But with no solid leads to go off, she would all too often let herself just get lost in her paranoid thoughts.

The number 32 bus pulled up at the bus stop. Described as a tin can on wheels you could hear the engine before seeing the vehicle itself. The once red and yellow paint peeling away to reveal great patches of rust. It had begun to rain again, as it frequently did lately. The sky above was so grey with rain clouds, it had made it almost dark outside. Bella didn't hurry from the shelter to the bus, any more than she usually would. She didn't mind getting wet. It was just life to her, and she didn't worry about things like rain. Her clothes and hair damp now from the brief exposure to the downpour, she stepped onto the bus in her quiet, yet self-assured way, showed her student card and took a seat.

Bella wasn't heading anywhere specifically. She knew who the bus driver was. Amy regularly took this bus during his shift, and recently Bella had been tracing Amy's steps. To be able to fit in all her extracurricular activities, Amy would stick to a strict routine. Bella had thought of all the people who saw Amy everyday, and Bill, the bus driver, was one of them, so he made it onto the list. Bill would have been on shift during the morning and afternoon school rush. More importantly, he would have been driving when she headed to her singing lesson after school, the singing lesson she missed. Bella calculated that Bill would see Amy two or three times each day. Bill had no wife and no family. He lived on his own and often, a faint odour of alcohol lingered around him. Any lead is better than no lead, and so she decided to ride the bus to check it out, although what she was looking for she didn't quite know.

Out of the window to her left, she watched town landmarks, houses, and stores pass by, the images made hazy by the condensation that was beginning to collect on the glass. Sat towards the front of the bus it felt busier than usual with people avoiding the

The Familiar Encounter

weather. She was at an angle whereby she could just about see Bill in the driver's cab, his meaty arms wrestling the large steering wheel, elbows sticking out. With a long, ear splitting screech of the breaks, he proceeded to stop slowly to let more people on board. When the automatic doors opened, the cotton wool-like hairs on the top of his head would waft in the breeze. Greeting everyone with a huge smile and a broad 'How are ya?' Bella found it curious that his smile would quickly disappear once the passenger had passed by and moved down the aisle. She watched him in the mirror, his resting expression becoming more of a scowl, with excess skin on his old face weighed down like the jowls of a bulldog, making his eyes appear tiny. He would snort and sniff every few moments, frequently wiping his nose along and up his arm with a grunt.

She rode the bus from her home stop through the busy town square and up through the tree lined avenues to the small estate off Hansen Road. All the while, Bella studied Bill carefully, looking for a sign, anything at all that would show this guy was fishy. When she had carried out research in the library, she hadn't found much on him, apart from realising he had been in the same year as her father in school. She had decided to dig deeper and had recently brought the subject of Bill up at the dinner table to provoke her father's opinion.

"Bill the bus driver is so friendly! I'd never taken the bus much before, but he had a jolly old smile on his face when I got on, which picked up my day." Bella's comment was out of character, but she could count on her parents not to pick up on this. She felt virtually invisible to them at the best of times, and now, with their focus on Amy more than ever, she could act any way she wanted, without worrying that they would question it.

"Oh, Billy! He was a real laugh in school - is he still the bus driver? He's been working on those buses his whole life. Hasn't changed a bit I'll bet!" Richard said, shaking his head to himself as if he were wondering where the years had gone as he always did when anything from his past came up.

"Did he like buses in school then?" Bella wanted to keep on the topic.

"Yes, he always used to have these little toy buses. The guys and I used to give him such a tough time in school. He was a weird kid really but such a laugh." her father recalled, stuffing a large fork full of pie into his mouth.

That was when Bella put a red mark against Bill's name in her notebook. Being bullied by her father as a motive was a stretch, but she needed something.

Eventually, the bus would turn around Bella thought, and head back towards her home stop. She could sit tight, get what she needed from the trip and then she'd be home, with minimum effort required. She didn't think she would draw attention to herself; she never drew attention to herself. But Bella could see as people were getting off and on at the various stops, Bill was looking over at her, he had realised that she wasn't getting off the bus.

"Hey... hey young lady, are you lost?" Bill asked while driving down Sycamore Avenue, changing gear sloppily causing the old engine to crunch.

Bella needed to think. Her plan had been foiled. She wasn't as invisible to everyone as she thought and she would now need to come up with an excuse to stay on the bus, having passed all the stops so far. She couldn't think of one.

"You got me! I'm lost, I'm heading for the diner", she said quickly, frustrated at herself that now she would need to change buses after all.

"You've missed the closest stop, love. You want to be getting off on Canopy Street in three stops time darlin'. That's the closest you'll be getting now on this bus." he said, followed by a sharp grunt while he cleared his throat.

She remembered she had some missing posters in her backpack, something her mother insisted she always carry and hand out whenever the opportunity arose. Bella figured that since she was now heading for the diner, she may as well hand a few out. It would save this massive farce from being a complete waste of time.

Looking at the time on her phone she realised it would be packed full of students by now and a knot formed in her tummy, and she had to quickly shake it off. She told herself that it could lead to something, and to just do it. It would take at least another 30 mins for the bus to come along home, so she may as well put the free time to good use.

Her prediction wasn't wrong, the diner was full of her classmates, but she got on with what she was there to do. As she began handing out the missing posters, she could sense the change in atmosphere. Part of the crowd in the diner was silent. She received more sympathetic looks than usual, as she worked her way around handing out the posters, trying to get in and out of this overcrowded extension of school as quickly as possible. Her ears pricked up as she overheard part of a conversation between a group of girls. One of the girls she didn't even recognise mentioned the words "...that's the sister of the missing girl", and the knot in her stomach cinched tighter as she realised people were starting to make the connection. Her incognito cover had been blown. Now she would need to be more careful when it came to working through her growing list of suspects.

She made her way over to the far end of the diner. Near the pool table, she handed a poster over to Scott Bowers. There was something about the way he was looking at her and it stood out as if he had seen a ghost. She knew who he was, one of the most popular guys in school. He was on her list, as were many of the Hanfield Heartbeats by default. But Scott's skin had lost all colour and his eyes became wide as he gawked at her.

She had never seen him up close before. There was no doubt that he was good looking, and of course, he had the charisma to match. Not that he ever spoke to her, but his confidence was something she had observed in class. However, this didn't explain the sudden look of horror on his face. His reaction to her posters was in contrast to the usual sympathetic small talk from people that she was used to.

Although she planned to keep looking into Bill, Scott was the highlight of her mission this afternoon. In order to grab some air and brainstorm after the stuffy diner, she decided to walk home. The rain was only very light now, and she smiled with the thought of her findings, having acquired a real clue for the first time.

IX
Those That Walk at Night

    He was riding his bike down the back lanes behind the school, along paths that students often used in the evenings during the summer months but were warned against after dark. He headed out through the open meadows, through poppies in flower, having a hard time in the breeze. He peddled faster following the trail through the forest. This part always seemed eerie to Scott. He would get a chill down the back of his spine at the thought of what remained undiscovered in the thick, dark woods. These thoughts were fleeting though, as he had other things on his mind today. He felt hesitant about this evening's plans. He had already agreed to volunteer with Izzy, but he didn't have any experience. As with the woods around him, it was the unknown he was unsure of.
    He would be meeting Izzy and other members of the 'Help a Hand' organisation at Cliff Edge Care Home. He had never realised it existed before, a large converted manor house outside the town centre. It had been well developed but was surrounded by the woods. He was running late, as usual. Pushing himself to go faster along the trail, he could hear crows cackling and smaller birds singing in the trees as he passed by. He had too much on his mind to enjoy the lovely weather, worrying that he wouldn't have anything

The Familiar Encounter

to talk about with the elderly. He'd have nothing in common with any of them.

Coming onto a straight flat country road, he knew he was getting closer. He could almost see part of the vast old-style mansion amongst the trees. Pedalling nearer, the full scale of the building was revealed. It was just like his internet search had promised. 'Cliff Edge Care Home is a stunning country mansion, set in the heart of Hanfield beautiful trees and wildlife.' The place had grand stone walls surrounding it leading up to a large, iron gate, ornately decorated with strange goblins and monsters, a detail Scott didn't question.

He couldn't see anyone around, and as the gate was open, he proceeded to bike along the dusty ground towards the massive front door. He was never worried about his bike getting stolen somewhere like this, so he stood it against one of the side posts outside, before climbing the stone steps and cautiously opening the door.

Relief washed over him as he heard Izzy's enthusiastic voice, and following her high-pitched sounds, he entered. As he rounded the corner from the entranceway, an older lady in light blue coveralls waved at him intensely to get his attention as she approached.

"So, we have another one!" She said while fishing for something in one of the large trouser pockets. "You'll have to sign in young man, volunteer or not!" She pulled out a pen and putting it into his hand she ushered him over to the far corner of the foyer towards a polished oak table.

"Of course, thank you." Scott looked at the book. Pages upon pages of columns. He could see from the previous names on the visitor log, that he would now be the final volunteer to arrive. Izzy's handwriting was unmistakable, big and bubbly, with little crosses above the 'i's and he smiled.

"You made it! I was beginning to get a tad worried!" Izzy walked over wearing a funky blue and yellow jumper, "...are you ready for some thrilling company!" Most would think she was being sarcastic, but she wasn't.

Izzy kissed Scott quickly, grabbed his hand and led him through to a room which probably covered a quarter of the entire ground floor. He had never been to a care home before, but he knew it was a common room of sorts. There was an original feature fireplace, and chairs were scattered around. There was an area with a chess table, some bookshelves, and over at the far end were some more comfortable looking chairs in front of a large bay window. Like the rest of the building, the room looked as though it hadn't been decorated for decades. There was a strong smell of antiseptic, and it reminded him of a doctor's waiting room.

He saw a petite lady over by the group wearing the uniform blue overalls. She had a badge on that read;

Cliff Edge
Candice Sommers
Team Manager

"...thank you all so much for giving up your free time to bring some companionship back into our patients' lives. Now don't be shy, feel free to initiate a conversation." With that, Izzy let go of Scott's hand and walked straight over to an old man sitting on his own. This sort of thing came so naturally to Izzy. It made Scott feel bad that he didn't know where to start. Looking around the room, he walked over to the closest bookcase and examined the kind of books on offer. They were mostly dull-sounding history books with a few classics sprinkled here and there. On the lower shelf of the cabinet was a stack of old, battered looking board games. He picked up the game of draughts, although he had no idea how to play. He was soon approached by Candice.

"I know someone that would love to play draughts, would you like to be introduced?" she said quietly.

"Sure!" Scott was beginning to think that this could be the longest couple of hours of his life.

"Mrs. Samuel used to teach at your High School. Follow me."

Weaving through the clusters of residents sat at tables attempting jigsaws, asleep with their mouths wide open, or simply staring into the distance Scott followed Candice over to the far end of the room where an elderly lady sat in front of the large bay window. She had a cup of tea and a crossword puzzle in front of her.

Her hair was grey, shoulder-length and frizzy. Her skin was very wrinkled, and the old chair she was sat in was swallowing her small frame. As she slowly looked up from her crossword, a sweet smile formed on her face.

"Mrs. Samuels, meet Scott. He's a young lad from the 'Help a Hand' volunteers' scheme. He would like to play draughts with you".

The Familiar Encounter

Mrs. Samuels didn't say anything, but her smile broadened, and her eyes sparkled above her rounded cheeks.

Candice turned to Scott. "Don't be shy, take a seat. Mrs. Samuels hasn't any family and has been with us for some time; she's our oldest patient by far at 102. Sit down, sit down!" Candice said before walking off and leaving him to it.

Scott stood there for a moment. The old lady looked very frail, she still hadn't said anything and given her age, it crossed his mind she may not even be able to hold a conversation. He noticed she looked at him as though he was familiar to her. He had never met anyone so old before and Scott questioned if she still had all of her faculties. She picked up her teacup, and her fragile arm shook as she slowly brought it to her thin lips, concentrating on only this.

"May I sit here?" Scott asked politely, but the silence was only broken by loud slurps of the tea rather than a response. So Scott took a seat opposite the old lady. He looked out of the large window beside him onto a vast garden. It had lots of plants and flower beds, and some smaller trees with bird feeders hanging from them. It was a strange thought, but he decided this would have been the spot in which he would have chosen to sit, if he were a resident. It was not a bad view.

Mrs. Samuels was now concentrating on putting down the small teacup. Scott could see that although she was still smiling, it was taking a lot of effort and he got up and leaned over to help her.

Scott noticed the crossword puzzle in front of her again. "You've got a few there. I've never been able to get my head around those things".

Mrs. Samuels smiled at Scott, looking into his eyes.

"Would you like to take a break from it and we can play a game of draughts? I've never played before, but I'm guessing if you're one of the oldest in here, you've probably played all those games a tonne. Would you like to show me the rules?"

Mrs. Samuels was silent but gestured toward the draughts set in agreement.

"I suppose I could just use the instructions on the box here." He set up the board awkwardly. "I'll be black."

Mrs. Samuel's hand reached for a counter and pushed it to one of the black squares on the board. They began to play, and as the time passed, it became clear she was very good at the game. Scott realised that he was enjoying her company, despite the fact they were only communicating through smiles and their moves on the draught board. He wondered if she was deaf or just unable to talk. Being so old he thought it was safe to assume that it could be a bit of both. He looked down at the draught board and compared his hand with hers, noticing her frail, skeletal fingers push the counters around, using as little force as possible. Her skin looked translucent, while his hands were solid and sturdy.

He saw a thin band around her right wrist. It was pretty but very simple—a silver dainty chain with a gold egg-shaped pendant on it.

"That's a nice bracelet!" Still feeling the need to make small talk he gestured towards her wrist as she looked up at him.

As he suspected, there was no response from Mrs. Samuels other than a smile, and taking her left hand, she stroked the egg-shaped pendant, as if thinking back to a distant memory.

The atmosphere in the large room was better than Scott had expected, and his fellow students were now all sat with someone, either chatting or playing a game. Izzy was dancing to a record at the far side of the room with the elderly man she had initially approached. She was smiling from ear to ear, being spun around in a ballroom dance. The record player would crackle every so often, but no one seemed to mind. He could think of other things he would usually be doing after school at this time of the day, but at that moment he was genuinely glad he had been convinced to spend time with Mrs. Samuels. He looked at Izzy with a sense of gratitude.

As Mrs. Samuels had reacted to his comment about the bracelet, he thought he should continue to talk, even if she wasn't able to answer him. It was as if he was talking to himself, but it would perhaps keep her entertained

"So, I'll bet you have seen some things being 102?" He made his move on the draughts board, and she watched closely as he did.

"I guess this place can get boring sometimes though." Mrs. Samuels looked up at him and smiled as if to agree, moving her draughts piece another square over.

"You're so far away from everything over here though, it must be quite peaceful... the garden looks like a great place." He moved his counter, and she jumped up slightly, pushing hers and knocking one of his off the board. She was thrilled to be winning another game.

His time at Cliff Edge was almost up, as he could see Candice make her way over to them.

"Okay you two, it's time for Scott to get home. The visiting hours are almost up." She walked on by leaving them to finish off the game.

"Well, Mrs. Samuels, it was a pleasure." He began putting the draughts counters back in the box, "Same time next week?" he asked, rhetorically.

She leaned over and grasped his arm, squeezing it gently to get his attention again. Scott looked at her, and she pointed frailly at the pendant on her wrist.

"This is from those that walk at night." It was the first time she had spoken in the two hours he had been sitting there. "Your answers are with them." Her voice was croaky and dry.

"Wh-what?" Anyone else would have assumed this to be the ramblings of a crazy elderly person, but it grabbed Scott's attention.

"They walk at night," she whispered, as Candice walked back over to them both.

"Okay Scott, have we said our goodbyes?" Candice asked. Mrs. Samuels smiled her big smile and nodded.

Scott didn't know what to say. He was now the one that was speechless after her strange words. He rose from his seat and walked with Candice to sign out.

"You did well with Mrs. Samuels. She isn't much of a talker, so some folk feel awkward around her. In fact, she's not said a word for years, but you seemed to connect and get along fine. I hope to see you again next week Scott. Take care." Candice was busy and didn't stay but went back into the large room to attend to someone else.

Izzy was waiting outside by Scott's bike. When she caught sight of him, she couldn't help but rush over excitedly, kissing him all over his face as she always did. Peck, peck, peck.

"WELL?" She got such a buzz from new experiences, her energy always giving Scott a lift, and he laughed.

"As surprised as I am at myself for saying this, it was actually... quite fun!" It was impossible to match Izzy's enthusiasm, but Scott always tried his best. He wheeled his bike alongside Izzy for a while as they talked. It was starting to get dark now and Izzy was full of stories from the man she had been chatting to for the last couple of hours. Scott listened and responded appropriately, but he kept his brief conversation with Mrs. Samuels to himself.

As they arrived at the bus stop for Izzy's ride home, they said their 'goodbyes'. They would see each other the following morning at school, and mounting his bike to ride home, he felt drops of rain on his face. Although it was still hot outside the rain clouds were setting in. *This weather! Make your mind up.* As he tried to beat yet another downpour home, he was unsettled by Mrs. Samuel's comments. He needed to know what she meant by 'those that walk at night'. There had always been something strange going on around the borders of Hanfield. He realised that from the moment he moved here. From Amy's disappearance to the unexplored woods, and the old history stories of strange creatures living in the woodlands always had the sense that there was something mysterious going on. Pedalling home along the back roads he recalled the egg-shaped pendant on her wrist and wondered what it symbolised, and he made a decision to visit the old library tomorrow at school. Maybe he would strike lucky and discover what Mrs. Samuels was talking about. He had so many puzzle pieces, but what did they all mean? He needed answers.

By the time Scott arrived home, his dinner was waiting for him. His parents had a simple routine. They maintained the wholesome tradition of sitting down together each evening to eat, and they had both eagerly awaited Scott's return.

"Oh, look Henry... he enters!" His mother commented, while getting up from her old, worn settee. His parents were retired working class. Scott's family home was quaintly decorated in keeping with his mother's taste for floral patterns, kitchen lino, and a fold away table and chairs, that appeared out of place

"I'll go ahead and reheat the cod." Scott's mother made her way over to the kitchen wearing a faded, ankle length dressing gown. She wasn't much of a cook and to reheat fish would soon prove to be a big mistake.

Scott's father, a retired Marine, decided to move his family to Hanfield on a whim. Many months ago, biting into an apple, he noticed the small sticker reading "Hanfield Fallen Apples", and doing anything to ease his newly retired boredom, he went to look it up. Reading about it as being one of the most peaceful towns, and being a quiet man, who didn't often speak unless he had something to say, he fell in love with the place. Scott's parents had a yin and yang type of relationship. His father was a man of few words, whereas his mother was a woman of many.

Serving up the soggy fish to both men sat at the pull-out wooden table, she kissed Scott on the forehead, as always.

"How was your day, pumpkin?" Taking her seat, she picked up the serving spoon, her intricate false nails with their purple diamanté reflecting the light and sparkling like disco balls, as she spooned a type of fluffy mashed potato with chives on to each plate. "I met this awesome old lady... feels weird saying that but she was so interesting! She was 102 and kept beating me at draughts." Scott told his mother and father, missing out the minor detail of Mrs. Samuel's intriguing comment.

"I'm so glad Pumpkin! Do you think you'll do it again?" as she transferred mash on to her fork along with soggy the cod, it was challenging to say which was which.

"I'll be going back with Izzy next week!" Scott said.

"Just you be careful!" his father warned, "I tell ya, it's getting too dark to be biking about through them woods." Parents around Hanfield had become worried since Amy's disappearance, especially now that summer would soon be at an end.

"Oh, Henry! The boy's doing some good!" His mother scowled in his father's direction for a moment, before shifting her gaze back to Scott, her expression softening into a smile. As an only child, he was the apple of her eye.

The following morning at school, Scott was feeling tired, and unsure if his dodgy tummy was down to his mother's cooking or the mystery going around in his head. The answers he needed weren't coming to him as he tossed and turned in bed all night. It seemed to him that the more answers he longed for, the more questions he had. There had to be someone out there who knew what was going on, who could give him answers.

He had football practise after school, so his only opportunity to do any research at all that day would be during lunchtime. His pre-lunch Chemistry lesson went by slowly, even with his lab partner Danny asking him for further girl advice every moment they had. Mr. Malick didn't yell at them this time.

They were experimenting on observing what happened to various items when put under pressure. As Scott tweezed the small, green leaf into the little machine, Danny started the timer.

"I don't know what to open with. Ya' know?" Danny whispered to Scott as they sat staring at the leaf beginning to wither.

"Confidence is key." Scott responded. "You gotta act like you're confident, girls like that... I think?"

"Yeah totally... so if I mention that I've liked her for the last three years?" Danny was clueless.

"No, Danny mate – far too much! Maybe say you think she looks pretty today." Scott was trying to focus on the experiment, and give Danny sound advice, but all he could think of was getting to the library.

The bell rang for lunch. As was the norm in practical Chemistry classes the boys hadn't finished tidying up their equipment after the science experiment.

"I've got to rush off. I'll owe you one, Dan..." Scott left, and headed straight for the school library before Danny could even react.

The library was somewhere he hadn't previously spent too much time, which was reflected in the quality of his schoolwork. He always prioritised socialising with Izzy and his friends. Scott knew they would be looking for him over lunch but would never guess he would be in the library, so he could conduct his investigation without distraction.

The library was distinctly older than the rest of the building. It was the original school, and it had been converted when they expanded the school to meet the demand of new families moving into Hanfield in the forties. It was anyone's guess how old the library was with its dark, shuddering wooden floors, and its dense, timber bookshelves arranged in narrow rows, that blocked out the natural light streaming through letterbox style windows positioned along the top of the walls.

While trying to navigate the large room, he walked along the rows, observing the categories marked by hand with a permanent marker.

Trying to make the most of his lunch hour he asked the librarian at the front desk.

"History of Hanfield you say? Er, yeah you wanna be looking under the General History section, or if it's a specific subject feel free to use our computers over there to the right. But please don't ask me how to use those... I'm for books only." The librarian laughed, pointing over to a row of old desktop computers seemingly from the mid nineties.

Sitting down at a computer, he first typed "Hanfield Egg Pendant" into the search field, and, after taking a few minutes to load the results, the screen displayed various newspaper clippings from over the years with unhelpful headlines;

"Hanfield Hens Laying Fewer Eggs!" and "Are Eggs Really Good For You?"

Finding nothing of use, he changed his search to "Those that Walk at Night", and waited......

"Hanfield Sponsored Night Walk!"

Scott huffed. This was harder than he first thought. He went on to search for some keywords; "Hanfield Girl Missing: Night: Egg."

Which brought up droves of articles about Amy Ferhulse. As Scott scrolled and scanned, he had the sensation of being watched. From the corner of his eye, he realised he wasn't the only one staring at his computer screen and turned his head to discover Bella Ferhulse, standing watching him.

His mind flashed back to the moment he locked eyes with her at the diner as she passed him the 'missing' poster. The similarity in her facial expressions made him nervous as Amy once had. This time Bella's expression wasn't as blank as before, she was scowling at him, and for a moment he wondered why. Looking back at his computer screen he realised.

"Creep much?" Bella asked, referring to his searching for Amy. "You weirdos obsessed with a young girl going missing make me sick." She kept her voice down, but her words were punishing, and he flushed red.

"This doesn't look good, but I can explain... I think?" Was Scott actually about to reveal all? What else could he do to excuse this action? "You see I knew your sister. I was..."

"Yes... and? Who didn't know her?" Bella cut in. "Explain yourself otherwise, I'm going to the police!" Still keeping her tone lowered, despite the threat.

"It's a long story! I don't think her disappearance is straightforward... this town is... weird!" Panicking, Scott blurted out his thoughts to her. But to his surprise, the two frown lines between her eyebrows began to lessen and she sat down on the seat beside him.

"Weird?... How then?" Bella questioned.

"Well firstly this whole massive forest, and all the stories of ghouls and such! I've never heard anything like it! Just weird stuff Bella... it is Bella, right? ...But yeah in comparison to other towns I've lived in, the place is spooky – and I've moved around a fair bit. No one seems to question or notice any of it!" As Bella didn't seem annoyed with him now, he decided to open up and get some thoughts off his chest. *Oh crap, this is not good.* Scott didn't think Amy's sister was the right person to be telling his suspicions to but what other option did he have? "It's all questionable to me. I can't help myself!" Scott paused as a student walked past "...and admittedly, I am curious to know where your sister is Bella. That's not a crime!"

Sitting back in her seat, she paused to think for a moment, before pulling her chair in closer to Scott. Her mood wasn't as confrontational anymore.

"I'm sorry for going off on you. I'm so used to people gossiping about my family... Come on then, tell me what you know, no judgment from me."

"You won't believe me." Scott was nervous to tell her the full details of what had happened so far. *She's going to think I'm a nutjob.*

"I will believe more than you think." Her mood had changed, and Scott was seeing a softer side to Bella. The twins were more alike than he first thought.

X
Family Secrets

Another day as the victim family. Richard was entirely fed up with feeling this way and his frustration had reached breaking point. He couldn't sleep at night, he couldn't concentrate during the day, and his wife wasn't making him happy. Yet another morning going through the motions of his usual routine before work. The tension with Dana was now unbearable, and would be even worse following an argument the night before; an argument he didn't even remember but would be punished for, nonetheless. But this was just the way things were now.

    He missed his quirky, happy Amy most of all when feeling this way. On these stressful mornings he wasn't able to shake the feeling that he had taken his daughter's positive energy for granted. Amy had qualities that he had disregarded but now missed more than anything. Her outlook on life was contagious, and it now appeared to have been the only thing that lifted the home's atmosphere, holding his marriage with Dana together. Now, all that was left was the glaring possibility that they were no longer right for each other. It was the marriage he would always refer to as 'magical' whenever anyone asked, but he now felt trapped and suffocated, and had done so for some time.

Turning off the shower he heard the coffee machine downstairs loudly grinding the beans. His heart sank realising Dana had woken up early and he would need to see her before leaving for work. Not what he needed before another long day in the office. He had hung today's suit on the wardrobe door, and as he began knotting the navy-blue silk tie, he decided to grab breakfast at the office and head off as soon as possible. He couldn't take the poison of her contempt towards him now. Richard hated feeling stuck, permanently dwelling on his rapidly deteriorating situation.

Entering the large kitchen to collect his workday lunchbox, walking through towards the fridge, he noticed Dana sat at the breakfast bar holding a cup of coffee between both hands, her elbows leaning on the surface. There was a fresh bowl of cereal laid out next to her for Richard. Noticing this, Richard knew all too well that despite it appearing to be a peace offering, it was anything but. It was simply an invitation to jump back into some sort of disagreement, it always was.

"Good Morning", Dana said bluntly, her eyes rising from staring into her coffee cup, watching the steam drift into the air.

Richard didn't need to look over in her direction to see she looked tired. He had heard her get up numerous times during the night. Her light red hair was unbrushed, eyes dark and puffy. Still in her peach and white pyjamas, he realised this to be her usual state when at home now, rather than the glamorously groomed, energetic drama teacher that everyone knew. Now she was merely the wife that took him for granted. The worry, sleepless nights and lack of makeup made her look much older, he noticed. He allowed his mind to drift back to past mornings waking up next to her when they would talk and laugh all morning. He remembered adoring her natural, flawless beauty. Richard felt a sadness wash over him as he recalled once feeling so happy. He wondered where it had all gone wrong.

He started to wish her a 'Good Morning' in return but stopped himself. He didn't see the point anymore. He continued to walk over to the large, American-style fridge and grab one of the three Tupperware boxes containing pre-prepared salsa salads, which he loathed. He stuffed it into his black backpack with his fresh gym-wear before zipping it shut. Richard didn't like having his routine disrupted but even the laid out cereal bowl didn't entice him. He didn't have the energy for any more arguments.

Silently walking out, he headed to his study. It wasn't looking as tidy as he usually liked to keep it. He had been busy preparing the necessary financial forecasting sheets for next year's plans. The work was complicated, and trying to meet demands with budgets that didn't stretch anywhere near close enough to cover all costs involved, was another source of stress for Richard. He gathered the papers from his desk to organise into his briefcase, and as an anxious knot materialised in the pit of his stomach, he sighed to himself.

Grabbing the black leather briefcase and placing it on top of his desk, he used the combination to unlock and open it. Just one glance revealed that something wasn't right. There were irregularities. Items had been moved. A profound dread and panic came over Richard as he pulled out a few papers. Searching for the most important file, his brow became moist, and his mouth dry. He stood in disbelief.

"No... no... what the...?" He murmured to himself as he frantically fingered through the handful of files and papers. Still, the essential file wasn't to be seen. "This is impossible!"

Richard stuffed the remaining papers back into the briefcase and walked out onto the spacious driveway where his Audi sat. Its navy-blue, metallic body shining in the bright morning sun.

He jogged over to the boot of his car, but nothing other than his golf bag sat there. *Where the hell is it?* Getting straight into the driver's seat, and causing the engine to roar to a start, he reversed, before screeching off towards his work office.

"It must be at the office... I've become sloppy lately. I'm so tired... Stupid, stupid..." Richard shouted to himself while weaving in and out of lanes, overtaking and undertaking, in a desperate attempt to get to his desk at work. The sweat on his forehead was now beading and he was deaf to other drivers beeping him over the sound of his heartbeat in his ears.

He pulled his car into the bay, grabbed the once precious briefcase from the passenger seat and marched up the stairs into the grey building. Almost knocking over the decorative leafy plants in the middle of the foyer, he ignored the beaming Stephanie as she sat at reception, wishing him a great day.

Unlike the home office, Richard's office at work was over-organized. He loved this office. In recent weeks it had become an even more important sanctuary, shielding him from the unwanted stares of his colleagues and the outside world. He understood that being the father of a missing child, he was a source of curiosity for the small town, and even more so with the rumours circulating of his suspicious involvement. But Richard didn't mind the gossiping whispers circulating about him because they weren't true. He would never harm his daughter. Often in the quiet afternoons, rather than mingle with others in the staff room as he used to enjoy, he would busy himself with organising files, keeping the computer's software up to date and filling his schedule, making his assistant somewhat redundant.

But he needed to find the file he had been keeping safe all this time. It was his secret weapon, and equally, the only item that could ruin his reputation and his career entirely. Opening all the drawers in his desk, he filtered through the papers, messing up his colour coded, alphabetically organised, sub-categorised system that he had so fastidiously created.

"Damn it! Damn it to hell!" He was shaking and started when a knock sounded on his frosted glass door.

"Hi there, Sir, did you need any help with anything?" Stephanie asked, clearly having noted his hurried entrance into the office.

"No!" He blasted before lowering his voice to use a softer tone, "No... thank you, Steph."

So keen to help she backed awkwardly out of the doorway until the clouded glass door had closed behind her.

Richard stood upright and, closing his eyes, he began to think. He started to retrace his steps in his mind, trying to remember where he would have left the incriminating file.

I had it with me before the meeting. I took it out and discussed it at length with strategy manager, Brian Whindipp. He told me to keep it quiet until the dinner with the Mayor, and so I kept it in my briefcase. I last saw it on Wednesday when my briefcase was opened in the copy room... the copy room! I must have filed it away with some other items.

Richard walked purposefully across the office. The workstations occupied by council administrators were only half full at this point, as his colleagues were still arriving for the day. Richard knew he only had a few files in that copy room. It would be locked away, but even so, the thought that the documents had not been in his possession for the best part of a week made him feel weak at the knees. He knew only too well that locks could be picked and accessed in no time by anyone who knew what they were doing.

When he arrived at the row of grey filing cabinets over on the far side of the small copy room, he shuffled through a few tiny silver keys before finding the correct one. He went over to the drawer praying he would find the folder nestled in amongst the various maps and figures of the town. He unlocked and opened the drawer, and there it was; HIGHLY CONFIDENTIAL 04-2019

As Richard pulled out the file, he felt a difference in its weight. His heart dropped, and as he opened it, he found a solitary envelope, his name scribbled on the front in a hand that he didn't recognise. He looked around him, suddenly feeling as though he was being scrutinised. His personal space had been invaded by someone, and that 'someone' had taken his private files.

He shoved the envelope into the inside pocket of his suit jacket and returned to the privacy of his office, to open it.

He sat at his desk: his mouth was dry, and he was sweating profusely now. His fingers trembled as he carefully opened the envelope. It held a single, cream sheet of paper on which was messy, hurried handwriting:

> Climbing your way to the top, keeping your head down,
> Getting a long way in Hanfield without a frown.
> The wholesome life to some,
> But dig deeper and it's numb.
> Meet me beneath the overpass outside the town tonight,
> Or all your darkest secrets, the townspeople will sight.

Reading the poem, he sat back in his chair and let out a shuddering sigh. He couldn't imagine who this person might be. He didn't recognise the handwriting, and although he could think of plenty of people from his past that would want to ruin him now, he couldn't imagine anyone that would go to these lengths. This was calculated and planned. He couldn't have foreseen anything like this. Surely it would have to be someone with access to the office, a colleague, someone he saw every day. Someone who had counted on him discovering it today. Maybe even a colleague he had had round for dinner? He found it hard to picture who this could be.

He had no idea what he was letting himself in for. It couldn't be a joke as the contents of the file were too important and only a select few knew of it. It had to be something more sinister. Being well practised at judging situations, he knew this was far more than a light-hearted mocking, and so he had to prepare himself for the worst.

Richard felt he could safely assume this was going to develop into blackmail. He remained seated as he asked himself what these secrets meant to him, and how much he was willing to pay to keep them hidden until the time was right for their revelation. Overwhelmed, he quickly stood up and slammed his fist into the wall behind him, causing the framed photo of him and Dana looking happily into each other's eyes on their wedding day, to fall and smash on the floor below. Then it hit home. Dana had done this. The poem was just her style, and she would be vicious enough right now, to realise the magnitude of the threat to Richard. Everyone in the office knew who she was. It would be easy for her to walk past reception without anyone batting an eye, and plant the envelope, perhaps even using Richard's very own keys, at night while he slept, uninterrupted. He could ask to investigate the CCTV, but he didn't want anyone asking too many questions.

He assured himself that he knew exactly how to handle her. She had worried herself sick with Amy's disappearance, and distrusting everyone, she was now out to ruin him. Things had truly gone sour in their marriage, and the sadness he had felt at their dying relationship that very morning, disappeared into a pit of fiery rage. He took out his phone and proceeded to draft a new text to the contact affectionately called 'My Apple', with a sneer on his face and a sly look in his eye.

'My darling Apple, I have missed how we used to be together. Meet me at our restaurant this evening. I will be finished with today's business by 6 o'clock. Always yours, Richard.'

He sent the message and carefully stowing the poem safely into his desk drawer, he continued with his work. He would not allow the issue to intrude further until he needed it to, he instructed himself. But this was easier said than done, and throughout the day, his stomach churned.

Lately there were times he had felt he was clinging to his sanity with the finest of threads. He felt as though he had stepped into an alternative universe; as if he was existing in someone else's reality, but it had to be a nightmare, his nightmare. He knew now that someone was after him, someone was out to destroy his world further, and maybe Amy's disappearance was all a part of it too. *It could only be Dana.*

As the clock hit 6 pm, he experienced a surge of anticipation. Leaving work, he got into his car, which was parked over two spaces due to the morning's panic. He drove to the fairly standard restaurant, located just outside of town. Always trying to convert a bad situation into an opportunity, he smiled smugly, to himself. He was going to get his revenge on Dana for crossing the line.

He parked his polished car alongside a black Mini Cooper with a 'fire truck red' trim. He sniggered to himself, hardly able to contain his excitement, it was *her* car. Entering the restaurant and making his way over to a woman at a table in the far corner, who was smiling seductively at him. He sat down opposite Ms. Rhompski, the Russian admin manager. She had also come straight from work to meet Richard as her long brown hair was draped in a messy bun. She wore a crisp white fitted shirt with a necklace hanging just below her collarbone, drawing attention to her cleavage. Her dark red lipstick matched her nail polish. There was an aura around Ms. Rhompski, which warned people not to mess with her. She was a different breed of woman to Dana.

They had met two years previously, when she began working as an admin assistant to Richard. It was a relationship that quickly evolved into a mindless affair. It had ended abruptly when Amy had discovered the two of them, before running away. Richard had become blasé with the secret, and they had been meeting at the family home.

They hadn't so much as texted since Amy had gone missing, but Ms. Rhompski was one of the few people who knew exactly what was in the missing file. Like Richard, she stood to make a lot of money from the plans and lose just as much if they were revealed early.

"My Flower!" Richard kissed Rhompski on the cheek twice, leaning over the table. A public display of affection he would never have chanced before.

"Aw Richard!" She grabbed his chin between her thumb and index finger, her nails pointed and sharp. "I'm so sorry about your daughter. I thought it would be best that I don't call given the circumstances."

"You are kind to say so, but Flower I'm not here about that." he admitted.

"I thought when I got your message..." She had a soft voice in contrast with her Russian accent.

"Look, Apple, I'll get straight to the point. It's been stolen." he said.

"What? Not the records? The data? Surely not the plans?" Her voice was less soft now. The waitress arrived with two glasses of champagne. She took a long sip of hers before putting it down on the table. "Do not tell me this."

"I was so careful, but they have been stolen, and that's just the black and white of it Apple. The good news is, I know who's taken them. But I need your help to get them back." He took his glass of champagne and raised it to salute Rhompski.

Ignoring his invitation to toast, Rhompski didn't break eye contact "Who? Who?" She asked bluntly, demanding like a furious owl.

"Dana has them."

"What?! Richard! You know I cannot go near her. She has been through too much. Why would she take them? Does she know about me?" The panic in her voice escalated and people around them looked over.

"She hates me. It took for Amy to go missing to fully expose her hatred but it's certainly here now. She must have found out about us. Or.... I don't know – I'm not here to speculate. I know it was her ok, the culprit left a poem which was entirely her style. She's probably been planning this for ages."

"Wait – a poem? What the hell?" Rhompski asked, she could be dramatic at the best of times, but her confusion and frustration were becoming clear to those around them in the restaurant, as she downed her drink.

"Never mind about the poem. All you need to know is that it was Dana. She has the file." Richard didn't have much time to explain, but as he took Rhompski's hand in his, he turned on the charm. He looked into her eyes and smiled, "I'm rather glad I need your help with this one. It gives me an excuse to see you."

"Stop it!" she commanded half-heartedly, holding his hand across the table. "Well, what is there to do? You need to ask for it back!"

"I don't know what she fully intends to do with the plans. It's too risky to presume she will just hand them over. I'm to meet her by the overpass later, so I think we should both go and we can explain. We will tell her everything. It'll be bigger than she expects, and she is in well over her head." Richard was speaking frankly now, taking a sip of the champagne.

"The more people that know, the greater the risk we face. We need to think." Rhompski said.

"There is no time to think, Cheska!" Richard interrupted. "I know my wife, and this is the best course of action."

Three glasses of champagne later, Richard had convinced Rhompski to go with him. The sun was setting quickly as they headed to the overpass.

"I wish things had been different. Do you ever feel that way?" Rhompski said from the passenger seat.

Richard was staring straight at the road ahead, but he took her hand and squeezed it. "I do live with some regrets."

"Maybe I should just be happy I met you." Leaning forward to reach for her handbag in the footwell, she pulled out a red lipstick and began applying it in the visor mirror, achieving a perfect result despite the twists and turns of the road. "And for the record, I do believe you will be reunited with your daughter."

As they approached the quiet road which would take them to the fateful meeting spot under the overpass, Richard slowed. He was looking out for Dana's car but could only see a few abandoned ones. This spot was popular amongst fly-tippers. His Audi continued along the single carriage road, the disused and poorly maintained surface causing a bumpy ride for the two of them. The sky had almost finished its transition from dusk to darkness, and up ahead, Richard could make out a slender figure dressed in black. The person was standing, as described in the poem, under the overpass.

Richard stopped the car. Removing his seatbelt, he held his hand out to Rhompski, instructing her to stay in the car until required. She sat back in the passenger seat submissively, while he opened the door and began walking towards the figure. The ground was full of potholes and rubbish thrown by careless drivers from the overpass. Wearing his expensive work shoes, he took care to walk slowly and carefully, placing his feet quietly on the ground. He had kept the ignition on, and the dipped headlights shone in the direction of the figure.

The noise of the vehicles thundering overhead, echoed across the area, and there was a slight smell of engine fluid and diesel fumes in the air.

It was a cold night, and as Richard moved nearer, he felt the hairs on the back of his neck stand on end in reaction to a passing breeze. His steps, however, remained as confident as ever, placing one foot in front of the other towards the dark figure not too far in the distance. He squinted now as he got closer, trying to make out Dana's face in the darkness.

The beams from the car's headlights had faded due to the distance and weren't quite reaching the person in front of him. This faint light and the dull glow of orange in the air from the overpass streetlights above, meant that the still, dark shape, in a hooded cloak, was barely discernible. As Richard edged nearer, he could now see that the individual was standing with their back to him. The lightweight material of the cloak rippling in the wind like bed sheets on a washing line.

"Good evening!" Richard shouted over the din of the echoes. It may have been the rough area or the darkness, but something was telling him to stop and stand a couple of metres from where the figure was standing.

It remained still, Richard knew full well he had been heard, and the lump in his throat returned. It was disconcerting that the person in the cloak remained unresponsive. If this actually was his wife, then her behaviour was extremely strange.

"I said, good evening... you wanted to meet me here?" he shouted, a little closer and a little louder this time, and yet nothing.

The Familiar Encounter

He squinted his eyes, trying to adjust to the darkness, and concentrated on the figure. For a second he thought it could be a statue draped in black cloth, and put there to scare people away, because as the wind caught the shape of the figure, he could tell the body was completely still, as if not even human.

"What the hell is this?" he questioned, looking around behind him over at the car. Nothing but a pair of bright headlights staring back at him, and he thought about turning around to go home. He was getting cold now, and everything about this scene told him he should leave, but he needed those files. They could not fall into the wrong hands, and he had to get them back.

He began walking the last few paces over to the figure in black, while it remained unresponsive. He slowly reached out his arm to touch its shoulder. He was almost sure it was a statue. It felt thin and bony yet hard and cold, like stone. Suddenly the figure responded. Richard snatched his hand away as the creature moved. It stood taller than him, with its head bowed at first, but as Richard stood rooted to the spot, its neck extended slightly as it exhaled a deep, ghostly breath. Its shoulders moved as they began slowly turning towards Richard, before the rest of its body followed.

Richard's original confidence had diminished entirely. He was dumbfounded while trying to catch his breath at what he saw. He held his hands to his mouth, gasping as the creature turned to reveal its inhuman form. Although the hood still covered a significant portion of its head, the light was just enough to illuminate its barely human face. Its chin was almost non-existent, and the lipless slit of a mouth was partially open, revealing rows of sharp, pointed teeth. The monster's cheekbones sat high and prominent as a frame for the most horrifying eyes Richard had ever seen. They were almost perfectly round, their shining depth like glassy black holes glaring back at him. It was expressionless, watching Richard, as he found his feet and began to slowly move backwards. For every few retreating steps he managed, the creature would take a significant step toward him. Richard moved back further, and the creature's spindly leg once again protruded from its cloak, with a stride much greater than any Richard could ever achieve.

"What do you want from me!" Richard finally blurted out between his terrified gasps. The creature suddenly reached him, its arms engulfing Richard before he could put his up to defend himself. It put its mouth to Richard's ear, its wet teeth grazing the skin as it spoke.

"You won't keep us out. You won't ruin what we have created."

Richard wriggled out of its embrace and fell to the floor. The creature lunged after him at speed and spoke right into his face this time, shouting. "You will not destroy it!" Its voice was broken and grating, as if it hadn't uttered a word for decades.

Richard lay on the floor, shocked for a moment. He could feel the cold, dampness of the ground beneath him, soaking through his suit and through to his bones. He could hear the wind howling through the overpass pillars, the thundering roar of the traffic overhead, and the distant sound of Rhompski's screams coming from the direction of his car. Suddenly the creature turned and bounded away, its long legs transporting it quickly into the night. Richard's head spun from the encounter but with one thing remaining in the forefront of his mind: the poem.

"*Why?*" he said to himself, attempting to crawl away, before everything went black...

XL
Their Minds

It was another warm day which made Monica all the sleepier. She was in class, fighting her tiredness and trying to engage her brain. Her nightmares were to blame yet again. They had been getting worse lately, and the images were far more vivid. Monica was frightened to fall asleep as she was guaranteed to wake up in the same cold sweat of panic over and over, and always before the whole dream played out. A falling branch, a scream or a sudden movement within the dream would wake her. The images she now saw were not so easily shrugged off as before. She found it difficult to fall back to sleep. Each time she closed her eyes she would see the creature catching up to her. Sometimes now, she would even see Amy Ferhulse in the distance shouting for her to run faster towards her.

But today she was excited to see her boyfriend Rick after school. She looked up at the clock above the chalkboard and felt happy her school day was almost over. He would be waiting for her outside by now. Between schoolwork and practising for the Summer Sling, she had not had the free time to see him lately, so she knew she needed to snap out of her zombie-like state before spending time with him. It would be much overdue quality time too.

She had kept the nightmares a secret up until now, but the worse they became, the more she wondered if she should tell him about them. They had been together around six months now, and she knew they trusted each other. Monica was not someone that opened up quickly to others, but she knew this was something she needed to share with someone. While she sat in her final class for the day, trying to wake up, she thought it would probably make her feel better.

Monica must have been rooted in her thoughts at this point as she had not realised the school bell had rung, marking the end of the day. Everyone else was already up and out of their seats, rushing bodies enthusiastically packing away their books in their backpacks. Monica jumped up from her seat and began quickly stuffing her things into her bag to catch up with the rest of the class, who were now filtering out through the door as fast as they could. In her rush, the removable casing around her pencil sharpener opened. Monica's navy cardigan was now covered with pencil shavings. As she picked the bits from her uniform, tutting to herself that she had always meant to throw that broken sharpener away, she found herself alone in the classroom.

While rummaging in her bag, she took out her hairbrush and quickly brushed through her thick mahogany coloured mane. It had developed a reddish hue from the sunshine the town had been experiencing recently, and she wanted to show off to Rick. Being moments away from seeing him again she had a skip in her step leaving the classroom. The hallways were empty and dark now that the school was winding down for the day, and she quickly bobbed along towards the exit.

Crossing one of the hallways which led towards the science labs, something caught her eye, making her stop in the direction of the exit and pause for a second. Right at the end of the hallway she had noticed Scott Bowers and Bella Ferhulse chatting. Two people talking wasn't something Monica would usually find cause to be distracted over, especially when Rick was waiting for her, but she had many subjects with the two of them, and they had never shown any indication that they were friendly. They weren't a likely pair to be seen together around the school either. Despite not being able to hear any of the conversation, she could tell they were in an in-depth discussion. Their body language told Monica they were familiar with each other and the meeting was planned and deliberate.

Bella looked over, and in that second Monica looked away and continued walking. *None of my business. I wonder if Izzy knows they are friends.*

She didn't know Scott particularly well, but he didn't seem the type of character that would hurt her friend with any infidelity. But being the sensitive judge of character that she was, she knew there was something off about their meeting. The discussion seemed intense. Somehow, it did not feel right.

Continuing out of Hanfield High, pushing through the large double doors out onto the front concourse, she saw another familiar face and forgot all about Scott and Bella. Rick stood by the gate leaning on the bonnet of his truck, a cheeky smile on his face. Rick was tall and had smart, shaved hair which was almost black. He had pale skin which had freckled over the summer. He was a hard worker, and you would usually find him in a rough pair of jeans and a top, covered with bits of plaster or paint. If he wasn't on shift at the supermarket, he would be helping out his father in construction. His hands were worker's hands, all dry and cracked. His good looks were not the reason Monica fell for him, although they didn't hurt. She found him to be kind-hearted and deep. They could sit in his truck and talk all evening long about anything and everything. He seemed to understand her like no one else ever had, and on an entirely new level.

Since the summer break ended, they had grown into a routine. Rick would always pick Monica up from school or dance practice, and they would end up driving for hours. Their final parking spot was usually in Forest's End, discovered hundreds of years ago, but now a popular spot for dog walkers and outdoor yoga lessons, as the area was so beautiful. Many small wildflowers would grow there in pretty patches. It seemed to be a clearing in the woods where rays of sunshine would gently seep through. It was much quieter than Fade Away Diner, and it seemed to be their little secret.

As Monica happily got into Rick's truck, she looked back at the school and noticed Scott and Bella still hadn't left, but then didn't give it another thought.

She had missed the smell of Rick's car. It was a mixture of old wood, the aroma of the slightly sweet, tree-shaped air freshener hanging from his rear-view mirror, and occasionally, the very faint musky odour of white spirit and cigarettes, lingering from a hard day's work. There were some old dry patches of mud on the floor and bits of wood shavings. The seats were worn having been gradually broken in by Rick's burly construction colleagues, and Monica liked the way she sank into them. It was the kind of thing he would get embarrassed about if she pointed it out, so she would always quietly enjoy the sensation.

"How's the competition prep going?" Rick asked while starting the raggedy engine of the truck, with a knack only he knew.

"We're so busy babe! I think we have a real chance of winning. Everyone is just so committed at the moment." Monica answered while putting on her seatbelt, noticing she was still covered in pencil shavings.

"Hanfield Heartbeats have won every Summer Sling for as long as I can remember. Dana Ferhulse must be running out of space for all the trophies she's collecting." Rick said, knowing this was Monica's first Summer Sling. Then he turned to smile at her quickly, "I've never watched one, but this year I've made sure to get tickets."

"You're coming to watch?" Monica's voice became slightly high-pitched as it filled with excitement. "Are you really!"

Rick laughed, "Do I seem like the kinda guy that would pass up on an opportunity to watch his girlfriend perform? I've got to see what you've been so busy working on!" he said.

"That's so thoughtful!" Monica was surprised, as it didn't seem like something Rick would ever consider going to, and it meant a lot to her that he would be there to support her.

As Monica watched the passing houses from the window, still in the first year of her new home, she felt so happy. Everything seemed to have come together for her in a lot of ways. Driving past houses outside the main square, she thought how cute some of them were, their gardens so meticulously designed and thought through, with summer blooms and flowering trees. Some of the houses or smaller cottages were all unique and special, not like the city where she was from, which was very grey and coldly regimented.

Out of town, the roads widened considerably. The grass verges became wilder, Trees began to appear as they entered the road that ran through a portion of the forest. She found them almost mesmerising as they drove past one after the other, almost identical in size and shape.

"... it's like Dad says, I need to get as much experience as I can if I'm going to be running the business one day." Rick filled Monica in on work, but he stopped, noticing she wasn't paying attention, "Erm... Mon? Am I that boring?" Rick chuckled to himself.

"Oh, I'm so sorry, I was listening. I hadn't noticed the trees are all such a similar size. They're all massive too!" Monica snapped out of her trance.

"So, the trees distracted you? Ok, I'm definitely boring you." He laughed again, but this time with a trace of concern.

"Yeah but, ugh..." Monica sighed: "I keep doing that, daydreaming. I keep getting these weird dreams... I've not been sleeping great." Monica felt slightly awkward confessing to the nightmares. She was afraid he might think she was strange. She went back to looking out of the window to hide her embarrassment at having finally brought up the one issue that had been playing on her mind.

"What are the dreams about Mon?" Rick sounded curious but concerned. His voice comforted her.

"It's weird, always the same thing... I'm running through the forest away from something - a man or an animal. - I'm unsure." She looked over at Rick to gauge his reaction, it felt good to finally say it out loud.

Rick was frowning thoughtfully. He moved his hand away to change gear, "I don't know much about dreams, but I have heard they are meant to mean something. You stressed about something? You have been working hard recently with school and dance."

"...I don't feel stressed, in fact, I feel happy with my life. I love school, dancing, and you," she answered, feeling better to have got it off her chest, but still none the wiser.

Rick looked over at her for a second and flashed a big grin, "Even when watching the trees is more entertaining?" he joked.

Monica laughed and gave him a gentle shove in the ribs, "I'll have you know that I come from a city with few trees, so they're quite exciting for me!" Monica played along.

She turned to look out of her window once more laughing when suddenly she saw a girl with bright red hair run through the trees towards the road in front of them. Monica grabbed Rick's arm, pushing his body to steer away.

"Look out!" Monica screamed, and leant over to push the steering wheel with such a force it made the truck move over into the oncoming lane.

"What? What!" Rick shouted, moving the truck back to the correct lane, just in time to avoid hitting an oncoming car.

"What the hell was that?" Rick demanded.

Monica sat slumped over in the worn seat, with her hands over her eyes.

"I'm so sorry! I thought I saw something – someone, run out onto the road just then!"

Rick sighed a sound of relief, "That was close!"

"Didn't you see that, that...girl?" Monica asked the question, but she already knew the answer having realised it was yet another figment of her imagination, as if her nightmares were now bleeding into her reality.

"No Mon? What girl?" he asked shakily, more concern in his voice.

"The girl... she looked exactly like... like Amy!" Monica was so sure it was her.

"It must have been a trick of the light. The shadows of the trees around here can be deceptive!" He held her hand again to comfort her: "Just maybe hold off from doing that again eh? I almost peed myself!" Rick joked to try and lighten the mood.

"Yeah, I guess so... Sorry. Like I was saying, I'm just not awake today!"

The weather was changing. Hanfield in the height of summer would have been sunny right up until 9 pm. But now the nights were drawing in, and the sun was slowly beginning to set much earlier. Monica was shaken up, but not from almost causing the crash. The girl running out into the road looked as real to her as Rick did sitting beside her. *What I saw was not a trick of the light.*

Seeing Amy made Monica recall when she first started with the Hanfield Heartbeats. She had quickly gained the impression that she would never stick it out, as the girls had seemed cold and arrogant at first. Amy had welcomed her with overwhelming enthusiasm, attempting to get to know her. Monica, being slightly cynical, first thought Amy as vapid as the rest of the group, and if it weren't for her mother being the coach, she would have shown it. But it wasn't long before Amy proved her wrong and made Monica realise that the group wasn't bad at all.

Amy had a certain something about her. It was something Monica couldn't put her finger on, but she had an elusive quality that seemed unattainable for even the most desperate of girls in the group, namely, Hannah. It had been almost thirteen weeks since she last saw her, but the pictures of Amy were still very much in evidence around town. Even so, Monica was sure no one else was having Amy enter their nightmares. Now seeing her in her reality, it filled Monica with dread that maybe her subconscious was trying to tell her something.

As Monica and Rick pulled into the entrance of Forest's End, they both noticed that the sunset was now at its most vivid, and the sky was a beautiful mix of pink and orange. The birds in the trees were loudly telling each other it was time for bed, as the noises from the surrounding forest picked up.

"In my favourite place, with my favourite person." Rick said, turning to Monica and smiling at her. "Thank you for making some time for me this week."

Monica looked up from her feet, having been deep in thought for a moment. She twisted around in the soft, partly collapsed seat and smiled at Rick.

The following day, Monica awoke feeling refreshed for the first time in a long time. She had slept through the whole night after Rick dropped her off. Talking to Rick had lifted a weight from her mind, and maybe he was right, she perhaps did have too much going on at school. *That relaxing evening was exactly what I needed.*

Feeling energised, she ran downstairs, hopping from the second to last step and skipped to pour herself some orange juice. She quickly grabbed an apple to eat on her way into school. Mrs. Ferhulse had asked everyone to be in first thing today for more dance practise with the competition being two days away. She had recently returned to work at Hanfield.

"You need more to eat than an apple!" her mother lectured as she hurriedly ran out of the house.

It felt like the season had shifted overnight, bringing a colder autumn, way before its due, and only having a couple of days more to practise before the competition, everyone was looking tired. But the mood quickly elevated, and the group became motivated the instant Mrs. Ferhulse walked in, clapping her hands to get everyone's attention as she usually would.

"Right girls! ...and guys! Only a couple more magical days of practise left! Are we going to make the most of it?"

The room responded with a resounding, "Yes", but this response was not good enough for Mrs. Ferhulse. Monica knew it wouldn't be. She knew the routine by now. Dana would always try and get the team energised.

"That doesn't sound like the enthusiastic response one would expect from reigning champions!" She predictably repeated the question.

The room responded with a much louder, "YES!" and although Monica was tempted to roll her eyes every time this happened, she had to hand it to Mrs. Ferhulse, it always worked. She knew how to engage with the group, boosting everyone's energy with just a few words of encouragement. The energy levels were now high enough for Mrs. Ferhulse to allow the warm-up to begin.

"Izzy, you were looking excellent yesterday morning. I want to try something very quickly with the pyramid." Mrs. Ferhulse said, weaving in and out of the group while they star-jumped. "I hope you don't mind that we restructure the pyramid Hannah, so I can see what Izzy looks like at the top. You can be second tier as your legs are longer. Go ahead and switch places."

Echoed gasps moved through the group. Right away, Monica looked straight at Hannah as inconspicuously as she could, to gauge her reaction. As she expected, Hannah looked furious. She could do nothing to hide her feelings but look down at her dance shoes. But Hannah was not the only one to react. Changing the positions so close to competition was unheard of. Dana would be taking a risk.

"Yes babe! Top of the pyramid!" Scott said, encouraging a suddenly shy looking Izzy.

Everyone got to their starting positions to begin this new formation of the dance, with Hannah reluctantly swapping places with Izzy.

"Don't fall now." Hannah whispered to Izzy with a false smile on her face.

Hannah was now positioned in front of Monica and studying her body she could tell all Hannah's back and arm muscles were tight with anger at the change. Karma had finally caught up with Hannah, and as they began to dance the routine, Monica hoped Izzy would shine and claim the top-tier position.

As they all performed the moves leading up to the final pyramid, Monica willed Izzy to pull it off. She deserved this recognition. Everyone moved impeccably. Their movements were perfectly synchronised as they performed the routine they had spent weeks learning, hitting each beat and step with definition and with the same enthusiastic smile on each member's face.

Then something strange began to happen in Monica's mind as she willed Izzy to find her confidence. Everything started to move in slow motion. She panicked thinking she was off time but no, everyone else was moving slower too. Even Mrs. Ferhulse, who was shouting out instructions and encouragements was sounding deeper and her words elongated as if time had slowed down. But no one seemed aware of this strange change in pace other than Monica herself. Assuming this was her lack of sleep over the last few months catching up with her again, she continued punching the air in time with everyone else, still hoping Izzy would shine. So many strange occurrences had happened to her recently that it was like she was now going through the motions, and she was able to adapt to the slow pace. Monica would be one of three girls from the group to perform turning jumps. Whenever they practised in the school's gym, Monica would always look out of the huge windows and focus on the oak tree in the schoolyard. A total of four spins were required for this part, and as she jumped up into her first, she looked out for her oak tree. Standing all alone like it was an imposter, like it did not belong in the middle of the tarmacked yard, but it was the point she used for spotting.

She had eyes on the tree, grandly filling the empty area with its large branches and bright green leaves, only something wasn't right. She saw Amy, coming out from behind the tree. She was far away and if it wasn't for her recognisable red hair getting caught in the wind, she wouldn't have known it was her. But it *was* Amy. Monica gasped with shock. Moving in the now acceptable slow motion, Monica completed her second turn, spotting to take in another view of the tree. Amy was closer, and even closer still on her third turn. By the fourth turn, Amy was pressed up against the glass. In that slow protracted moment, Monica witnessed the expression on Amy's face as they made eye contact. It was a look of mocking amusement, not a look she had seen before. She broke eye contact with Monica and seemingly winked at someone else behind her.

Monica was able to look back at the window once she had finished her final twirl, and Amy was gone. She had disappeared again. With no time to react, her attention was quickly drawn back to the ending of the routine. She got into position, still grinning like everyone else, helping push Izzy up, propelling her to jump, finishing on top of the pyramid. Mrs. Ferhulse was quiet for this edited ending as she observed, her brow furrowed in concentration. Monica had no idea how well executed this was, but watched Dana Ferhulses' face change from avid attention, to rapturous appreciation, her eyes wide with happiness. Monica was now plastering on the energetic dancer smile, but this time it was a very genuine, real grin.

"Izzy!! What do I say! Superb!" Dana shouted in astonishment, "Hannah, you really do look more comfortable there on second-tier darling, you understand, don't you?"

Monica knew this would have killed Hannah inside. They were still holding the pyramid formation.

"Izzy doesn't have much experience at the front, so as long as you're sure it won't cost us the competition." Monica could hear that this was spoken through Hannah's gritted teeth as she struggled to remain calm.

"Izzy has no experience in this position, and yet she so belongs up there. Well done girl!" Dana said encouragingly to Izzy.

"If you are sure, coach, I don't want to step on anyone's toes, so to speak!" Izzy had such a bubbly personality until you put her in the limelight, then her uncertainty in herself seemed to emerge.

"You know me. I wouldn't dream of having a last moment change before such a huge competition unless I were sure it would benefit us tenfold, and I am sure. So, Izzy you are our new top tier, congratulations!" Mrs. Ferhulse said. Only Monica seemed to know this would feel like daggers to Hannah, as the group offered congratulations to Izzy while packing up to get ready for classes.

"Wow! That would be amazing, coach!" Izzy exclaimed, "But Hannah, are you sure you don't mind?"

"No issue with me." Hannah answered under her breath, unable to crack even one of her fake smiles this time.

"Hannah is so busy with so many other projects Izzy!" Mrs. Ferhulse appeared thrilled and completely oblivious to the thunderstorm of fury now raging in Hannah's mind.

Monica noticed that as Hannah walked off towards the changing rooms, she was looking curiously out of the window. *Did Hannah see Amy too?*

XII

Ms. Henrys Hidden Life

Ms. Henry hurriedly struggled to open the door to her home. The door was relatively old, and the lock had become temperamental. Eventually, it swung open. Walking purposefully through to the kitchen, she slammed the grocery bags onto the countertop, and she gasped as she hit her head on one of the cupboards above her.

Ms. Henry wasn't like the usual mothers you would see around Hanfield. She didn't go to the salon every other week to get her facial and nails done. Her hair had always been a deep brown colour, only now there were wiry stands of grey poking through which she was content enough to leave. Ms. Henry did not wear makeup and would always get her brightly coloured, flowing clothes from thrift and charity shops around town. It would be fair to assume Ms. Henry was a 'free-thinker' in the way she appeared and behaved.

She unpacked her groceries into the huge fridge freezer, which didn't quite integrate with the décor of the rest of the kitchen. She enjoyed the original features of the old house, such as the dark stone worktops and the brass coloured sink, but her daughter insisted on new, high market items in the home, such as an ice dispenser within the fridge, and a smoothie maker for her morning shakes before she headed off to dance practise. Their house portrayed the story of two very different personalities living under the one roof. Upon closing the fridge door, Ms. Henry smiled to herself as she noticed the photo of her, aged of twenty-three holding a three-year-old Hannah Henry. Both were laughing at something happening behind the camera, and it transported Ms. Henry back to a simpler time. She loved that photograph and insisted it be kept on the fridge, one of the few sentimentalities Hannah would allow her mother, despite not cherishing it in the same way. Today while she had a few moments she took it from the fridge and gazed at it for some time. However, if she thought about that photo long enough, she would find the memory bittersweet. At the time the photo was taken, she was embracing being a single mother. Recently she had wondered if Hannah's father had stuck around, would the girl have still got so out of control. But no, it was better this way, Ms. Henry thought. She knew it was from her father that Hannah had inherited her dominant, narcissistic personality flaws. It wouldn't do for her to adopt his manipulative behaviour as well.

    Ms. Henry caught a glimpse of the clock on the old, creamy coloured cooker beside her and let out another gasp. It wouldn't be long before Hannah was home from school, and Ms. Henry had a long-standing routine of practically being her personal assistant. Putting away the remaining groceries as quickly as possible, she pulled out a couple of slices of bread, and began making a sandwich, ready for her daughter's arrival.

    With her strict schedule, anything Hannah could think of to save herself time, she would have her mother do for her. Now heading upstairs, she prepared Hannah's outfit for her singing lesson that evening. There were a few varieties to choose from, but she had certain types of outfits for various after school activities pre-approved.

    It was getting colder outside, so she picked out a cream cardigan to go over the pale pink top, a matching cream mini skirt to be worn with her light autumn boots. Folding the items neatly on Hannah's bed, it would often cross Ms. Henry's mind that it shouldn't be this way, but she didn't know how to handle her daughter's terrible mood swings. Being such a peaceful person, she didn't believe in ever raising her voice to Hannah, and even if that's what she needed, it was far too late now.

Ms. Henry would justify this daily routine as doing her part to help her daughter achieve her dreams. Hannah would often make her feel like a hindrance, and it gave Ms. Henry a sense of purpose to be helpful to her daughter in this way. However, deep down, she knew it wasn't right. Now Amy had disappeared. Hannah's moods were getting worse, and the truth was Ms. Henry didn't believe her daughter could sing or dance as well as some of the other students at the school. She had come to realise this hard reality over the years of watching plays and competitions. There was a time when Ms. Henry loved hearing and watching Hannah perform. But as the years went on and the more desperate Hannah became for attention and acclaim, and to pursue this career path, the quicker any joy seemed to slip away. There was no way Ms. Henry would ever dare to share her real thoughts with Hannah. She had become obsessed with performing.

Once she had finished preparing everything for Hannah's arrival, she hurried out to the garden. Ms. Henry had a 'happy place' beside the trees, and she had often found solace and quiet here, while Hannah was home. As much as she would like to find out how her day had been, she had been told so many times by her daughter not to bother her while she was resting before singing lessons. These days it was hard to tell what sort of mood her daughter would be in when she returned home. The rare days that Hannah came back in a good mood were Ms. Henry's favourite, as they would converse almost like they used to, and for those few hours she would feel like she had a proper relationship with her daughter again. However, they hadn't had a 'good' day for a few weeks now.

More commonly, Hannah would come home and stamp her feet, slamming the door behind her and screaming, as if she were possessed by something horrible. Years ago, when it first began to happen, Ms. Henry would have a secret joke about it to herself. She would laugh that Hannah had come home as someone else, someone whom she had affectionately named Mildred.

Mildred was the nasty cat from a cartoon Hannah would watch as a child. Ms. Henry remembered that whenever Mildred the cat appeared on the screen, Hannah would cower away, frightened of the character. As Ms. Henry laid down her aztec print blanket on the slightly overgrown lawn, she smiled thinking back to the time Hannah would want cuddles and protection after seeing Mildred. She sat on her blanket, facing out onto the vast forest, and crossing her legs, she closed her eyes, preparing to meditate. Relaxing, she listened to the light breeze, gently making the trees sway, causing the leaves to rustle soothingly, helping her mind focus completely on the environment around her.

Meditating at least twice a day Ms. Henry felt this was a great way to reduce stress but also keep in touch with the land and her fellow earthly creatures. Growing up in Hanfield, she knew there were others living in the forest surrounding the town. She believed the stories people would tell about spirits and grey coloured demons inhabiting the woods. She could feel presences out there. She knew they weren't something to be afraid of, as others had described tales of horror and destruction from many years ago. Still, Ms. Henry worked in the apple orchards for the majority of her life. Every few years or so, she would catch a glimpse of something in the distance, through the trees. These sightings would always happen around the end of summer, and the image would always be o a human man. It would walk differently, with a much longer stride, and its back would be so curved that it would almost arch over on itself. When she was younger, she had tried to show others what she had seen many times. But now she knew, unless they had a connection to the supernatural, they could not feel or experience these beings in the same way.

Just as Ms. Henry knew others lived out in the forest, she could also sense that the sweet girl Amy was also out there somewhere. But she sensed that Amy did not want to be found. It was a strange concept that she had to wrap her head around initially. Ms. Henry had always been one with nature, and whatever the winds and whispers of the trees told her she would still respect, even if it made no sense to her at the time.

Concentrating on her breath, breathing deeply in and out, she sensed nothing, only the wind picking up across her bare arms and ankles. She heard the sound of a bumblebee near her, and in the distance, she heard some children playing football. Then she sensed her, stretching out her mind to feel what she was feeling; an internal struggle with a yearning to belong again, but with a need for solitude and the connection with the forest. Ms. Henry was so attuned to her that she could almost feel the mud beneath her feet, and the branches scraping against her skin. She couldn't tell what Amy was doing out there but had an overwhelming feeling that it was meaningful whatever it may be, and that was good enough for her.

Something caused Ms. Henry to lose concentration, as her ears turned back to the sounds around her and those of the house. She thought she heard a window smashing, and she got up quickly to run back into the house to investigate. The front door was wide open. She turned to enter the kitchen before a plate narrowly missed her head and smashed against the door frame. Her carefully prepared sandwich was all over the floor along with several other glasses, mugs and other plates from the kitchen cupboards. Ms. Henry hadn't seen Hannah come home in such a state before. Her face was bright red and was screaming wildly, while violently throwing the kitchenware towards the opposite wall.

"Hannah! What happened?" Ms. Henry spoke calmly in a bid to try and lower Hannah's aggression.

Suddenly a bowl came flying over towards her, hitting her in the hip and smashing on the floor.

"Argh... that was painful!" She slowly made her way over to Hannah. She needed to control the situation before it got out of hand, "Come on now, please calm down".

"That bitch stole top-tier! She stole *my* spot!" Hannah screamed.

"You are only going to damage your voice for your lesson later screaming like that," Ms. Henry warned, despite wincing from the extreme pain in her hip bone. She removed the ceramic mug from her daughter's shaking hands. *Mildred has certainly arrived today!*

"Why must everything go against me?" Hannah moaned, beginning to break down.

"It's not the end of the world!" Ms. Henry said, "Mrs. Ferhulse is probably trying to give everyone a fair chance at it."

"I am the better dancer. Why does she have it in for me?" Hannah shouted.

"Sometimes these things happen, and it's like we spoke about the other day – getting so worked up won't help." Ms. Henry would always try to make her daughter see the bigger picture, as she knew down the line, things may not work out the way she planned.

"But it's not fair! I work harder than Izzy Briggs!" Hannah said.

"Things will always work out for the better, trust me, and be gracious about this." Ms. Henry rubbed Hannah's shoulder to comfort her, but she shrugged her hand away, as she always did.

"No, I did that the entire time with Amy. This is supposed to be my time to shine. Izzy should be getting some bad karma for doing this to me. I'm going to help it along." Hannah began to walk out the kitchen, "Then maybe she won't be able to perform at all at the Summer Sling." She laughed cruelly as she walked upstairs towards her bedroom. It was almost time for them to set off to her lesson.

Her mother stood in the kitchen, surrounded by broken things, shards of glass and lumps of ceramic scattered along the hard floor. There were marks on the wall where items had hit it with such a force, but the one thing she was concerned about being broken was her daughter. Hannah had never threatened harm to anyone before, but somehow Ms. Henry believed she would be capable of doing something to another student at the school. A reality, which for some time, she had not wanted to admit to herself.

Cleaning up the mess in the kitchen, Ms. Henry ignored the pain from her hip. She had become used to aches and pains in her body over the years. When Hannah suddenly morphed into Mildred, she would sometimes kick and hit her mother. She would bear the brunt of many of Hannah's worst days, all the while thinking to herself this was simply a phase her daughter was going through, hoping that she would grow out of it. But it seemed to be getting worse each day, to the point that 'Mildred' had become the more prevalent of her daughter's personalities.

On the outskirts of town, in a large manor house out in the countryside, lived the very best singing coach around. It was someone Hannah had insisted upon, and despite it costing a considerable amount of Ms. Henry's small salary from the apple orchards, she agreed to it. Of course, Hannah's voice had hardly improved, but Ms. Henry was trapped. She didn't want to anger her daughter any more. Although she felt sympathy for Hannah most of the time, it was now starting to become apparent that her daughter's dreams were unattainable.

But one thing Ms. Henry was sure of, she needed to broach the earlier threat Hannah had made. The twenty-minute car journey out of Hanfield to the manor house, seemed like the perfect opportunity.

"Violence is never the answer you know Mil - I mean, Hannah," Ms. Henry said.

"Do you think I'm that silly? That stupid?" Hannah snapped back.

"I don't, but I have to follow up on your threat back there." A sense of relief came over Ms. Henry as perhaps the comment slipped out in anger. *In the heat of the moment.*

"I'm far too clever to get my own hands dirty. The rest of the group along with the coach think I'm agreeable to it. They haven't the first idea what a big mistake they've made!" Hannah said calmly from the passenger seat, typing on her mobile to one of her many school friends.

"I know you don't believe this, but trust me, everything happens for a reason. Don't you do anything to that innocent girl!" Ms Henry warned.

"Or what? Are you going to say something? Are you going to stop me?" Hannah paused, waiting for her mother to answer while Ms. Henry remained silent, "...I didn't think so!"

Her mother waited in the car for Hannah to complete her overpriced lesson. She usually went for a walk along one of the lanes near the large house. This time however, she remained in the car bewildered at how out of control her daughter had become. She had evidently been blind to the extent of her daughter's deterioration, and she was horrified that Hannah would now want to interfere with someone else's success rather than wish them well. It was not how she had raised her.

She suddenly had a change of plan. Needing fresh air, she left the car and she proceeded to venture down a smaller lane, one she had not discovered before. With the weather beginning to turn, she noticed some red leaves up ahead, contrasting against the lush green backdrop of all the other bushes and trees. The path was muddy and unkempt, but she was curious, regardless, and continued to walk ahead, admiring how pretty this area was. The further she walked, the more overgrown the pathway seemed to get, but this did not deter Ms. Henry.

The Familiar Encounter

Arriving at the small tree, she was amazed. She had not seen a tree like this one before. Its leaves were thicker than any other she had seen, and such a deep red so early into autumn. The bark of the tree looked aged as if it were ancient, but it was no taller than her.

"I've never seen any such thing!" she said out loud.

She reached out her hand and went to touch one of the waxy looking red leaves when everything around her shifted. It was suddenly nightfall in the forest. She took her hand away from the leaf in shock, and time reverted to the present, as if nothing had happened. She stepped back, to look at the tree, confusion on her face. She reached out to touch the leaf once more, and once more it became night again. Ms. Henry kept her hand there. She felt some light rain and a rather strong wind upon her. The area looked the same, but she could see something more. The forest was palely lit with the glow of the full moon above and coming towards appeared a thin man of average height, wrapped in a dark cloak. It was just like the figures she had seen many years ago from the apple orchard.

Between the trees, in a narrow clearing, she could see the creature was lunging forwards on its unusually long legs. As it made its way closer, she began to make out the details of its face. It had no colour to its skin. With the cloak's hood covering the majority of its face she could only see its broad pointed chin and narrow neck. Ms. Henry was frozen with fear as it made its way over to her in the dark. She hadn't ever been so close to one before.

"I have a gun!" Ms. Henry blurted out, "Wha-what do-do you want?"

The figure lunged further this time and was now behind the small tree. This close she could see its long nose, and its pale skin threaded with small blue veins like a map of some busy city. Its mouth swung open to reveal wet, razor sharp teeth which shone in the moonlight.

"We have hoped to respond to you for quite a time." The creature was well-spoken, but its voice sounded raspy, "We hear you frequently."

She could not find any words, and even if she did her mouth did not seem to be working. She remained still, unable to take her eyes off the hooded monster with its perfect English.

"You are correct to be concerned. Your child has the capability to seed many evils. But her power is not yet fully known to her, an advantage you must use now to destroy her," the creature informed Ms. Henry in the same monotonous voice. It was neither feminine nor masculine.

"But she is my child. I could never!" Ms. Henry could not believe what she was hearing, what she was doing or where she was, "I could not destroy anything."

"She was not ever yours. Look back and recall." The creature turned its head to look behind it, as if it were in a hurry, "I must depart. Look back and recall!" The alien repeated itself before turning around to lunge into the night.

Instantly, Ms. Henry was surrounded by daylight again, but her skin still felt the cold from the night's air, and the vision of the creature was burnt into her mind. She no longer felt afraid, just puzzled by its message. She wished she had asked more questions and had longer with the creature.

As she turned away to walk back to the car, the tree had returned to its original, leafy green tone.

XIII
Izzys' Break

Looking around her she asked herself what should change about the bedroom to make it more 'boy-friendly' - as her friends in school would say. She moved her vase full of freshly picked daisies from the window and on to her desk, then refolded her pyjamas to place carefully on top of her pillow. Arranging her stuffed animals in order of size at the head of her bed, she suddenly realised that she was probably much too old to have any stuffed animals at all. Blushing slightly at the thought of Scott discovering her love of the teddy bear, octopus and monkey she had slept next to since she was a child, she grabbed all three, kissing each on the head and placed them in the storage box on the top of her wardrobe. Izzy then looked for small details to change, but finding none she proudly grinned to herself; much better!

Izzy was in a great mood as she always was whenever the sun was shining outside, and the birds were chirping. In fact, it was rare for her to ever be in anything but a great mood, but today was different. It was the last Friday of the summer, which meant it was the big day. It would not be standard lessons today at school; it was the Summer Sling event and competition. Since Izzy had recently moved up to first tier within the Hanfield Heartbeats she had mixed emotions. Confidence was not Izzy's strong suit, but she always focused on the positives, and Scott would be visiting for dinner with her parents that evening after the Summer Sling.

"This is just the perfect day!" she said to her mother as she skipped along the landing to head to school.

"Have a great day, and break a leg! I will be rooting for you in the audience!" Izzy's mother had been thrilled at the recent news of her daughter being promoted to number one on the dance team. As far as she was concerned it was long overdue.

When Izzy arrived at school that morning, it was chaotic. Some of her classmates were decorating the corridors with bunting, and others were rushing around trying to find out where they needed to be. Today was the climax of the whole year, and for a moment, Izzy paused and smiled as she took it all in. But then, someone she did not recognise from a lower year approached her.

"Don't just stand there... here!" The girl handed Izzy a pile of papers with 'No Access' written on them in large letters, "These need sticking to the classroom doors, so the parents don't go walkabout and end up lost."

The girl heard her name called and rushed off. Still in a world of her own Izzy smiled, staring down at the papers, when another classmate who was rushing by, bumped into her, knocking the pile of papers from her arms. They went everywhere, and she hurriedly tried to collect them all from between the legs moving all around her.

When Izzy had finished collecting each one, she noticed in amongst the jostling crowds a pair of legs paused in front of her. She knew who it was by the smell of the perfume in the air and her graceful, self-assured stance. It was Hannah Henry, and Izzy cheerily got up off the floor to greet her.

"You feeling confident?" Hannah asked stone-faced, glaring along the corridor rather than looking at Izzy.

"I'm a bit nervous but very excited. Do you have any tips for me?" Izzy asked.

Hannah responded, turning to look at her, "Since we've all worked so hard over the year on this routine my only advice would be not to mess it up."

Watching Izzy's pupils dilate with anxiety at her words, Hannah was satisfied and sashayed off down the corridor, her presence intimidating her fellow students who parted like the red sea, to let her through. Hannah had fed into Izzy's reservations.

While working her way down the corridor sticking the signs to each classroom door as she had been instructed, she saw Monica leaning against one of the door frames. She was texting on her phone. Izzy thought she always looked so fresh and relaxed. There was no way anyone would shove 'No Access' signs into her lap. Monica was like chalk to Izzy's cheese, their personalities contrary to each other, with Izzy being so excitable and highly energised and Monica who only spoke and reacted when there was a real purpose to do so.

Izzy began taping up one of the signs on the classroom door next to where Monica was standing.

"Hey Mon! How ya feeling for later? Pretty good, I expect!" Izzy asked.

"Hey! I feel pretty good! How are you feeling, is the more important question?" Monica put her phone away in the back pocket of her skinny, stonewashed jeans.

"Well y' know... to be honest, I'm wondering if I should just let Hannah do it," Izzy said reluctantly. "She's so much more experienced than I am... and everyone has worked so hard. I don't want to let the team down!" Izzy knew she could speak honestly to her friend while she played about with the roll of tape, nervously picking at it, trying to find the beginning.

Monica's smile dropped into a look of concern, "No! Don't say that! You'll be fantastic. Hannah may be more experienced, but she doesn't have the talent or stage presence that you do! Trust me!"

Monica had asked Izzy to trust her, and she did. Her words felt so genuine.

Izzy smiled, "Thank you, Mon."

"Now let us get these needless signs up quickly so we can go mess around in the gym!" Monica giggled, "...you just know the parents will be wondering about it in the classrooms regardless!"

Izzy laughed along with Monica as she began to help. Hannah's attempt at getting to her had not penetrated deep enough to make Izzy act upon it, despite the usual nervous excitement kicking in.

They moved along to the gym together where they were sure the rest of Hanfield Heartbeats would be, psyching themselves up and preparing their 'look' for the big performance.

An especially enthusiastic Mrs. Ferhulse stood in the central doorway of the separate gymnasium while the girls made their way over. Monica and Izzy caught sight of her tell-tale red hair and baby pink velour tracksuit, a look only someone as gregarious as her could ever get away with.

"Come quickly, I have your outfits girls!" Mrs. Ferhulse shouted over the football field as the girls excitedly picked up the pace.

"Scott didn't ring me back last night so maybe he's also nervous. Hopefully, he'll be in the gymnasium," Izzy told Monica expectantly.

A pang of guilt set in for Monica upon Izzy's mention of Scott's name as she recalled the moment she saw him in what appeared to be a heated discussion with Bella Ferhulse, in an empty school corridor. It was a couple of days ago now, and she had told herself it probably looked worse than it was. She felt like a bad friend for a moment, but knew telling Izzy would risk her performance later on that day. It was probably nothing, but alarm bells were quietly ringing in Monica's brain. Why would he not have rung her back?

"It's so typical of a guy to shut off contact before a big day, I mean isn't he meeting your parents today? He's probably so nervous!" Monica worked to shut down any concerns in Izzy's voice.

"Good point Mon. He'll be putting so much pressure on himself to make a good impression, but they'll love him – how could they not?"

Upon arriving at the sports hall, Izzy was on the lookout for Scott, while Monica headed for the pile of dance uniforms in the corner of the room.

"Have you seen Scott?" Izzy politely interrupted a conversation Danny was having with one of the other dancers. She longed to have one of Scott's pep talks before preparing for the show.

"You know what Izzy, I think I saw him head towards the library first thing!" Danny screwed his face up thoughtfully.

"Oh! Really? I do hope he gets here on time. There's much prep to be done!" Izzy said, trying to avoid sounding too disappointed.

She headed towards the changing rooms with her uniform. The package was lighter than she expected and had the words 'Miss. Isabella Briggs XS' written across it. It was now beginning to sink in, and she couldn't wait to get out there. The outfit was in her hands, and it was real.

Izzy ripped the plastic casing with her fingers and marvelled at the outfit. The Hanfield Heartbeats uniform was mainly deep red with a dark blue ocean trim. The girls wore a pleated armless mini dress, while the two boys had wide-leg trousers with vests. Izzy loved her dress, and she twirled around the women's changing room, practising her high kicks. The sound of the performance music playing clearly in her mind.

Before she knew it, they were well into having warmed up and running through the routine for one final time. The atmosphere in the room was alive with anticipation and excitement. She kept Monica's words of encouragement running through her mind the entire time.

"Okay everyone let's get your final stretches in. Backstage in thirty minutes sharp!" Mrs. Ferhulse echoed across the sports hall and leaning over to Izzy she gave her a motivational nudge and whispered, "You'll smash it girl!"

Izzy looked up from concentrating on a stretch and smiled at her coach. Behind Mrs. Ferhulse were the large gymnasium windows and through them she noticed cars beginning to arrive, and minibuses full of the opposing dance groups from other schools.

Backstage each group had their own area, clearly labelled. It was less than an hour before the Hanfield Heartbeats were due to perform, and the excitement was building. The various groups would always quieten down slightly just as a new group was set to dance, to observe their performance with curiosity.

Finally reunited backstage, Izzy happily sat on Scott's knee chatting with him, when a teacher approached them, "It'll be the Hanfield Heartbeats next!"

"Remember everyone; smile!" Mrs. Ferhulse offered her final bit of advice to the group before ushering them into position. Everyone was tense.

As the curtain went up, the stage lights were brighter than Izzy remembered, and this worked to her advantage as she couldn't make out any of the audience beyond the first couple of rows. A moment later and the catchy dance music began, and just like that, the dance routine they had all rigorously practised repeatedly over the last year was now going to be judged. Izzy felt full of energy, and any doubts about her skill had now totally disappeared, she was doing what she loved the most.

Halfway through the routine, they approached their positions for the first of three significant lifts.

During the first lift, Izzy felt terrific while she was flung in the air by both Danny and Scott. Keeping a big smile plastered to her face, she caught a glimpse of a couple of camera flashes from the audience, before disappearing from view behind the girls who would support her in landing. The next lift was slightly tricker, as four members of the group including Hannah lifted her to hold a position for three seconds, before being lowered again. It seemed to Izzy that it happened so fast, but as planned she was raised by all four girls, the widest smile remained glued to her face. A couple more camera flashes from the audience felt like a quick pat on the back 'well done'. But before Izzy could tick off another lift as well-executed, a body appeared from nowhere. All she saw was a quick blur of royal red and blue, and instead of being lowered by the girls she was quickly pulled by her waist. She tried to resist but the figure caused her to land about half a metre from where she needed to be. Some audience members gasped. They had been through the routine so many times, Izzy knew exactly where she needed to land, and this was not it. Breaking character for a second to get her bearings she noticed the wooden panel where she should have landed was missing, leaving a wide, open hole in the stage. Izzy wasn't being sabotaged as she first assumed, but saved. The thoughts of a guardian angel crossed her mind. Still, there was no time to dwell; she smiled her biggest smile and gave everything she had to the remainder of the dance, finishing up at the very top of the pyramid to rapturous applause. Izzy made sure to take it all in with tears in her eyes at what a magical moment it had been for her, and no matter the final result, she was thrilled.

As the Summer Sling continued on, Izzy was able to make her way to some seats at the back of the hall to watch the other performances. She had felt such a high from being on the stage. She didn't have a care over the mishap with the flooring at all. Looking around she was glad to be sat between Scott and Monica, and some of the other members of Hanfield Heartbeats were also nearby, enjoying the remainder of the event, but Hannah was nowhere to be seen.

"Where did Hannah go? I don't think I've seen her since the performance!" Izzy enquired, having had a genuine interest to see what Hannah thought of the performance.

"She's in the choir closing the Summer Sling," a voice stated from the row behind Izzy.

"I'm surprised you didn't remember Izzy!" Monica giggled, "it's all she's been talking about for weeks!"

Izzy wasn't one for laughing at other peoples expense. However, she was still euphoric from the adrenaline, and she giggled along quickly before stopping herself. She realised that Scott wasn't laughing. In fact, he had been quiet the whole time.

"Is everything okay Sweetie?" Izzy whispered to him while the headmaster introduced the next act.

"Oh yeah, I'm fine." Scott flashed Izzy a quick smile.

She could tell something was up, but once more assumed it must have been the pressure of meeting her parents later that day. She hadn't expected him to be this nervous, as he was usually so outgoing and got along easily with everyone.

Eventually all groups had performed, and the final act was getting ready, but not before Mrs. Ferhulse walked on to the stage to announce the winners of the dance competition. Izzy told herself she would not get too invested in this part, but she couldn't help it. The palms of her hands had become sweaty, and she began to fidget while Mrs. Ferhulse ran through the names of all fifteen dance acts that day.

Monica went to grab Izzy's hand as it was a tense moment for all of them. They had worked so hard to get the performance perfect.

"...and the winner of the Summer Sling this year is...." Izzy closed her eyes in anticipation "...The Disco Divas!! Well done!"

For a moment Izzy was hopeful they would win, but her heart dropped because this meant that the incorrect step had cost them the competition. *She* had cost them the competition. Scott put his arms around her while she simply sat there, speechless. The first loss Hanfield Heartbeats had faced in years, and it was all down to her.

"Izzy! Seriously don't worry about it! The competition was so tough this year! It happens, and we will do better next year!" Monica's words didn't seem to help this time, but Izzy smiled at her anyway.

A moment later, the attention shifted, as the headmaster came back on stage and began to speak about Amy. He described her as being one of the most promising students he had seen walk through the old school's corridors for some time. He spoke of her friendly personality, and finally, he pointed out that everyone should take a flyer on their way out today. He welcomed the choir to wrap up the Summer Sling. Hannah walked onto the stage with such confidence, thanked the headmaster and took centre stage while Mrs. Ferhulse shed a tear from the side-lines.

"Amy was my best friend in this school. She helped me get through the tough times, and she celebrated with me during the good times. I hope that wherever she is she's celebrating for me now..."

"Oh please," Monica whispered to herself, while Izzy felt humbled and inspired by the speech, like much of the room as they listened to the choir.

Izzy thought the choir sounded beautiful and was the perfect end to the Summer Sling. Despite feeling like so much had happened since she disappeared, she missed Amy. She sincerely hoped Amy was not lost forever. People were beginning to get on with their lives now, as most of the community had assumed the worst.

With the Summer Sling over for another year, and while many parents and friends filtered out of the doors, she took Scott's hand.

"They will love you, try not to worry," she attempted to reassure him. He smiled at her and quickly kissed her, still it somehow didn't feel the same as it had done before. Something was seriously wrong, but before Izzy got a chance to react, her parents walked over.

"Ah, so this is the guy we have heard so much about!" Izzy's father was short and round. He went to shake Scott's hand while Mrs. Briggs embraced Izzy.

"You were amazing darling!" she said, hugging Izzy.

"I don't feel great having not won," Izzy said.

"But it's a team effort and if you ask us the girl you replaced... Hannah is it? She let the team down, not you," her mother said with a cheeky grin.

"I thought you were all fantastic!" her father chuckled, rolling his eyes at her mother's spiteful comment.

Upon arriving back home, Izzy was feeling much better after having received a lengthy pep talk by her parents and some kind words from Scott during the car journey towards their polished, red brick home. To Izzy's relief, Scott was now beginning to come out of his shell a bit more.

Her family home was always immaculate, and the place was bright and airy. Her parents were middle class and had a separate dining room which her mother had laid ahead of time, earlier that day.

"Make yourself at home Scott, what would you like to drink?" Mrs Briggs asked from the kitchen.

"Oh, I don't mind!" Scott answered politely.

"He likes cola!" Izzy shouted back to her mother from the living room, "Have a seat! Don't be so shy, silly!" Izzy teased, but she was beginning to feel slightly frustrated that his mood was so changeable. She wanted to press him for an answer as to why he was acting this way but decided against it. It wasn't the time or the place.

As the day turned into night her parents and Scott got along brilliantly. He made perfect conversation with them and spoke fondly of Izzy. They laughed about the earlier performance but also discussed more serious topics. Izzy could see her parents loved Scott, which was all she wanted from the day. So, despite things seeming slightly off with him, she felt her mission was complete and she had almost got through her big day.

Eventually, Scott looked at his chunky sports watch and said his 'goodbyes', thanking Mrs. Briggs for the meal and excusing himself perfectly.

"But I thought you were going to stay for a while longer." Izzy said with a half-smile and glaring disappointment in her voice.

"I've got so much schoolwork to do Iz. I promise I'll call you over the weekend! Thanks again for having me, Mr. and Mrs. Briggs!"

Izzy was left feeling drained and disappointed with the events of her day. After waking up with such excited anticipation, neither the competition nor the evening with her parents had gone the way she envisaged. She padded up the stairs to bed, realising that Scott hadn't even seen her bedroom that she had spent the whole morning perfecting just for him. She sighed getting into bed, utterly deflated and ready to have this Friday over with.

With the covers pulled over her head and her eyes closed she chose to change the subject of her thoughts to something else. Izzy remembered something she had picked up at school earlier, the flyer about Amy Ferhulse. She hadn't even had a chance to read it yet and so, like a quickly distracted puppy she jumped out of bed to grab it from her backpack. As sad as it was, the flyer acted as a welcome distraction from the day's events and getting back into bed, she opened it up to read.

Inside were photos of Amy, including one that Izzy had taken herself at a school fundraiser where she and Amy had participated in raising money for the school's football club to travel overseas for a big game. They'd had so much fun that day trying to complete a world record in star jumping. Izzy laughed to herself remembering it. Written in the leaflet was a brief paragraph about Amy and what she had meant to the community, a description of her appearance, and ways people could continue to help the family find her.

On the rare occasions when Izzy was trying to get to sleep in a bad mood, she would close her eyes and picture all the things that she loved about her life, her parents, her friends and Scott. Her mind was beginning to relax, with everything going dark, and she felt comfortable in amongst her fluffy pillows and airy duvet, letting her bad day slip away as she drifted off to sleep. A breeze brushed her cheek. She opened her eyes to see a figure standing over her. The room was dark, but as her eyes adjusted, she knew it was a person. The streetlight from outside lit just enough of the figure for Izzy to make out a bright red tone to the girl's hair, and with that Izzy gasped loudly.

"Amy!"

XIV

Her Window

Bella found it *utterly intolerable.* It was the morning of the Summer Sling. She knew if Amy were still around, she would be taking hours to get ready for this day. Bella, however, was happy with her basic tartan skirt and 'Smashing Pumpkins' t-shirt for school today.

In recent years, the school had a rule that if you were not participating in the event, you would still have to attend school despite not having any classes. So, she continued to gather her books, intending to stay in the library for much of the day. The thought of sitting in the school's assembly hall watching dance after dance was her idea of *'Hell on Earth'* as she had so dramatically described it the year before, when her twin sister, Amy, had attempted to get her to join in with the rest of her classmates.

Bella loathed the idea of it now, even more so because she knew it would be centred around her sister's disappearance. As much as she wanted to find her sister, she didn't like it being thrown in her face by people who didn't even know her. Plus, she wanted to keep up her low profile – the least amount of people who knew who she was, the better, as far as she was concerned.

With her father having left for work early that morning Bella knew she only had to avoid her mother, who would be on the warpath to get her to "join in for your sister". Bella proceeded to sneak out the back door and climb through the thick hedgerow in the garden.

Arriving at school on time, she headed straight for the library. Making no eye contact, a strategy she had perfected over the years, she managed to avoid being roped into helping anyone with the preparations. If anyone ever did approach her, she would scowl at them until they moved on. Simple, but effective.

The library was much quieter than normal, but she still sat at her usual table, right in the back behind some large bookcases. It had always been her spot. It was the quietest.

She began with some homework she had meant to do for some time. Her schoolwork had been taking a back seat since Amy's disappearance. Her priorities had changed. She was compelled to get answers, and this made it difficult for her to make any time for her studies. It wasn't something Bella ever worried about anyway, but with her mother's return to school she was on her back about it.

A few sums into her Maths project and it wasn't long before she became bored and pulled out her notebook. It was the one in which she had been writing obsessively since she decided to start her investigation into Amy's whereabouts. She flicked through the long list of suspects. They were all scored out now. On the most recent pages was a doodle of an extra-terrestrial-like monster. Bella was none the wiser, but it was something that resembled the creature which had confronted her father at the overpass, and Ms. Henry outside town. It was a rough sketch, but she also had various scribbles of notes on the opposite page.

It seemed she had a new prime suspect, and having recently befriended Scott Bowers, it had excited her that she may finally be on to something. He had some interesting facts as he had told her all about Mrs. Samuels, and maybe it would soon be time to pay her a visit.

She didn't trust Scott completely. Bella was too clever, and she knew guys like Scott well. They were the type of guy who would have picked on her in primary school, and now upon getting older felt like any one's business was his business. He was easy on the eyes, and he knew it. Bella thought Scott had a pretty face, the kind of guy to end up in a boy band that all the younger girls would swoon over and have posters on their wall whether they had any real musical talent or not. The sort of guy Amy would have fallen for. But she needed him right now. Bella was unsure if he had told her everything he knew, but he seemed very keen to keep discussing his findings with her, and she thought perhaps she should confide in him about her big discovery.

Bella could hear the loud footsteps of a man walking over the old wooden floorboards of the library, and she knew it would be him. She was slightly surprised at his being there, because he was in Hanfield Heartbeats, and the Summer Sling was like Christmas Day to them. She knew her mother would have told them all to be preparing from the crack of dawn, but lo and behold Scott's head popped around the bookshelf. His golden blonde hair was dishevelled and untidy, but he still pulled it off.

"I'm amazed you're not in the hallway by now sweet-talking the judges!" Bella joked with Scott. She knew she would not have had time for him if the circumstances had been different, but as it was, she had become quite fond of him, and felt required to downplay his presence.

Scott laughed, "It's a flying visit Bella. I really should go, but I just wanted to catch up ahead of the weekend."

Bella closed her notebook as he moved closer to sit down next to her. She marvelled at how Scott still seemed so committed to finding out what happened to Amy, being someone who didn't tend to generally put much faith in others. He had managed to prove her wrong many times.

"I've been thinking, and I'm convinced we're on to something. I don't know if you have plans for tomorrow night, but I wondered about heading out to the forest at nightfall to check out what Mrs. Samuels meant about whatever 'they' are," Scott spoke so enthusiastically about finding Bella's sister, it warmed her cold, cynical heart, and she wondered right there that maybe Scott could be a friend *she* could finally trust with what she knew. "What do you think?" Scott whispered quietly, pressing for an answer and clearly in a rush.

"I think... I haven't been entirely honest with you," Bella said, leaning into Scott to keep her voice right down. The library was empty, but she still needed to be careful.

"Oh?" Scott looked over his shoulder then back at Bella.

"You might not remember, but I rode my bike past you and Izzy the other week," Bella reminded him.

"Yes, you almost knocked us over!" Scott remembered.

"I was heading out towards the home of someone I suspected would want to hurt Amy, an older man who used to work in the school as a caretaker. He was on my list. When I found out he lived in a small house right out of town, in amongst the forest, I thought I might be on to something. I thought that's where Amy would be. I was desperate to find out, and so I cycled out that way," Bella explained.

"Yes... Go on," Scott no longer looked as though he was in a rush to get away, hanging onto what Bella would say next.

"When I arrived, it looked more like a hut and the lights were off. No one lives there. I remember feeling disheartened that I had ridden all the way there. It was a pain to get to in the end as the road stopped, and I had to ride through woodland. It had been another waste of effort. But then I swear I saw something," Bella grabbed the bottle of water out of her bag, her mouth became dry at the thought of telling her secret to someone.

"What did you see, Bella?" Scott was eager to know.

"I don't even know what to call it," Bella sighed, "It was so misty outside and so dark, and something moved past me like a flash. It scared me, so I grabbed my bike and went home. I thought it was just an animal, or that I was so desperate to see something when I got there, that maybe my eyes were playing tricks on me, but then when you started telling me about the pendant I thought..."

"Bella... what was it?" Scott stared at Bella, mouth half open with his brow furrowing over his blue eyes as he concentrated.

"It looked like something from the sea..." Bella quickly opened her notebook again and turned to the doodles, "It's probably better if I show you..."

Scott grabbed the book, holding it up to his face with both hands. "What is that?" Scott asked, "...and this is what you think took Amy?"

"I don't know, but the more I listen to you, the more I think it's a possibility that I wasn't seeing thing," Bella looked away, cringing, having opened herself up to Scott's judgment.

"'Things that walk at night' Mrs. Samuels told me. It checks out, the pendant she had!" Scott put the notebook on the desk to the side of them. He reached out and carefully touched Bella's cheek to turn her head back, "Thank you for telling me."

Bella couldn't take her eyes away from Scott's, and in that brief moment his hand felt warm and soft. His stare was lingering on her for what felt like forever, and she thought he might kiss her. *Am I going to kiss him back?* He began to lean in even more, and just as Bella was about to close her eyes for a kiss, Scott pulled her hair.

"Got it!" Scott shouted. Bella opened her eyes to Scott holding some of the hedge from her back garden, the one she had hauled herself through earlier that morning.

Feeling herself going red, she turned away to take out some of her schoolbooks, hoping this would be the conversation finisher, and give Scott the cue to head off to his friends. Bella was confused. *Do I like Scott in that way?*

"So anyway, I'll see you tomorrow night? We can maybe find one of those skinny-looking guys!" Scott got up and grabbed his backpack.

"Sure!" Bella said nonchalantly, flashing Scott a brief smile, before pretending to study.

Bella knew she could have wished him good luck at the Summer Sling, but he had plenty of people to wish him luck already, and she was careful to keep on topic. They were never going to become lifelong friends, he was just a tool to aid in finding out what happened to her sister, and perhaps it was time to keep reminding herself of that more often.

The more Bella sat in the empty library thinking about Scott, the more agitated she became. *Why did I do that?* Her whole being was against people like Scott, and she had got all the information he had on the matter. She didn't need him anymore, and she certainly didn't need his help in the forest tomorrow night.

The Familiar Encounter

Getting back to her research, she pulled out a book she had taken from the community library. It was called 'The Hanfield Histories'. The way it had been illustrated had drawn her to it, with ghouls and goblins on the cover. As she quickly flicked through, it appeared to be folk stories rather than real history about Hanfield. She opened it and began reading each page to see if anything at all seemed relevant to what she had seen and heard so far.

A few hours went by, and just as she was beginning to lose hope and think she would be better off concentrating on her schoolwork, something on the next page caught her eye. A sketch of the pendant Scott had described to her days ago.

Tentascope Chain; The tribes of the historical Crimpets would use this to identify humans who were aware of their existence. The ancient tribe having fallen to Earth and said to be from a burnt-out star or a moon that had been attacked. The small number of survivors are said to reside in the miles upon miles of Hanfield forest, though no known sightings are confirmed.

It wasn't much to go off, but it was something, and any sort of something was huge to Bella after the long run of bad luck. This was one of the biggest leads she'd had since starting her quest for the truth, and she needed to find out more.

"Mrs. Samuels!"

She spoke loudly enough for the librarian at the front desk to send her a scolding, "SHHH!"

Bella was excited. She knew Mrs. Samuels was staying in Cliff Edge Care Home, which was a distance away, so she would need to leave now. She stopped herself for a moment to consider if perhaps she should wait and tell Scott tomorrow. Mrs. Samuels had already opened up about it to him, so maybe he could still be of use. Then she snapped out of it and realised deep down that this was just a curiosity for him. Once it blew over, he wouldn't even say so much as a 'how are you?' to her in the corridor, and with that, she decided to stay with her reclusive ways and go it alone.

Bella headed off in the direction of the exit. Passing the entrance to the hallway, she could see everyone was watching the final choir. The posters on the wall outside the hall had a photo of Hannah Henry and Amy laughing together, with bold letters above it which read 'For Amy'. Bella rolled her eyes as she usually did about anything involving Hannah.

"Oh yeah, for Amy... or yourself, Hannah?" Bella asked the inanimate poster.

She was leaving school slightly early, but no one was around to see her. They were all doe-eyed over Hannah right now which was fine by Bella. Using her attention-seeking as a welcome distraction, Bella left by one of the side exits. She caught the first bus heading in the correct direction. She needed to think of how she could walk into the building and get a seat with Mrs. Samuels specifically.

Bella had been pretty good at sneaking around other people's homes before, back when she was working through her list of suspects. She had an unusual skill in creeping around and stalking those she needed to collect information on. It wasn't legal, but it got the job done.

With the remainder of her journey, she began jotting down questions she would ideally like to ask Mrs. Samuels if she had the opportunity. *Why the hell are there actual aliens in freakin' Hanfield?* She figured she would present her questions a little less directly than that.

After Bella got off the bus, it sped off, leaving a mist of soot from the disused road behind it. She walked the distance to the grand old house, slotted randomly in the middle of nowhere and surrounded with trees.

When she caught a glimpse of the house, she turned right towards some thicker foliage. Being careful not to use any clear pathways to approach the building she went around the long way. This was not like sneaking up on your average house. There were so many windows and her tartan skirt would be visible to staff in the greenery.

This was not going to be as easy as she thought, and she cursed herself for her stubbornness in disregarding Scott's usefulness. She would be less detectable by the staff members as soon as she was up against the house. Taking cover behind a small bush and looking round for ideas, she had a brainwave. She had recently watched a movie where the main character used false shrubbery to sneak up on someone. It seemed silly, but she grabbed two potted plants from the edge of the garden by the greenhouse and held them out in front of her. It wasn't a perfect disguise by any means, but it meant she had some camouflage. She paused to giggle for a moment. *If only Amy could see me now.*

Running as fast as she could from behind the bush, straight over to the red-brick wall, she pressed her back right up against it. Standing between two large windows while she caught her breath and discarding the plants, she listened out for anyone who may have seen her, but she could hear nothing. Bella continued to peep in one of the windows. It looked to be the dining room. It was getting on for teatime, and there were plenty of elderly people in there. But she didn't have eyes on her target and realising she had no idea what Mrs. Samuels looked like, she used the information she had and looked out for someone who was a combination of:

1) Female
2) 100 years of age
3) Wearing the egg-shaped pendant

Like a real-life version of 'Guess Who' this seemed to be getting harder. She kept her back up against the wall and ran past a couple of windows, praying no one would have seen her in those few exposed seconds. She now found herself between another two large windows, another part of the care home, it seemed to be the kitchen and it was full of staff. Just as she was feeling as though she had no luck at all, her ears pricked up as she heard one member of staff start talking. She was standing in front of the window looking out, just inches away from Bella.

"Mrs. Samuels has been slowing down a lot recently, that's only half her food she's eaten again today," she sounded worried.

"What do you expect, Kathryn? She is ancient. She barely moves from that living room window, so it's not as if she's using up the energy," another care assistant replied.

That was the clue Bella was missing; she would find her in the living room window. Now she just needed to wait for the sound of all the staff leaving the kitchen to run past the window. She sighed while waiting, annoyed and frustrated. These old windows were so low to the ground there was no space she could use to crawl past.

Looking out onto the grounds of the care home while she waited, it seemed quiet and peaceful. The garden had plenty of little spots to sit and watch the bird feeders and the flower beds. Beyond this, the woodland was thick and dark, surrounding the entire grounds. It was only connected to town via that one rough road.

When the chatting from the kitchen seemed to quiet down, Bella decided to make her move over towards the next set of windows. This time they were slightly smaller frosted windows which she assumed were toilets and she kept moving. She was relieved to see she was now next to a common room window. From the outside, Bella could hear some old jazz record playing. Feeling brave, she quickly peered in through the window.

She saw no sign of Mrs. Samuels right away. The first thing she noticed was how dark the room seemed to be, with elderly people sitting around playing card games or listening to the music. Some had cups of tea while others were fast asleep in their chairs. The room was tastefully decorated. It looked warm and welcoming, with a massive open fire not far from the window she was peering through. Scanning the large, comfortable room, Bella squinted as she noticed a woman looking out through the opposite window, her pure white hair drawing Bella's attention. She could barely make out the woman, but Bella thought it likely that she was the woman she was looking for. She continued to make her way around the building again, sneaking past windows, quickly and nimbly. The sun was beginning to set now, making it much easier for her.

When she got to the final window, she wondered how she could get Mrs. Samuel's attention. How would she speak to her through the glass? *Damn it!* Annoyed that her last-minute plan had not been well executed, she now wondered if she should even try to make herself known to the old lady at all. It seemed like she was finally on to something, and after all her other investigations, it was the worst time to become sloppy. She had let her feelings for Scott get the better of her.

She continued to peer through the window. At the very least, she wanted to try to see the pendant to back up Scott's story, and she moved closer. The old lady with the white hair sat at a small deep mahogany table right in front of the window. The table was varnished and polished to a deep shine and Bella could see the reflection of the sky in it. Mrs. Samuels sat away from everyone else. She was reading a book while wearing tiny reading glasses and using her long, thin finger to point and follow each line. For a moment, she looked to be engrossed in the book, concentrating too hard to see that Bella had been standing in the window, but then her finger stopped following the story and paused. Mrs. Samuels looked up, slowly replaced her reading glasses with another pair and looked right at Bella, who was now standing in full view. Bella had initially been smiling slightly so as not to scare the old lady, but her smile disappeared when she realised that she had already met Mrs. Samuels before.

XV

The Nightmare

Richard's hands and knees were now bloodied and sore as he made his way over to his car, unable to get his legs to work from the shock of his encounter. The further he pushed his body, the brighter his car headlights seemed to get, so bright his eyes could barely take it. The sound of Ms. Rhompski screaming along with the speeding cars from the overpass were getting quieter, the yellow light from his headlights was now a blinding white. He could no longer hear anything. Falling face first into the mud, Richard fainted.

Richard felt something running up his arm, it felt cold and steady, but not uncomfortable in the slightest. It was a silky feeling, and it calmed him while he sat there feeling it move. Eventually he looked down, and to his terror, found a snake, draping its black and yellow body around his arm. Richard shouted out in horror, and the snake recoiled for a moment before opening its mouth wide, exposing its sharp fangs before darting forwards towards his face.

"Help, Help!" Richard sat up in bed, having awoken from the nightmare to find Dana sitting on the side of the bed, stroking his bare arm.

"Hey! You're dreaming!" Dana grabbed his shoulder to make sure he had indeed woken up, "You have a temperature, you're sick."

Richard took a moment to focus on Dana, who wore the same furrowed brow she always seemed to have whenever she looked at him. He knew, looking around him, he was awake this time, as his dreams were never as dreary as this, the grey bedroom they shared in their dull marriage.

To anyone else, it would look as though Dana was caring for him, stroking his arm lovingly. But this was nothing other than her taking the opportunity to patronise him. She always took joy in calling him a child in their arguments. But she was right about one thing. As Richard tried to muster up a thin smile for his wife, he realised his head was throbbing, his hands were all sweaty, and his entire body was chilled and aching.

"Why do you care?" Richard asked without any expectation of a legitimate answer from Dana, as he lay back down in bed and rolled over.

"It's not like you to miss work... you're still my husband, after all," Dana spoke with an undertone of frustration in her voice. She regretted bothering with him at all.

With the mere mention of work, Richard hauled himself out of bed and began getting ready, grunting with the effort of heaving the shower doors in the ensuite.

"...and he's back," Dana whispered under her breath.

He would still rush to work despite feeling as though he had the biggest hangover, just moving around made his head feel worse. His whole body felt awful, but he had to get into the office as soon as possible. He hated for anyone to see any weakness in him.

When he arrived, it was worse than he envisioned. Some members of staff had already approached him on his walk from the car to his office, asking if he was okay. Richard didn't quite know how to answer that question, because with his life falling apart around him, he was not okay, and at the moment he knew he most definitely did not look okay either.

"Mr. Ferhulse, Mr. Ferhulse!" Steph followed Richard as he stormed towards his office. He assumed she was another one wanting to see if he was okay and decided to continue walking and avoid her.

"Wait!"

He stopped and spun round to face her, outraged by her interest in his wellbeing.

"What? I don't see why everyone is so concerned that I've walked in a couple of hours late. I don't feel well, end of topic," he spoke with a raised voice out on the main floor, and people at desks nearby stopped typing to listen.

"I was going to say... erm, you had some letters left at reception for you... glad you're feeling well enough to come in today Mr. Ferhulse," Steph smiled at him, nervously.

Richard felt embarrassed having jumped down her neck. He sheepishly took the wad of mail from her hand and quietly thanked her. *They will all think I'm an ass.*

Sitting down at his desk, he had locked the door to his office to save any further unpleasant conversations. He exhaled in pain as he rubbed his head with one hand and his back with the other, the painkillers he had taken before leaving the house were not working.

Just as Richard was waiting for his computer to start up, he began sifting through the large chunk of mail Steph had handed him. The dates were from that morning, yesterday and the day before... and the day before that.

A sinking feeling came over him as he realised, he had been off sick from work for a lot longer than he ever knew. He quickly opened his calendar to double-check whether his terrible suspicions were correct.

"How?" Richard asked himself in disbelief. It was a Wednesday, and he had not been at work since the previous Thursday, "Almost a flaming week!" he shouted as he simultaneously stood up from his desk in surprise. He had lost the entire weekend and start of the week. He dreaded the thought of how many meetings he had missed, "...and golf with the Mayor!" he exclaimed staring at his calendar.

He picked up the phone on his desk and began dialling his home number.

"Hello?" Dana answered

"I've been off work for almost a week!" Richard shouted, "How?!"

"Why are you asking me? You disappeared, I thought you had left me... us," Dana sounded genuine, "Then you turned up last night and went straight to bed as if nothing was wrong."

"I don't remember anything Dana! You didn't think to look for me?" Richard was confused and furious.

"Nothing would surprise me about you anymore. You had left, and I was glad!" Dana snapped back and hung up the phone.

Richard slammed the phone down in rage. He needed to calm down and think rationally. He was sweating profusely because of his high temperature. His mind felt foggy as he tried to remember where he had been. Last week he was out for burgers after work with some colleagues. It could have been food poisoning, but that wouldn't account for the number of days. One thing he did know, he needed to catch up on piles of work. His rational brain was coming in to play to make a survival plan as he looked helplessly at his diary, and all the missed meetings and deadlines. *I'll simply get through this work today, and at some point it'll come back to me.*

Prioritising catching up with the mountain of work, he chipped away trying to ignore his headache and fatigue, managing to put out the worry of where he had been over the last few days from his mind.

He decided to cancel all the meetings for the rest of the week to catch up, and delay speaking to anyone regarding his whereabouts. His colleagues behaved friendly but were anything but, they would push for answers when he didn't have any, and perhaps someone knew where he had been – someone had to. But for now, it was time to get his head down and work.

Conducting as much damage control as possible, he worked well into the night arriving home in the very early hours of the morning, ready to get a few hours of much needed rest, hopeful that he would shake off the sickness. He hadn't spoken to Dana since their earlier, explosive phone conversation. He had often wondered what the repercussions would be if he just left one day. Richard had thought about it long and hard when things started to become frosty between them. He would think about moving away and starting fresh, knowing however, that he could never actually do it. But he always imagined people would care, Dana especially. But now he knew the truth, it was quite the opposite. *I was glad!'* he heard Dana's voice on repeat in his mind while he lay in bed looking up at the ceiling, Dana, lying right next to him sound asleep. *She was glad I had gone. Amy's disappearance was the cake, and Dana's resentment was the cherry on top, followed by sprinkles of career-ending slip-ups and...*

As his mind ran into issues at work, he recalled the biggest one of all – *the missing file!* He hadn't thought about it all day. Now this consumed him. *Did I get it back?* Richard huffed and rolled over in uncomfortable frustration. He was tired, in pain and couldn't even remember if he ever located the file. *I'm sure I did?... Did I? It was gone, and I was going to get it back. But where was it?* Trying his best to piece things back together, he couldn't grasp that part of the puzzle. *It's been a week, if someone had it, the contents would inevitably have been leaked by now.* It seemed like a rational conclusion to quieten Richard's mind enough to rest, which was what his weakened, aching body needed, and he soon drifted off to sleep.

Waking up, he felt refreshed and humbled. It was a beautiful Sunday morning, and he could hear Dana and Isabella laughing loudly and uncontrollably downstairs at something. It made him smile; he was curious about what it was that made them so happy and so strolled towards the stairs in his blue and black pyjamas.

From the stairs, he could see a considerable amount of the bottom half of the house. It was an open plan with a large hallway opening up into the kitchen and dining area, and on the opposite side there was the living room. The rooms were all decorated a peachy cream colour with large windows letting in the bright rays of the morning's sunshine.

The girls were just out of view, and so he followed their laughter expectantly. Approaching the living room, he picked up a third voice, it was Amy's.

His heart almost burst out of his chest as he turned that final corner to reveal all three of *his* girls. Almost like the last few months hadn't taken place, the three of them sat on the floor, still also in their pyjamas, huddled around the iPad in hysterical laughter. Richard stood there watching, whatever they were looking at was holding their attention, and he took it all in. He was beyond happy to have his family back together. Amy's happy energy had returned, and everything was going to be ok.

Dana was first to notice him standing there, and she shot him a big smile and mouthed, 'Good morning' coyly, as his daughters continued to mess around on the floor. He joined them, moving to embrace Amy, but something wasn't right, she was freezing, so cold it gave him a shock, and he jumped back.

"Are you ok, Dad?" Amy asked in confusion, still half giggling with Bella. Richard stared at Amy for a moment, noticing her big smile and feeling her presence. How he had missed her.

But something stole his gaze. His eyes shot upwards from the floor and over to the far end of the room. Behind his wife and children, his eyes came to rest on the figure stood in the dark doorway between his office and living room. A chill came over him. The character wore a black cloak. Its shape was only vaguely distinguishable to Richard. His eyes were fixed on it, but no one else seemed to notice as they joked together. The figure was concealed well within the dark doorway. It stood still, watching them from the shadows.

Despite its stillness, he could see it was a person, and another cold chill washed over his entire body, lingering down his spine.

"Guys... I want you to go outside," Richard said calmly. The instinct to protect his family had kicked in.

"What? Haha!" Bella said, dismissing him.

"Go outside!" Richard repeated.

"Your Dad's right, we should get ready and head out to enjoy the weather today! We're not sitting in our PJ's all-day girls!" Dana said supportively, unaware of the strange man standing only metres away from them, still watching intently.

Richard forced a smile and nodded in encouragement to the twins until they got up and walked away. This was good enough for Richard. He needed them away from whoever this man was in their home.

"You too!" he said to Dana, forcing a light-hearted smile. She looked confused for a moment but smiled back, shrugging her shoulders and getting up.

"If you're making coffee, bring one up for me, would ya?" Dana asked while heading upstairs, in the same direction as the girls.

There was something about the intruder that made Richard feel afraid. He got up from the floor and tried to focus on the figure in the doorway before approaching him.

"What do you want?" Richard asked, "I'll call the police!"

The figure stood upright after leaning on the door frame to watch them, and in doing so, moved into the light. It began to laugh, only very slightly at first but became increasingly uncontrollable as it went on. It was male, but it didn't sound like regular laughing. It was forced and unnatural.

"What the hell's wrong with you?" Richard quizzed confidently, now feeling braver, assuming the guy was not as much of a threat as he first thought: "Are you a nutter from the hospital? I should call them".

Richard turned his back to get the phone from the hallway while the guy continued to laugh uncontrollably. However, the tone itself was changing, it was getting higher and higher in pitch. Richard stopped in his tracks, as the noise the man was now making was that of his two daughters laughing. He was mimicking their laugh.

Richard was tall and had always been active, and he felt outraged that the moment he was reunited with his lost daughter, this guy had decided to invade their home and try to intimidate him. Richard was livid listening to the man copy his daughter's laugh. He took it as a threat.

"You're to leave my home right now!" Richard turned towards the figure and strode angrily over to him. He was still laughing, "Who do you think you are?"

Richard attempted to grab the man's arm as hard as he could to drag him through the house and out through the front door. But upon making contact, expecting to feel the width of a regular arm, he found it was thin and skeletal, more like a narrow tree branch, but hard, like it was bone. As he paused, Richard looked to the cloaked man's face who had now ceased his laughing. He was close enough that he should have been able to see a face looking back at him... but couldn't. He adjusted his grip to accommodate for the much thinner frame.

"Come on, let's go," Richard said.

The figure wouldn't budge as he tried to walk him out. Richard increased his force, and used both arms, but the man still wouldn't move. He was becoming increasingly frustrated as he knew his daughters and Dana would soon be ready for a day out, and this stranger was going to ruin it all.

He heaved with everything he had to try to force the man to leave, but suddenly Richard was sent flying towards the kitchen counter as the figure abruptly disappeared into thin air.

A second or two after crashing headfirst into the counter, Richard awoke with a deep inhalation of breath back into reality. It was another dream; he could tell right away as the familiar feeling of misery and anxiety engulfed him. Looking around, he was no longer in the dazzling brilliance of his dream, nor in his bed, but instead, was sprawled on the floor downstairs.

He had been wrestling with a couple of Dana's favourite designer jackets along with the umbrellas hung up in the cloakroom. The headache was returning with a vengeance as Dana appeared at the top of the stairs.

"Who's there?" she called out, turning on the light.

"It's me... it's just me," Richard said with a sigh. It had all been a dream, he thought despairingly. The happy wife and most of all, Amy's' return, were all just an agonising dream

"Do you know what time it is Richard?" Dana shrieked at him: "I really was glad when I thought you were gone. I can't do this anymore. You're not the person I married. I want a divorce." Not waiting for a reaction, Dana turned the light off and turned on her heel, back to the bedroom, leaving Richard in the dark.

Richard let his back slide down the wall of the cloakroom, to sit dejectedly on the floor. He wasn't surprised Dana had asked for a divorce, but he couldn't help but let the tears flow, as he lowered his head to his hands in torment. For a brief moment he had believed that Amy had returned, and everything was as it should be; that they were all one big happy family. He needed her home; they needed her home.

Everything in my life has fallen apart, but I wouldn't care one bit if Amy would just come back.

XVI

Amy's Return

Hannah had woken up at 5 am to prepare for the Summer Sling, just as the morning sun was beginning to rise. Every colour was filling the sky as it turned from night to day, but Hannah paid no attention to this when opening her curtains, catching a shot of her reflection in the glass window she posed, and played with her hair.

Her mother wasn't awake yet, and she resented this. *Mother should have my morning smoothie ready for me. I should not be wasting my time like this.* Clattering about with the chopping board and blender, she whizzed together her favourite banana and apple smoothie. Usually, Hannah would have a more substantial breakfast to start her day. But on competition days, she never liked to have a full stomach. It wasn't so much nerves as it was excitement; this was the feeling she experienced when competing ever since she could remember.

Still, today was different. She had loved the idea of performing and competing in the school's events, for a long time, but now she felt it was beneath her, even more so recently, as she knew her talents had not been appreciated by her mentor, Dana. *The world has gone crazy*, Hannah thought while sucking on her super thick smoothie, and pacing the cold kitchen floor. However, despite this, she still felt that old familiar excitement ahead of today, heightened by her planning and scheming.

She had a lot of strong feelings, albeit none positive, over Mrs. Ferhulse's decision to change up the lead in the troupe at the last minute. She felt it was a personal attack on her, and this was the final nail in the coffin when it came down to Hanfield as a whole. None of these people appreciated what she was doing for the community. Not one person seemed to see her for the super talented asset she was to the town. Her enthusiasm for dance had been temporarily diverted with thoughts of sabotaging Izzy today. Hannah scrolled quickly through her phone, not on her social media apps but on the notes she had made to ensure that today's plan went smoothly. She was passionate about everything she undertook, and this was no exception, everything was planned out precisely.

"Then you'll think twice before trying to upstage me," Hannah muttered out loud while grinning at the plans.

Despite being classed as friends, Izzy was someone she would often look at, and think *how sad*. Izzy had no sense of style. Hannah thought she was pathetic with her volunteering and her photography club, and she was certainly no match for her in anything, let alone dancing. This made the change in lead dancer even more insulting. Thinking back to the humiliation, she clenched her fist, digging her long, manicured nails into the palm of her hand. Here it was, the day of execution with the plans right in front of her. Her excitement was for sweet revenge and nothing else. She had been channelling all of her anger into this day.

"Oh no, you're not coming to watch today!" Hannah instructed, upon seeing her mother appear holding one of her nicest dresses and carrying the iron.

"Of course I am, I love supporting you... now, why on Earth would I not attend?" Ms. Henry responded.

"You embarrass me, is that a good enough reason?" Hannah said while using the bare wall to stretch out her hamstrings.

"I think every student in that school feels that way about their parents watching them!" Ms. Henry spoke rationally despite Hannah's words hurting her feelings. She knew there would be no point in getting offended, or even in showing her dismay. It had always been wasted on Hannah.

When it was almost time for Hannah to leave for school, she went into her wardrobe to pull out the dance outfit. Unlike everyone else in the group, she had managed to get hers ahead of time to be able to make adjustments to the fit. Putting on her altered uniform, the red and royal blue tones suited her tanned skin and golden blonde hair. She'd gone heavier on the eyeshadow and added a red lip to match the outfit, always putting careful thought into her appearance to ensure she looked outstanding all of the time. Even if she were now in the background, she would still make sure she stood out.

Getting off the school bus, having left her mother behind, she was to head over to the sports hall. This was where Dana had instructed they all meet for their usual motivational pep talk before the competition.

On the way Hannah paused having spotted Izzy down the hallway. Izzy was smiling through her muddle as always. She hadn't collected her uniform yet for the competition while Hannah was already wearing hers. Hannah wasn't sure if she should feel further insult at being replaced by someone so clueless. *That figures*, Hannah thought, watching as Izzy looked bewildered moving past the busy hall. Hannah smiled to herself as she strutted in Izzy's direction. She had acted pleasantly regarding the position swap in front of Dana and the team, but she had no intention of keeping this up when alone with Izzy.

"Feeling confident?" Hannah stood towering over a shorter, slightly overweight Izzy.

"Do you have any tips?" Izzy asked, smiling politely, as if she were too innocent even to notice Hannah's negative tone.

Hannah smirked, "Since we've all worked so hard over the year on this routine my only advice would be not to mess it up," she shrugged while Izzy's happy face dropped.

Content she had tortured Izzy just enough to plant the tiniest seed of doubt into her mind, she walked off, round to another busy corridor heading towards the girl's toilets to check her makeup quickly. The way the other students looked at her when she walked into a room made her feel powerful. The mirrored wall in the toilets was busy, as was everywhere else in the school right now. But aware of her presence, and with no words spoken, the other students began to gradually clear out. The room was spacious, with two rows of toilet cubicles and a host of mirrored sink areas, with the entire room tiled in a vintage avocado green.

"Thanks, girls!" Hannah said, taking out her makeup bag.

Looking at herself in the mirror for the 100th time that morning, she poked and preened her hair and face. After running her fingers along each eyebrow, she took out her eyelash curlers. A cold chill ran through her as she took the silver curlers in her hand and clamped them onto her lengthy, black lashes. *Urgh, this old draughty school.* The bathrooms were now empty and eerily quiet considering the day's event.

"Dong!" She heard a loud, sharp noise coming from the other side of the room, from one of the cubicles in the second row, as if someone were banging on a cistern. It made Hannah jump so much a couple of her precious eyelashes were pulled out by the curlers.

"Who's made me mess my lashes up? You're going to be in so much trouble!" Hannah shouted, staring down at the curlers in frustration.

No one answered, but Hannah knew someone else was in the room. She could hear them moving against the silence of the otherwise empty school toilets.

"Who's there!" Hannah demanded, throwing her curler down and storming towards the second row of cubicles.

With no lights or windows at this end of the room, it was much darker. The water dripping from one of the taps was the only thing breaking the silence in the room. *'Drip, drip, drip'* echoed off the shiny green tiled walls. Hannah looked towards the very end cubicle from where the noise had come, and with every laminated door ajar, it seemed she was all alone. With another cold chill hitting the base of Hannah's spine, she turned around to head back to her mirror. Time was getting on!

'Dong!' Another loud, echoing noise coming from that toilet again, louder this time, making Hannah jump once more.

Frustration mounting, she turned back around to investigate again. To her shock, she had turned to face someone. A horrible image, enough to make her really react this time. Hannah brought her hands to her mouth and retreated until she hit the cold, hard wall.

"No... it's... it's not," Hannah stuttered in disbelief, "Amy?"

Amy nodded calmly, studying Hannah with her eyes.

"But... but you're dead!" Hannah looked at Amy as if she were a ghost, her illusions completely shattered

"I don't think that was ever confirmed," Amy stated, walking towards her old friend, "You've not been very kind while I have been away, unlike the friend I used to know... or thought I knew."

Amy was just as Hannah remembered her, the orangey-red hair vivid against the green room, and her fair porcelain complexion, luminous in the space. Only Amy now looked thinner, her face slightly gaunt, and staring into her eyes, Hannah could tell she was very different to how she once was. As Amy approached her, Hannah remembered to adopt her confident role.

"Well gosh, I think I'm just in total shock, sorry!" Hannah composed herself. Standing up properly, she dusted herself down and opened her arms to go in for a hug, "I'm *so* glad you're back."

Amy pushed her back up against the wall. She was no longer blind to her attempts of manipulation.

"You don't fool me, and you don't know what I've gone through to get here... I want to warn you, if you harm Izzy today I'll be coming for you," Amy threatened. Looking into Hannah's eyes the entire time she saw the hatred in them and could feel the evil emanating from her.

Hannah was aware that Amy's skin was ice cold, her breath making faint clouds in the air as she spoke.

"Okay, whatever!" Too frightened and in shock to protest, she conceded, hoping Amy would back off.

"I hope you've understood me. You need to stop this," Amy warned, standing back up properly and heading slowly out of the toilet doors, having put her hood up over her head. Hannah stood in silence for a moment. Her heart was beating out of her chest as she attempted to process the quick exchange. It had all happened so fast she wondered if it had really taken place at all. She headed out the toilet doors a few seconds after Amy, expecting to see a commotion in the corridors as people realised that long lost Amy had returned. But there was nothing, no sign of Amy at all and no scene of note. Hannah could see Izzy and Monica chatting and laughing together further down the corridor, and she felt a rage build up inside her all over again.

You won't be laughing for much longer. Hannah shrugged the entire encounter off with a flick of her hair as she went back to doing her makeup. She needed to rush now as it was almost time to begin preparing for the competition. Parents would soon be arriving and taking their seats to watch, and although she was intending to sabotage the whole routine, she didn't want to arouse suspicion by carrying herself any differently. Leaving the toilets, the corridors, not long alive with students, were now empty, and Hannah felt the cold, chilling sensation once more. She could hear the event was well underway now and walked that little bit quicker. Mrs. Ferhulse would be panicking by now that she wasn't there already. Heading out of the school doors to cut across the playing field towards the sports hall, she caught sight of someone running out of the school library, and despite the distance, she could tell it was Bella Ferhulse. She would recognise that train wreck of gothic outfit anywhere.

"We were about to send a search party, Hannah!" Dana joked sarcastically in front of the now prepared Hanfield Heartbeats, "Now that we're all here, let's take it from the top."

For the final practice, Hannah begrudgingly got into position behind Scott and Izzy. Right before the dance music started, she overheard a moment between the couple.

"So, where were you?" Izzy whispered.

"Finishing off some work in the library," Scott answered quickly.

In that instant, hearing those words, Hannah realised something juicier than ever. *Scott and Bella together in the library?* She knew Scott and Amy would have ended up together by now, had she been around, so maybe Bella was the consolation prize that Izzy didn't know about.

Heading out on to the stage, Hannah was positively buzzing with excitement at the prospect of getting her own back on Izzy. Her rage would finally have its outlet. Having spent countless hours on hatching this plan, it was about to be the moment of truth.

During the performance, she wanted to execute her steps perfectly, so that no one would suspect she had done anything to make Izzy fall. She envisioned everyone assuming it was just an unlucky accident, and so when the music started and the routine was underway in front of the bright lights, she smiled that little bit wider in the knowledge of what was about to happen. Barely able to contain her malicious exhilaration during the second lift, she took pleasure in noticing the floorboards of the stage were about to collapse. This was the moment she had been waiting for. On the final lift Izzy would fall through the stage, and at worst ruin their chances of winning the competition and be humiliated in front of the entire school. At best she would go away with an injury, *so she can't ever compete with us again.*

Just as it was about to happen, and Izzy was about to land from her third toss in the air, Hannah couldn't help but look over to watch. As quickly as a flash, someone appeared from the wings; a blur, which seemed to be wearing the same uniform as them, with the red and blue flashes so as to blend in amongst the group. Izzy was guided to safety by the individual, and although she looked puzzled, she continued to perform the routine, regardless.

It was Amy. She's ruining everything! Everything is going wrong for me! She could feel a deep anger inside of her surging to the surface. Her heartbeat quickened as she began to get hot with anger. The routine was over, and Hannah couldn't even hear the sound of applause. Everything was silent, while she focused on trying to keep it together. Rushing into one of the old dressing rooms, she smiled through gritted teeth knowing she was due back on stage with the choir in a few moments. Hannah slammed the door behind her, quickly locking it.

The room was filled with some smaller gym equipment and props from past shows. She grabbed one of the folded fabric banners and screamed into it as hard as she could. She stomped both of her feet with anger – yet another plan was foiled, and she couldn't take it anymore. This was supposed to be *her time,* and yet she was still being overshadowed. Amy was somehow still messing with her life.

Anyone else would have heeded the threat Amy made in the girl's toilets, but not Hannah. She was now too broken, too vexed to care. As she went to shove her face back into the large banner to scream again, she started to feel differently. As she stomped her feet and yelled, a real burning heat ran through her entire body. Hannah stopped what she was doing and lifted her head. Everything in the room was a blur, and as she looked down at her hands, she could see her fingers had become longer and thinner, and her nails were extra sharp and pointed. Her mouth felt strange, and she instinctively ran her tongue over her teeth, to find they were all as sharp as glass. Slowly dropping the banner and walking over to the mirror she looked at herself. The rash on her back had spread, and she scratched at her skin, panicking. The whites of her eyes turned a sharp blood-red. Her vision was still blurred, but she kept scratching, and as her eyes adjusted, she gasped loudly. Under her grotesque, sceptic skin were scales, *like a snake*.

"Knock, knock..." A loud banging on the door made Hannah turn around gasping again.

"Hannah Henry? Hannah? Are you in there? You're due to take the stage in 5 minutes! The choir is ready!" Hannah recognised the voice as one of her teachers. As she turned back around to face the mirror again, her appearance had reverted to normal, no red eyes, no shark-like teeth, and looking down at her now regular hands, she began to laugh maniacally, as a sudden surge of power came over her.

Emerging from the closet, and feeling better than she ever had done, she gave her performance, as heartfelt and as sincere as if she meant her tribute to Amy. She saw that even teachers and parents in the audience were shedding a tear and knew that not one of them had a clue she had been speaking to Amy earlier. No one had the slightest idea of the hideous monster inside Hannah, that had taken over.

XVII

A Few Crimpets

She began to rise from her tiny safe place and peered out into the woods, paying attention to sweep off the dried mud from her skin and clothes as she did so. Upon exposing herself, she looked upwards to find a horrifying figure. A now wide-eyed hobbling beast stood before her, approximately ten feet away, staring directly at her. No facial expression except the tiny eyes being larger in a moment that both startled them both to a pause. The disjointed mouth of this being let out a blood-curdling grunt before throwing its entire body weight into a lunging, horrifying dive toward Amy's direction.

With no fight left inside her, Amy cowered behind her arms, palms facing out towards the monster, closing her eyes as hard as she could, too frightened and too broken to even let out a scream. At this moment she knew she wasn't going to go home despite her best efforts. Bracing herself to be tackled to the ground, she felt helpless, but as the seconds ticked by, she wondered at the delay in the attack

Turning her head back to face its direction and glancing over her still raised hands, she was surprised to see the creature was paused

The Familiar Encounter

only a couple of feet away from her, the bush she had used as cover was now the only thing between her and it. It was still, as if it were a statue, and still too frozen with fright and exhaustion she didn't know what to do as she looked around clueless.

"Are... you *alright?*" Amy asked awkwardly.

The creature didn't react, unable to move apart from its beady little eyes darting around in all different directions. Amy recognised panic in them. She had never been able to study their faces like this, but its skin looked as wrinkly and rough as it had always felt whenever they would maltreat her, with a green tinge to the pale greyness.

"What *are* you?" Amy mustered the courage to ask it, while continuing to study it curiously. But it didn't have the capability to understand her or answer, and it didn't take long for the realisation to surface that she could actually make her escape.

Amy slowly backed away, as she didn't dare turn her back on the creature. She kept going until she gently bumped into a tree. Taking a deep breath, she prepared to begin running and hiding all over again, in a bid to get home. On the exhale she whipped herself around with the intention to sprint away, but the tree she had just been leaning on wasn't a tree at all, it was a person.

"Oh!" Amy stepped back from the man instinctively.

"It's a Fangrog, awful things... nasty body odour," the man said.

"Oh..." Amy darted a look at the creature again before turning back to face the man. Stunned at the confrontation, and hearing someone speak to her, she spoke tentatively, "...and who are you?" The man, who was dressed in all black, was much taller than her and very slender. In the shadows, she couldn't make out his features, but after her initial wariness, she was relieved to have bumped into someone who could potentially help her.

"My name is Franumbro, but you can call me Frank. I live here in the forest and was pleased to have caught sense of you Amy." Frank said, in perfectly articulated English.

"How do you know my name? Have we met before?" Amy was starting to worry that perhaps this guy wasn't good news.

"We were aware of you. You ate one of *our* apples. We did try to obtain you for a few days, but unfortunately, the wretched Fangrogs seized you first. I must say it's fortuitous to meet you like this, so you must forgive my excitement," Frank said, his monotonous tones seeming to contradict his words, "We must go now. I can only hold the Fangrog like that for a short while. You'll be appreciative of their strength if nothing else, and you must be weary." Frank turned around with one quick sweep of what Amy could now make out was a dark cloak.

"Hang on, what apple? I've never met you before in my life, and I've certainly not eaten anyone's apple!" Amy stated in confusion, but Frank slowly moved away, appearing to glide with his long strides, over the forest floor. "Hey! I'm speaking to you! I'm not exchanging one tormentor for another. You got that?" Amy was frustrated and wary, Frank seemed harmless, but she wasn't taking any chances after hearing his strange words.

"Come with me now Amy Ferhulse, it's time to leave this area," Frank looked back over his shoulder at Amy. It was hard to make out in the dark, but for a moment, she could have sworn his head had pivoted completely. Before she could react, the monster behind her began to gurgle and growl, no longer forced to be still. Amy gasped and looked to Frank for help as he was the least frightening of the two beings, but then it went dark.

Amy woke up alone in a bed, in a bright room, lit by the morning sun in full beam. She knew before even opening her eyes properly she wasn't in her own bed. The sheets felt thin and coarse against her skin. She looked at her arms and hands first, and noticed they were no longer covered in cuts or mud. She sat up in the strange bed to see that the entire room was decorated in different shades of earthy-toned greens and browns. A small room with a chest of drawers, a single bed and a chair. With the door on the opposite side of the room, she was surprised to see that every wall had a large window but no curtains: a straightforward, basic bedroom.

"Where am I?" Amy asked herself, the last thing she remembered was meeting Frank in the woods, and now she was here.

Getting out of bed, it felt strange to feel the hard, even wooden floor beneath her feet. She had been so used to bracing herself for standing on small twigs and sharp rocks for weeks. Noticing the chest of drawers had a hand-held mirror on it, along with a hairbrush and hairbands, she smiled. A simple pleasure she had longed for during the initial few days that she was missing. Amy went over, and in doing so noticed the view out of one of the windows. She wasn't in a house, or an apartment. Amy was elevated in the air within the canopy of the forest, or, as it appeared from this height, a vast jungle. Immediately, she felt very unsafe in the room. It didn't seem unsteady, but she thought that if any of the wooden planks became loose it would *not* be good. She went to open the door, and this confirmed she was indeed in a small room, built into a huge tree, with no way to get down.

Slowly backing away from the doorway to avoid falling out and plunging to her death, she noticed herself in the mirror laid out in front of her. Her skin was still as fair as ever, with full red lips and most of all, thick auburn hair which had always been her trademark.

"Hello, old friend!" she said to the hairbrush, giggling cheerfully to herself. She proceeded to slowly work through the knots that had built up over the time she had spent sleeping on forest floors and crawling through overgrown bushes. Eventually she managed to get her hair into a tidy French braid, *ah that's better.*

Noticing the black, oversized dressing gown she had on, she tutted. Leaning over to look inside the drawers. Two were empty but the third held a solitary apple. Without hesitation, she took a bite of the apple, having something sweet and juicy after all this time was heavenly. But she was interrupted by a light knock on the door.

Oh, what now! After weeks of boredom in the forest with the Fangrogs, the last few hours had been very eventful. It crossed her mind that had anyone told her she would be in this position last year she would have thought they were crazy, but now here she was, not even surprised at being sat in a tree, enjoying a ripe apple as if it were a bar of chocolate. The light knocks were repeated. *At least this jailer is polite.*

"Yes, come in," Amy said while munching on the apple, cross-legged on the end of the bed, trying her very best not to think about how high up she was. The door opened slowly to reveal something so peculiar, so unusual looking, that she remained where she was, only instead of continuing to chew on the apple, her jaw dropped open. Again, it looked like some sort of monster, only not as frightening to her as the Fangrog. Despite her surprise, she managed to remain calm while gazing upon it.

Although it had very long legs, it shuffled into the room from a thick tree branch. Its body appeared to be an elongated human shape, but it had disproportionately long legs to its short torso. It had white skin that shimmered brightly. But what was so unique about this creature was its face. It was hairless, with eyes very high on its forehead. It didn't appear to have ears or a nose, and the lipless mouth was half-open revealing rows of sharp teeth. Yet despite its unnerving appearance, Amy remained calm, because the creature's eyes looked so unbelievably kind and gentle. They were large and round, and reminded her of a horse's eyes, a deep hazel colour with long lashes, as holes into the creature's soul.

"I saved you from probable death earlier." It was Frank. The previous night he had appeared far more human like. The cloak had disguised his strange figure and his face had been in shadow.

"I guess you look quite different." Noticing how slender he was, she looked down at the large apple in her hand, "If you don't mind that I've already started on this, but you can have the rest." She held her hand out, offering it to Frank.

"That won't be necessary. I don't eat as you do." Frank spoke very matter-of-factly, but still noticed Amy screwing up her face while looking him up and down. "We Crimpets absorb what our bodies require through the soles of our feet. We can go about our day and not concern ourselves with trivialities like food, so long as we can still use our absorption pads." He lifted one of his long, skinny legs up to Amy's face for her to see that the bottom of his feet were gelatinous.

"Ew, that's gross Frank! Okay, okay, no apple for you then!" she said, now turning her nose up at the food like as if she had been put off.

"Last night I'd never heard of a Fangrog... and now you - a Crimpet, what *are* you?" Amy asked curiously.

"It is said that Crimpets came from another planet similar to Earth. Only, we are a far more evolved version of humans. We have been studying humans for many years, and many factors have confirmed this. Our bodies may look strange to you, but they have been optimised over time. Our sense of auditory perception is different, along with the limited requirement for a sense of smell or taste. We sense danger in other ways. We arrived many years ago and it's a mystery as to why. However, we thrive here in Hanfield forest, as I'm sure you can tell. But as for Fangrogs, your guess is as good as mine," Frank explained.

"*'We?'* so there are more of you scattered around the forest?" Amy questioned further.

"We made this area our home a long time ago. Come with me, let me show you around." Frank turned and began shuffling out of the door, in the same manner in which he had ended the conversation and abruptly walked off, the previous night, when they had first met.

"You've got to be joking!" Amy let out a short chuckle at the thought of climbing down from her elevated situation.

"I'm aware of the concept of joking. However, this is not a time for jokes. Please, follow me, and I'll show you everything," Frank continued to shuffle out.

"I can't climb down from here!" Amy got up from the bed in protest, "I'll fall!"

"It is quite simple. This particular room has been adapted for yourself, as we have been preparing for your visit. Come now, or be forever trapped up here," Frank intimated that there was a significant threat, but Amy could tell he was a gentle being. *Maybe I've gone entirely crazy from being in the woods for so long.*

Amy walked over to the doorway again to look, and this time noticed there were footholds chiselled into the tree. The distance between each foothold was short, which she found quietly amusing. They had accommodated the shortness of her legs in the construction of her shelter and her access route. She was afraid of falling and had come to feel safe in the little pod within the trees, but she needed to make an effort, and ultimately, she was very curious to see the rest of the tribe.

Frank guided her down. His long fingernails dug into the bark of the tree easily. Amy climbed down hesitantly having very little to hold on to apart from the footholds and random bumps or small branches coming out of the tree, By the time she arrived at the bottom it had taken almost an hour. Nonetheless she was happy she had made it down in one piece and felt reasonably proud of herself. She looked up at Frank with a satisfied smile on her face.

"There!" she said delighted, rubbing her hands together.

"Come now, much time has been wasted," Frank stated, not acknowledging her accomplishment, and walking off again towards a hut.

"Why am I up in the trees if you all live on the ground?" she shouted at him while he continued to walk off, gliding away with much larger strides this time. Frank mumbled something and Amy ran to catch up to him, "I couldn't hear you with you walking so damn fast!"

"It is so the Fangrogs don't take you again. We are hopeful that they can only climb so high," he told Amy while she ran alongside.

The hut they had arrived at was earthy looking, constructed of mud, leaves and wood. It blended well within the landscape of the forest. Amy noticed another handful of these huts scattered around. She gasped as she caught sight of some movement.

"Clic clic clic." The Crimpet at one of the doorways made some unusual sounds while hiding most of its body inside the hut. Only its long fingers and half its face could be seen, its huge eyes following her as they continued to walk.

Arriving at the larger hut, Frank lifted his arm to point at it, signalling Amy to walk through into the cabin first. Amy had become braver than she ever thought she could be over the last few weeks, and without even looking back at Frank, she politely knocked on the door and awaited a response.

"Knock, knock, knock." Whoever was on the other side of the wooden door knocked back.

"Are you... trapped in there? May I come in?" she asked, confused. She knocked again.

"Knock, knock, knock." Again, the individual inside didn't respond to Amy's questions. She wondered if this was a custom they had and so she knocked again.

Frank huffed loudly from behind Amy, "Just open the door! We don't adhere to the human ways."

Amy pushed the dark wooden door open. It made a creaking sound as she did so, and the Crimpet on the other side of the door ran lightly away. The room had some maps pinned up on the wall, a fireplace and a large table. It was pretty dark apart from some sun seeping through the two small windows either side of the door. Amy noticed the windows were not made of glass, but instead from a transparent plastic sheet, which would have made it impossible to see inside. There were two other Crimpets in the room, and they both looked exactly like Frank. One wore the same black robe as Frank had, and the other was slightly taller and was now hiding behind the robed one.

"Hi there, I'm Amy!" she said as she stepped inside. It was a strange situation, and she had no idea what to expect.

"Clic clic, clic clic clic... clic clic," the Crimpet in the robe gestured with its arms as it made some strange noises and stared blankly at her.

"I am the only one who knows your language. They are not familiar with encountering humans. It was my job to observe and take note," Frank explained while the robed Crimpet began to communicate with the other standing directly behind it.

"So, what are they saying? Is that why I'm here? So you can *'take notes'* about me?" Amy asked.

"No. You are here because we identified that you had consumed one of our Krytons. No human has ever done this before, and so we need to observe what happens," Frank explained, but Amy's attention had been taken by one of the maps on the wall.

"I live here! Can you take me back?" she was now pointing to a square on the map along her street in Hanfield, "Are we far?" Amy had so many questions she needed to ask.

"It would be too dangerous for now," Frank said, at which point he turned to the other two and spoke a language she had never heard before.

"Why is it dangerous? I don't understand! I have not eaten anything of yours!" Amy was beginning to sound frustrated. The other Crimpets started communicating and chirping together in a high-pitched tone.

"The apple you ate was not an apple, it was a Kryton. We have been here for many years and live a peaceful life. But we did have powers which we could use against those that would seek to harm us, in order to defend ourselves. But over the many years we realised we do not require such powers. Holding them made us feel tense here and so we found a way to relinquish them. The apples you see in the orchards in Hanfield are fine, but some, a very few, deep in the forest, are Krytons, orbs of energy disguised as apples, and you consumed on," Frank stated, "you and two others... but we have not been able to locate them, to get to them. The Fangrogs got you, and we think they were somehow trying to utilise the power."

Amy took it all in silently. She knew she had felt differently for some days before getting taken by the Fangrogs, as if she didn't quite belong anymore. It had been disconcerting as she couldn't fathom why. As she digested Frank's words, she remembered one of the last times she was over at Hannah's after school. Ms. Henry had made apple pie for her, Hannah and Monica after they had finished dance practise.

"Surely I would know about it if I had eaten one of these Kryton things?" Amy said, looking down at her hands. As she did so, memories began to flash through her mind, seeing her father with another woman and running away into the forest. Upset and angry, and sitting on a rock far from home, she wept into her hands. When she had finished crying, she looked up from her lap and noticed everything around her had died. The grass was brown, and the trees were withered. No more green bushes or leaves. Everything within a perfect five-metre diameter circle around her had become barren land, and she couldn't help but question if she had done that herself. Deep down she knew she had. That was when the Fangrogs had crept up and taken her.

Frank snapped Amy from her realisation: "Evidently not. You must learn how to control, and possibly call upon the power if required, to defend yourself if the need arises."

"So, the way you made that Fangrog freeze like that... could I do that?" Amy asked.

"We will be putting you through very many tests today, and then we can see. You may be able to stop the evil one you call Hannah." Frank said to Amy's surprise.

XVIII

The Accident

"Amy!" Izzy blinked her eyes rapidly. For a moment she thought that maybe she was still sleeping, and it was just another 'Amy' dream, only she had never experienced one so realistic. Amy stood next to the end of Izzy's bed, looking over at her with a big smile. To Izzy, her bed felt real, the cold chill that had just prompted her to open her eyes in the first place felt real, and every part of Amy was just as Izzy remembered. She blinked some more before sitting up in bed and looking around, "Amy, is that really you?" she asked in disbelief.

"Hey Izzy, it's good to see you!" Amy whispered so as not to wake Izzy's parents.

"What! No!" Izzy couldn't believe her eyes, she rubbed them with both hands and proceeded to jump out of bed to hug Amy, "I can't believe it's ..."

"Stop!" Amy held her hand out to stop Izzy from coming any closer and in doing so Izzy felt a wave of cold come from Amy: "Sorry Iz, but you have to be quiet. I must leave soon, and I don't want anyone to know I was back. No one can know."

"Are you in trouble? Where have you been? You know everyone has been looking for you for months now! We had the Summer Sling in your honour today! People think you're dead Amy! Oh, and guess what? I managed to get the lead in Heartbeats! Would you ever have guessed it?" Izzy tried excitedly, to fill Amy in as much as possible, in an enthusiasm overdrive.

"I know Iz, I saw you dancing, and I can believe you made the lead," Amy smiled.

"You did? You should have said! No one is going to believe this..." Izzy was practically jumping up and down with excitement.

"But I'm here to warn you," Amy cut across Izzy in a bid to get her point through. "Something is going to happen to you, I don't know what but I get these visions now... and well, all I can say is ignore it, whatever it is, ignore it... be your usual Izzy self!" Amy looked around as if she was in a rush to leave.

"Amy, are you okay?" Izzy looked concerned now, noticing she had lost weight, "Where have you been?" she asked again.

"It doesn't matter. I shouldn't even be back, not yet anyway. I had to warn you. Promise me you will be careful Iz!" Amy said, her big blue eyes staring right into Izzy's puzzled face.

"Oh, I know I'll go and call my parents; we might need to tell the police you're fine as they are working so hard to find you!" Izzy said, backing out of her bedroom, "Wait there, don't move!"

But when Izzy returned to her bedroom with her father and turned the lights on, there was no sign of Amy. She was no longer standing at the end of Izzy's bed as she had been moments earlier.

"Amy? It's just my dad!" Izzy shouted as if Amy would hear her, but Amy was long gone.

"Darling, today must have been more stressful than we had ever known," Izzy's father said with a sigh, "Try to get some sleep and relax. You did great today." He rubbed her shoulder and turned the bedroom light back off on his way out. Amy had been missing for weeks now, and barely any of the Hanfield locals believed she would ever return.

Izzy got back into bed feeling deflated, even more so than before. She could have sworn Amy really was there. It was her in the flesh, she was not seeing things.

I do so want my friend Amy back now, Izzy thought, doubting herself. She would have loved to have heard her voice and caught up with her. She really needed her friend's advice, as Scott's strange attitude all through the day had worried her. *Amy would know what to say, she always had the best advice.* It was true - Izzy had never been out with a guy before. She didn't like to worry about Scott. If only she could pick up the phone and speak to her friend Amy about it, her mind would be put at ease. Amy was always good at that sort of thing.

A new day began, a Saturday, and because Izzy had been so preoccupied with her sudden lead in the Summer Sling, she had completely forgotten to make weekend plans. She would usually see friends or Scott on Saturdays, and spend Sunday catching up on homework and spending time with her family. She had slept in longer than she had meant to this morning, but upon checking her phone, she had no messages from Scott, which made her heart sink. She had officially slept on it, and things were still feeling weird to her.

'Scott, is everything okay? Call me, love from Izzy.' She sent him a text, and for a while she stared at her phone, hoping it would ring right away, but it didn't.

She opened the Hanfield Heartbeats group chat. It was a reasonably new one Hannah had put together after Amy's disappearance, with everyone on the team included in order to schedule rehearsals and social events. There were a couple of messages from some of the girls.

'We tried our best, and that's all that matters, there's always next year!' Most of the messages were encouraging and focused on the team effort, but only Hannah had added something unkind; the blind emoji followed by the poop emoji.

There was a direct message to her from Monica, *'Izzy Bizzy! Plans for today? I'm thinking the park!'* but for once Izzy didn't feel like socialising. She decided she would stay in today for when Scott called her, trying to remain optimistic that he would call her soon and reassure her that everything was fine. She couldn't put her finger on what had changed his mood, but she had a bad feeling

Still in her pyjamas, she wandered down into the kitchen where her parents were both chatting and drinking coffee. The whole house smelt of roasting coffee beans and toasting tea cakes, the smell that would always remind her of a Saturday morning.

"How are you feeling this morning, sweetie?" Izzy's mother asked. There was a clear sense of concern in the air following last night's 'Amy' outburst.

"Yeah, I'm good thanks... you know what's so funny about last night was, I think I was sleepwalking! Sorry that I woke you both up!" Izzy laughed, trying to make light of having told her parents that Amy was in her bedroom.

"Okay sweetie, well you do have a lot going on at the moment. It may be worth thinking of taking a step back from dancing for a while," her mother suggested, in her worried tone of voice.

"Give up dancing? No way! I'd had a really tough day as you said mum but to give up dancing would be wrong. It was one blip and like I said, I could hardly help it if I'm sleepwalking, can I?" Izzy argued. She couldn't lose dancing at a time like this, as it would be the only thing worse than tanking the lead in the Summer Sling. Not showing up for any further rehearsals right now, was not an option for her.

Izzy's mother, who was leaning back on to the kitchen worktop waiting for the teacakes to cook under the grill, looked at her father who was sitting at the breakfast bar. It was evident to Izzy they had been having a long conversation about last night's events before she had finally emerged from bed that morning. Both had their hands wrapped around their coffee mugs, looking very dubious about her sleepwalking admission.

"Because you know sweetie, no one would blame you if you had thought you'd seen Amy. I'm sure you miss her very much," her mother said.

Izzy couldn't talk about this right now, and quitting dance was not an option. She jumped, feeling her phone vibrate in her hand, which she had been clutching ever since she had sent her message to Scott.

'Let us all get together for lunch today at Fade Away Diner! Spirits need lifting after yesterday's massive fail!!' Hannah had written into the group chat. Izzy was disappointed it wasn't Scott getting in touch.

The Familiar Encounter

"That was Hannah Henry... she wants the whole team to get together for lunch today. You see? Dancing is a great community, and I've got nothing to worry about!" Izzy smiled, and although she didn't want to go anywhere today, she needed to pretend everything was okay so her parents would stop worrying.

"Oh, okay." Izzy's mother looked over at her father again with a more optimistic expression while her father shrugged, "That's good to hear!"

On the weekends, she would always have fun with her makeup, getting out her colourful eye shadow pallets and laying them on the bathroom counter. Today she picked a similar pink to match her trainers. It was a beautiful day, so she planned on wearing a sky-blue skater dress. The nagging feeling that something was wrong played out in her head while she got ready. *This is just so unlike him. I wonder what I've done wrong. Maybe he will be at lunch today. Maybe he's playing football. Maybe he hasn't even thought about it yet.* Izzy worried while brushing and blending the pink into her eyelid. Her parents sometimes overreacted but she also worried about having seen Amy like that. *I honestly thought she was there.*

Deciding she needed some air and time to think, she headed out early to walk to the diner. As summer was starting to come to an end, she took a few deep breaths when she got outside, feeling the warm breeze and the sun on her skin, trying to absorb the day as much as she could. There would not be many more gorgeous sunrises, or long days, or walks outside wearing summer dresses to enjoy. It was always something she missed during the depths of Hanfield's dark winters.

When she arrived, she spotted two full booths over in the corner in front of the windows. The usual group was there with Hannah in the middle of one of the tables, busy chatting and laughing. It took Izzy a moment to adopt her usual happy expression, as she was disappointed to see Scott wasn't among the group. Walking over towards her friends, she double-checked her phone once more to make sure she had no missed calls or messages from him, but there was nothing.

"Well if it isn't the girl who cost us the trophy!" Hannah shouted over, having spotted Izzy. With at least half of the diner having heard her and turning around to stare, Izzy blushed, and her smile faded, "I'm joking silly! There's no blame within a great team like ours," Hannah scoffed while a couple of the teammates laughed making the sentiment sound sarcastic. Izzy joined them and sat on one end of the table, overlooking the diner in the hopes Scott would walk in soon, and things would get back to normal.

"Hey guys, have you ordered food yet? I was so enjoying the walk here in this weather I hadn't even realised I was running late!" Izzy admitted, putting her backpack down to one side and adjusting the length of her dress.

"There are a couple more latecomers we're waiting for, but I've ordered a milkshake," one girl said. Fade Away's milkshakes were a much-loved item on the menu.

"I feel so awful about yesterday everyone. I guess I wasn't ready for my moment, I'm not even sure what happened," Izzy admitted awkwardly to the rest of the team, addressing the elephant in the room.

"That's okay Iz-" one of the other team members started to say, when Hannah interrupted:

"But we should really learn from our mistakes. I think we can all agree that *I* belong front and centre forever now. It's just not fair to other, less experienced members of the group, to have that kind of pressure put on them." Everyone nodded along including Izzy, as Hannah spoke. She was also wearing her summer dress, only hers was white with a pink floral design all over it and fitted perfectly. Hannah's hair was straight with a side parting and a matching pink flower hair clip to keep it in place, "Especially if those certain members cannot deliver the goods come crunch time," Hannah added looking all around the table while she said it.

Before anyone had a chance to say anything further, Danny and Monica arrived, chatting and laughing together as they sat down.

"I found this one waiting for a bus over on Melbuller Road, so Rick pulled over, and he squeezed into the van!" Monica laughed and poked fun at Danny. Upon seeing Izzy, Monica sat in the same booth opposite her, "Hey... you never responded to my message this morning!"

"Oh I... I genuinely just forgot, I er, didn't sleep very well last night, so my mind's been more coo-coo crazy than usual!" Izzy joked light-heartedly, feeling bad about not getting back to her friend.

"Okay, well you're here now, so I get to spend time with you. nothing lost!" Monica said.

The waitress came round to take everyone's orders. The uniform was in keeping with the American fifties style of the diner, which was a white and red striped a-line dress, and this particular waitress was in Izzy's English class. Izzy was always totally surprised by how well her friend took everyone's food orders by memory and would gasp in amazement when she repeated the entire order, before heading back towards the kitchen.

"So easily impressed Izzy!" Hannah laughed from one end of the table, while Monica looked on with a frown. Izzy giggled, self-consciously, "and speaking of easily impressed, where's Bowers at?" Hannah's laugh had turned into a smirk.

"Oh erm, I'm not sure Hannah! Playing football probably," Izzy shrugged innocently.

"You mean you don't know where he is right now? He hasn't told you?" Hannah asked, while a curious, wide-eyed Izzy looked on.

"What are you doing, Hannah?" Monica snapped, her thick dark hair flying as she quickly swung her head around to face Hannah, "She said she doesn't know, now leave it alone."

"I'll bet Monica knows where Scott is," Hannah gave a polite smile back at Monica

For the first time in a long time, Izzy felt speechless. She didn't know what was going on, but she knew it wasn't good. The lump in her throat got bigger, and her stomach tied itself in a knot while she turned her attention to Monica, still clasping her phone on her lap under the table, although now something was telling Izzy she wouldn't hear from Scott.

"What Mon? Do you know where he is?" Izzy managed to squeeze out a few words, puzzled, while every inch of her body clammed up with anxiety.

"I don't know. Maybe he's waiting for the same bus Danny was going to get on?" Monica laughed a little, throwing out some possibilities, but Izzy wasn't laughing.

"Oh God Monica, if you *must* leave me to break the bad news to the girl!" Hannah said theatrically, while smirking, "He's been secretly seeing Bella Ferhulse, and he's been with her since late last night!" Hannah was now unable to hide the pleasure she was getting at the expense of Izzy. She grabbed her friend's strawberry milkshake and started drinking it from the striped paper straw with an air of satisfaction.

Izzy felt her whole world come crashing down, while realising that something inside had told her things had been off with Scott since yesterday. Her hands became clammy, still fidgeting with her phone under the table. She could feel herself welling up to cry, but also couldn't quite believe the Scott she fell in love with could do this to her. She couldn't believe he could seriously sit and have dinner with her parents last night and then go hang out with another girl. Everyone on the table was silent, staring at Izzy for a reaction after Hannah's revelation.

"It's not true. He wouldn't do that to me," Izzy spoke in defence of Scott despite it not looking good.

"I'm afraid so, and if you must know he had been in the library with Bella yesterday, he was almost late for the show... almost couldn't peel himself away from her to make it to the competition," Hannah added salt to the wound to stir things further, in between taking long slurps of the milkshake.

Izzy could not believe what she was hearing. *How does Hannah even know this... and Monica!*

" Monica? Do you know anything about this?" Izzy looked at Monica, while the rest of the table remained silent at the scene unfolding in front of them.

"Iz... I had seen them together," Monica admitted, "but they just looked like good friends... I didn't want to worry you."

"How long ago was this?" Izzy's voice shook, asking questions she didn't want to know the answers to.

Monica sighed, "A couple of days back." She winced as she spoke, knowing this sounded worse now after Hannah's involvement.

"So, everyone knew this was happening apart from me?" Izzy raised her voice. She didn't wait for an answer, she could feel her eyes welling up. Grabbing her backpack, she got up and left the diner before bursting into tears when she got out of the door. She heard Monica shout for her, but she needed to be alone.

Izzy felt angry and embarrassed, as if her friends had turned their back on her and betrayed her. She was always someone who saw the good in others, no matter what, and now she didn't know what to think. The fact that it all seemed to be common knowledge, was more humiliating to her than anything she could have imagined. Monica was coming out after her, so she started to run. She didn't know where she was going, but she couldn't go home to her already worried parents. She needed to think and calm herself.

I'm so stupid! Why did I think someone like Scott would love me? And everyone could see it apart from me. Running faster and faster with tears pouring down her red cheeks. Izzy had instinctively headed towards Hanfield's apple orchard. It was somewhere she often came on her own to find peace. Because of the nice weather, there were a few families about, some couples, and others taking their kids out for some countryside fun to pick their apples. No one seemed to notice Izzy as she continued to run down one of the rows of trees, her heart breaking and pink coloured, eyeshadow filled tears running down her face.

Eventually, out of breath and devastated, Izzy arrived at the very end of the orchard. The sun was still beating down onto the trees, and the area looked quiet enough for her to be alone for an hour or so. Her light dress would get ruined with a grass stain, and this was usually something she would be mindful about, but not today. Taking off her backpack which contained her camera and a jacket, she brought it onto her lap, hugged and buried her head in it. Weeping into the bag like it was a friend's shoulder, she thought of all the sweet times she'd had with Scott and cried even harder that all the happiness he had given her, had disappeared with deceit and lies. Izzy couldn't help but wonder what Bella Ferhulse had, that she didn't. Bella was quiet, unapproachable and the total opposite of Izzy.

Hours later, Izzy woke up, her head still resting on her backpack, confused for a moment about where she was. Her heart sank when she realised none of it was a dream. She must have cried herself to sleep. Still sat next to the forest on the edge of the orchard, it had got dark, and her phone battery had run out from checking it so often during the day. Getting up from the ground, she rubbed her puffy eyes and began the walk back home. Her parents would be worried about her by now, and she was very much ready to share her sorrows with them when she got in. She was, however, thankful that the air was still hot from the day's sunshine. As she began walking quickly from the end of the orchard toward home, something caught her attention.

Izzy looked to her right, back to the edge of the forest. Something was glowing subtly in amongst the thick foliage, a yellow glimmer, lighting up the green of the leaves. She stopped walking and turned towards it, squinting and rubbing her eyes some more. Maybe she was still half asleep.

"What is that?" Izzy asked herself. It was unlike fire as it began to change into a more intense orange, and then red. It didn't look particularly welcoming, but she was feeling rebellious and curious after her terrible day and so she began moving towards it.

The closer Izzy got, the larger the light became, and she could make out further details, the shimmery, glittery sparks coming off it, so much like fire and yet not. Not knowing what it was didn't scare her, it confused her. She got closer to it and paused, realising she had crossed the orchard line and was now in Hanfield's vast forest, a place she knew she wasn't supposed to be. There had been warnings each morning in school, following Amy's disappearance, telling people they shouldn't venture into the forest alone. She looked back to where she had come from. She could still see the clearing of the orchard, her safety line.

The light had become so bright that it was beginning to hurt her eyes, and having arrived at a thick gorse bush, she paused to rummage in her backpack for her camera to take photos. Putting the chunky Polaroid camera to her face she focused on a few shots.

"Click... buzz!" The camera made a loud noise as it ejected the instant photo, which fell to the floor. Izzy moved the camera a bit and with full concentration, took another, "Click... buzz!" Allowing the picture to fall again, not wanting to lose the perfect shot while in focus, she tried to avoid removing her eye from the lens. About to press the shutter to catch another photo of the glowing red light she paused, thinking she had heard some heavy thumping footsteps, but as this was followed by a hard breeze making the trees clatter together, she thought nothing of it.

"Click... buzz! Thump!" The photograph got caught in the breeze this time. It was flying, dancing and as if by magic got taken up into the canopy of the trees. Izzy fell to the floor next to the other two polaroid's, her camera still clasped in her hand, as a group of hobbling, pale white creatures surrounded her, dragging her into the light.

XIX
Scott & Bella

Leaving Izzy's house, Scott couldn't help but feel he had disappointed her in some way. Was it something he had said? Had he not been supportive enough after the competition? Maybe he embarrassed her in front of her parents. She wasn't her usual bubbly self all evening. She would always ask Scott how he was doing or if he was okay, but today it was like she was in overdrive trying to make sure everything was good, and then it wasn't. Her face dropped, and he noticed some sadness in her eyes when it was time for him to head home.

He'd never had a girlfriend before, so it crossed his mind he maybe should have asked his friends what their experience of meeting a girl's parents was like, but Scott hadn't felt nervous at all before tonight, he'd had too much on his mind. Izzy's parents seemed like ordinary, friendly people, but having known her all this time he had pictured just that. He knew someone like her didn't become so kind-hearted without having similar parents. As he thought about the evening, there had never been an awkward moment, a successful meeting he'd assumed. But the way Izzy had just looked at him didn't make sense, and he couldn't shake it from his mind.

It was late, and yet the sky was still glowing a dark red when he stepped outside. Izzy lived on the other side of town from Scott. It had crossed his mind that he wished he had his bike so he could get home quicker, but then who was Scott kidding, he wouldn't be going straight home, he had already taken his phone from his back pocket and proceeded to text Bella Ferhulse. It had only been a few hours since he last saw her in the library and yet at the time, he hadn't wanted to leave for the competition. He couldn't get their mission out of his mind. He had wondered if she'd have any updates, since he had seen her. He hadn't stopped thinking about the sketch of the man she'd shown him all day. *It was something from space, alright.* It had the same look of the things he had seen in comic books and the UFO documentaries he would sometimes watch with his dad.

'Just come from Izzy's house, where are you? I'm thinking we should explore the forest tonight instead. We're dealing with aliens and just look at that sky!' Scott sent Bella the text, the excitement brewing inside him, hoping she would be game for an adventure. The new revelation from that morning had given him the confidence he wasn't just chasing something that did not exist.

He noticed Bella had read the message, and although it was a Friday night, he knew she would most likely be at home reading or writing. He took a small detour on his walk to go past the Ferhulse family home. When Amy first went missing, he had attended many dance practice sessions in their garden, and he knew he was in the neighbourhood. All the houses around here had the same grand appearance. Cherry blossom trees lined the pavements, their pink and white petals were dotted around the roads as the trees had begun to shed.

'Busy tonight - let us stick with tomorrow.' Bella's short and blunt reply was not unusual to Scott. Most of the students at school would say she was cold or mean, but Scott knew better. Bella was independent, and she wasn't comfortable relying on anyone else. She was an island of her own. Scott did, however, wonder what she could be doing right now that was more important. He'd just arrived at her house, but as she didn't want to hang out, his being there was probably creepier than it was helpful. This didn't stop Scott from slowing his pace. Curious as to what Bella could be doing instead,

he peered in the general direction of the house. It was set back at the end of the short driveway. He noticed no lights were on apart from what he knew to be the kitchen and the study. With the curtains open and the light illuminating the rooms, he saw some filing cabinets, and more noticeably, Bella's father sat at his desk with his head in his hands. He looked upset. Feeling intrigued, Scott slowed down some more to focus. He watched as Mr. Ferhulse rose abruptly from his seat and began shouting. The muffled noise of his voice could be heard from the street. Scott could now see that he was on the phone, and very angry.

Don't be so nosey, she's busy, go home. Scott snapped out of it and picked up the pace to his usual speed. Heading home, he couldn't mistake the feeling of someone watching him. The strange figure that Bella had drawn, had disturbed him, and so, the chilling feeling of eyes upon him in the night, prompted him to shift gears and start jogging instead. He told himself that the sooner he got home, the more sleep he could get, and the longer he could stay out with Bella tomorrow night.

He must have arrived home and gone straight to bed, as when Scott woke up the next morning he noticed he hadn't closed his blinds properly, which wasn't unusual, but this time the morning sun coming through burnt his eyes awake. He didn't realise at first, but the buzzing noise from his phone was what had stirred him initially. It lit up and buzzed again. The first thing he noticed was Bella's name showing up. She was calling him. The second thing he noticed was the time read 4:35 am. It was positively sunrise, and his eyes felt it.

"This had better be good," Scott grumbled, answering the phone, still half asleep.

"We have to head out now... right now to find my sister. I know where she is!" Bella shouted, "Are you in?"

"It's 4 am Bella. I thought we were heading out to find her tonight... y'know *'those that walk at night'* the clue is in there," Scott said, he was always grouchy in the mornings, and his voice faded off as he began to doze again.

"...and I'm telling you I know where she is! This is massive... actually, no, I knew you didn't *really* care, I don't know why I even bother sometimes!" Bella hung up.

Scott rolled over, sighing loudly at yet another Bella mood swing. He closed his eyes but then became uncomfortable at the thought of her going out into the woods alone. He suddenly had an image flash in his mind, of her being yet another missing Ferhulse, and it would all be his fault. He huffed loudly again, prying his eyes open to be greeted by the bright morning light and he rolled slowly out of bed, rubbing his face and trying to muster up the same enthusiasm he had possessed only a few hours earlier.

Grabbing yesterday's clothes up from the floor where he had dumped them, he called Bella back. Holding the phone between his shoulder and ear while he jumped about his room putting his trousers on. Still coming to his senses, he could hear that she had picked up. Scott liked to think he knew her enough by now to imagine there was a 50/50 chance she would still want him out with her today, but she was stubborn and quick to write people off.

"Sorry Bella, I'm not the most energetic in the mornings at the best of times. I'm up, where am I meeting you?" he asked, still hobbling with one leg in his trousers.

"I'll meet you by the orchard in ten, so hurry up!" she spoke directly and then hung up, but Scott could hear a slight upbeat to her voice, and he smiled smugly. It was the slightest hint in her tone giving away that she was pleased he had called her back. Now dressed and starting to wake up himself, he was happy that he had too.

Sneaking out so as not to wake his parents, he grabbed his bike from the porch and began cycling over to the orchard. It usually took him ten minutes to ride over to that area of Hanfield, so he stepped on it. It didn't take him long to warm up, pedalling as fast as he could with his curiosity spiking at what Bella could want to suddenly share or investigate with him.

Scott's imagination ran wild with the vision of him and Bella discovering Amy and being able to help her return home. He envisioned her starting back at school, and how thankful her family would be. He had been desperately looking into the conspiracy surrounding her disappearance for some time. Still, it wasn't until this moment that he believed he was in with a genuine chance of being able to find her. *Unless we're too late.* Scott saw hope as a good thing, while opinions circulated around the town that she would not be found alive. Scott had seen something special in Amy during their brief meeting in the supermarket on that stormy day. There was no doubt about it, she *was* extra special.

Arriving at the orchard, Scott tossed his bike into some thick bushes by the entranceway. He couldn't see Bella and started to become anxious that she had set off without him. She certainly didn't seem to be in the mood to wait today. He checked his phone. Five minutes late, so he jogged on in. Through the metal archway which had been twisted and moulded into pleasant, swirly shapes to reveal the beginning of the rows of trees. It was totally deserted with no sign of Bella. The sound of blackbirds singing, and wood pigeons cooing, filled the otherwise quiet time of day, He had never been here during the morning, and it was magical the way the birds were so busy communicating. It made a lonely hour feel full of life.

"Bella? Are you here?" Scott broke the tranquil setting by calling out for her, still feeling a reservation of worry that she may rush into something dangerous on her own.

Just as he opened his mouth to call out a second time, she appeared from behind the trees in the distance. Scott wasn't one to notice the smaller details, but he noticed right away that Bella was wearing the same clothes she had had on yesterday in the library.

"You were out all night? Your outfit?" he enquired.

"*Your* outfit," she casually pointed out while walking over to him, that Scott was also wearing yesterday's clothes.

It was a fair comment and Scott decided not to say anything more on the matter. Still, he could tell she had been up all night. Her hair was unusually messy, and as she got closer, the dark rings sitting under her eyes became more apparent.

"So why are we here? Did you see, you know... it, again?" He didn't quite know what to call the figure in Bella's notebook that he had thought so much about since the day before.

"A Crimpet! It was an alien, and I know for sure they exist. I don't know how many there are, but they are in that forest and..." Bella spoke passionately before pausing and looking at Scott for a moment: "Scott, I can trust you, can't I? I need someone I can trust right now, but if you're going to lose your head, I'm giving you a fair chance to tell me and step away from all of this. Ask yourself, do you really want to know what's been going on? Because it's stranger than we ever imagined." Bella studied Scott's reaction with her big, and now bloodshot eyes.

"Are you kidding me? I'm in. I'm all the way into this, and trust me I have no one to tell. Bella you can trust me!" Scott gave a comforting, yet uneasy, smile to Bella, hoping this would put her mind at ease.

Bella whispered, "I did some more research and well... I couldn't help it... I went to Cliff Edge to see Mrs. Samuels... huh Mrs. Samuels." She chuckled and rolled her eyes repeating her name as if it amused her, "The old lady... she handed me this." Bella pulled up the sleeve of her sweatshirt to reveal the egg-shaped pendant on a thin chain, wrapped around her wrist.

Scott leaned in to take a closer look, "Mrs. Samuels *gave* you this? It's the exact one I asked her about when I volunteered."

"It's a Tentescope chain. Those aliens, well, the Crimpets, they gave them out to the very select few humans that know of their existence... kinda like a club, I guess," Bella explained to Scott.

"Why would she give this to you? She barely spoke when I met her," Scott said.

"She barely spoke to me either, it was a quick exchange. As soon as I saw her through the window, I knew exactly who she was. Don't ask me how, but I recognised her face right away," something made Bella pause. She held back as if what she was about to say would make her sound crazy, as if what they had been through already wasn't mad enough.

"Go on, who is she? Your long, lost Granny?" Scott half-joked, while still admiring the bracelet around Bella's wrist.

"She was... she is me!" Bella raised her eyebrows while waiting for Scott to react, "I mean it's impossible, but she is... me that is, I knew it when I saw her."

"Aw, man! If aliens exist, it makes sense that time travel would too!" Scott exclaimed excitedly. He felt lucky she was sharing her experience with him.

"I guess so yeah! Anyway, it wasn't like she confirmed it, all she said was to visit the orchard at 5 am. She said it through the window to me while she passed me the Tentescope chain. Her voice was croaky and quiet so maybe I misheard her," Bella looked around. Their presence didn't affect the birds as they picked and prodded at fallen red apples, shining on a bed of thick green grass covered in the morning dew.

"Yeah, nothing out of the ordinary here. Perhaps she said 5 pm?" Scott suggested, favouring the prospect that he may be able to return to bed.

"It's possible. But since we're here, we may as well have a look. Let's walk around the perimeter!" Ever dedicated to the cause, Bella took off walking, heading up towards the end of the orchard, "You coming?"

Scott couldn't decline, although he had liked the idea of going out hunting aliens at night, somehow going on a patrol during the early hours of the morning seemed redundant to him. Not one of his comic books at home talked of the hero defeating the evil monsters and getting home in time for breakfast. Still, this was real life, and he couldn't let Bella go alone, no matter how strong-willed and determined she appeared.

They walked along, their eyes peeled for any subtle movements, but only catching glimpses of rabbits quickly scampering away, having been disturbed by their presence. Not before too long, they saw the very end of the orchard. A few times Scott had opened his mouth to make small talk, but Bella would quickly put her index finger to her lips signalling for him to be quiet. It was only now he thought that if they did come across anything, how were they planning to fight it off? Neither had any knowledge on how to get away from these things, let alone how to kill them, but luckily it looked as though the search would prove fruitless.

Arriving at the end of the orchard, he thought it was time for them to turn around and head home, but Bella gasped as they both turned to face a clearing to their right. Scott could already see the woman, but Bella still tapped on his arm anyway to make sure. She had wild curly hair and was sitting cross-legged on a colourful towel, her eyes shut and her palms resting on her knees. This wasn't the big find Scott was expecting, but still, it beat coming across an angry alien. Bella and Scott looked at each other, unsure how to proceed.

"Hey you!" Bella shouted as patiently and polite as ever.

The Familiar Encounter

The woman gasped loudly, having had a shock, an awkward frown on her face showing she had not been expecting any disturbances. Scott's cheeks reddened for frightening a random stranger.

"Come on, Bella, lets go," Scott whispered under his breath, but to his horror, Bella began to walk towards the woman. "What are you doing?" he asked the question, but he knew what she was doing. Bella was enthused having met Mrs. Samuels and received some answers, and now she felt as though she was hot on the trail of finally finding Amy.

"What are you doing here?" Bella asked, continuing to walk over to the lady, who was now getting up from the ground, looking slightly outraged at the question.

"Hello there. It's a lovely morning, isn't it? I'm meditating," the woman responded with a surprisingly accommodating tone, despite the intrusion, "You're Bella Ferhulse, aren't you? ...and you're Francis Bower's son?"

Oh no, she knows my Mum, I'm going to be in so much trouble! He stood where he was, metres away from the woman, while Bella walked right up to her.

"Yeah? What of it?" Bella had been used to anonymity for far too long, and people recognising her recently had provoked her defensive attitude to surface a little too frequently.

"My daughter is in your year at school. Hannah Henry. You're friends, aren't you?" Ms. Henry asked. She wasn't what Scott imagined when he thought of what Hannah's mother would look like. She appeared kind and gentle, whereas Hannah was intimidating and loud.

"Absolutely not, you're thinking of my sister," Bella corrected Ms. Henry without even flinching. Bella spoke to every stranger with the same abrupt tone, and it wouldn't matter if you were her headteacher or best friend, she would challenge anything she didn't agree with.

"Yes, of course, I'm getting confused," she nodded and smiled in agreement, "It's a lovely place to clear one's head. How are you and your family holding up?" Ms. Henry looked genuine in her questioning. Scott had seen others ask Bella similar questions all the time, but Bella's answer was always the same.

"Great thanks, just brilliant. I mean, what family doesn't have its share of drama?" she asked sarcastically. This usually made the enquirer feel so awkward that they wouldn't dare enquire again. Seemingly satisfied that Hannah's hippy mother wasn't holding her sister hostage, she turned around to walk back in Scott's direction.

"Wait there... your bracelet..." Ms. Henry stepped barefoot off her towel and onto the cold grass, with Bella continuing to walk off unphased, she ran in front of her. Lifting her baggy grey t-shirt to show her a small tattoo on her stomach. "It's the same... where did you get that bracelet?"

Bella looked at the mark dubiously. It wasn't a tattoo, more like a branding with the outline of the scar making the same shape as the pendant on her bracelet.

"Someone gave it to me recently..." Bella spoke truthfully without wanting to give away too much.

"Have you seen them? You have, haven't you? I knew I wasn't the only one!" Ms. Henry said, "I experienced an encounter with one... not long ago, in the woods. It approached me, and that evening I noticed this." She ran her finger up and down the mark on her skin before turning to look at Scott. "And you too? Is that why you're both here?"

Bella looked around uncomfortably, unsure what to say. She had been very strict up to now, only letting Scott in on the information she had gathered.

"Yeah... Bella saw one from a distance, and now she has this bracelet," Scott spoke up now, walking over to them both. Bella shot him a less than impressed look. Still, he didn't care, Ms. Henry sounded genuine, "The lady that gave Bella this pendant told us to come here this morning."

"She told *me* to come here this morning," Bella corrected Scott angrily, positive he had said too much.

"What woman? What else did she say?" Ms. Henry questioned.

"Your turn now. What was your encounter with the Crimpet like? It hurt you?" Bella asked.

"It actually told me my daughter is... evil. The way he said it was so earnest, yet so disturbing... I haven't stopped thinking about it since," she said with a look of pain in her eyes.

"You must be about the only person in Hanfield that needs an alien to tell you that!" Bella said.

"Bella!" Scott cringed at Bella's rudeness, "Ms. Henry... have you noticed a change in Hannah?" Scott interrupted Bella's insolence.

"I have, yes. She's changed so much. She spends all of her time out of the house nowadays, but she won't tell me where she goes. Don't get me wrong, she's always been... determined, but now it's as though she's angry at everyone, as if she's been wronged by everyone. But what am I supposed to do? I'm at a loss! That's why I'm here actually, meditating helps me see things and feel things others don't. I think it might provide me with the answers." Ms. Henry sounded conflicted, "I shouldn't say this, but the way she's been so hellbent on filling Amy's shoes... I sometimes wonder..."

"You think she's had something to do with my sister's disappearance?" Bella asked calmly.

"Does that sound so awful for a mother to think? Sometimes she gets this look in her eyes..." Ms. Henry looked as though she was holding back tears with her confession.

"It's okay, we won't tell anyone... will we Bella?" Scott nudged Bella, but she remained silent.

"Would you both care to join me in meditation? I think that's why you've been told to come here," Ms. Henry asked.

"I guess so," Bella agreed, turning to find a spot on the grass on which to sit.

"I'm not sure it's for me," Scott said insecurely. Meditating in the orchard sounded utterly pointless to him. It wasn't the action he had expected.

"It's easy, come on now!" Ms. Henry tugged at Scott's arm, "Please, I believe this is meant to be!" All the while Bella was already sitting cross-legged on the damp grassy floor. It was two against one, and eventually Scott agreed.

Scott had no idea what he was supposed to do here, so he simply copied Bella and Ms. Henry, who both sat silently with their eyes shut. He started to notice his breathing. He could feel the condensation from the grass soaking into his jeans. It was cold but not uncomfortable. He could hear the light breeze wandering through the leaves on the apple trees all around him. As he started to relax his eyes became tired again, and he thought about how he couldn't wait to get back into bed. He would need to contact Izzy first though, and he was reminded of the look on her face when he left her last night. She was worried. *But about what?* He had been so wrapped up in his own project with Bella, that maybe he had accidentally been neglecting her. He realised she had been one of Amy's closest friends and he hadn't heard her speak about Amy for weeks. Maybe she was struggling but not saying anything. It was so easy to take someone as unequivocally happy as Izzy for granted. She *never* complained.

Scott thought if he concentrated hard on this meditation, maybe some answers would present themselves to him. Still, he hadn't had any encounters with the Crimpets, and he barely knew Amy. He certainly hadn't met his future one-hundred-year-old self through a care home window. In fact, the only thing he had proved to be useful for, was to be a wall that Bella could bounce her thoughts and ideas off. However, somehow, he was incredibly curious about Hanfield's forest regardless, and the community of other lifeforms beyond what he knew.

He thought about what Amy would have experienced bumping into one of them in the forest, maybe being lured in by something, eye-catching and unusual. He imagined a bright light in the distance, enticing her to walk further and further away from civilisation. She wouldn't have even thought of the dangers ahead, not until it was too late anyway. Though when he imagined it, it wasn't Amy he saw. Instead, he saw Izzy's face, and that was when he knew she was in trouble.

Scott opened his eyes, facing both Bella and Ms. Henry, who opened their eyes at the same time. All of them in that split moment had the same profound look.

"Hannah Henry is my *sister?* You and my Dad?" Bella shouted at Ms. Henry.

Scott didn't know what Bella had seen, but he could tell she had discovered something just by the look on Ms. Henry's face, and if what she had seen was true, he needed to get out of there and find Izzy. Without a word, he got up and ran, intending to jump on his bike and ride to Izzy's house. He needed to make sure she was okay. The green of the trees blurred past him as he made his way down one of the middle rows, when something made him stop dead in his tracks. The red hair, the pale skin – it was Amy, and she stood between the trees in plain sight, her striking looks, prominent against

the forest backdrop. Scott's phone sounded in his pocket, and he was so on edge that he jumped out of his skin before pulling it out, his hands shaking.
'Scott, is everything okay? Call me, love from Izzy.'

XX
Divorce

He knew his head hadn't been right for a long time. A lot of people had questioned the way he had conducted his life after Amy had left. Richard had continued to go to work as he always had, he continued to play golf with his bosses and still made every one of the council meetings. Keeping up appearances despite your daughter going missing fuelled gossip and theories. People talked, and one of the widely believed rumours was that Richard had had something to do with it all.

This rumour was untrue. Richard didn't have it in him to ever commit such a crime, especially against someone as dear to him as Amy. But this did not mean Richard was a good man. For many years he had taken his wife Dana for granted. His disloyalty to her even went as far as infidelity when he met Ms. Rhompski, and eventually the behaviour that had initially felt wrong, had become habitual, and despite in recent weeks having not had any real communication with her, he believed Dana knew somewhere deep inside of her. It would be one of the reasons she had now asked for a divorce.

In his career, he'd had to overcome various obstacles. Some were greater than others, but he always took them in his stride. With an unshakable level-headedness and practicality, he would tackle each problem, and usually come away better off than before. Being an optimist, he liked to think of negatives as an opportunity to improve himself and his life. The divorce would be no different.

With Amy gone and Bella almost always out of the house, it was usually just the two of them. Now they would reside in separate rooms. Richard had no issue sleeping in Amy's old bedroom. It didn't feel strange to him, in fact, it was a surprising comfort being surrounded by Amy's pink walls and possessions. Even so, he would still lie awake devising his plan. He liked to think things through thoroughly and weigh up the risks involved. On this particular evening, he decided to get up out of bed and do some preparations.

Richard wasn't sure where Dana was in the large house, as she kept to herself entirely now, barely acknowledging him. Despite this, he crept carefully into his office. He still held enough respect for his soon to be ex-wife not to want to disturb her if she were asleep already, plus he didn't want to attract any unwanted attention. Taking one of his favourite whiskeys from the cupboard along with a clean crystal tumbler, he downed the first nip and poured another right away to take over to his desk. It was the beginning of the weekend, after all.

He brought out some old plans. Something he had put hours of time and energy into at one point, 'a real golden nugget of an idea' he would call it. It involved clearing much of Hanfield's unused forest and turning it into an industrial estate. When he first came across the idea, he couldn't believe no one had thought of it before him. But having somehow misplaced the main plans, he had become totally indifferent to its continued development, and he couldn't put his finger on why. But if Dana was to demand her due in the divorce (and he knew she very well could do so if she had any evidence of his affair with Ms. Rhompski) he needed to find a way to replenish his funds.

He knew the plans wouldn't go down well with the locals of Hanfield, but then, he wasn't popular anyway. With the profits he could make off the back of the plans, he could move away and start afresh, in a new town where he wasn't viewed as the 'man who probably murdered his daughter'. Walking away with a clean slate seemed very attractive at the moment, having realised that Hanfield didn't have that much to offer him anymore.

Looking down at the glass of whiskey next to his keyboard, he made the decision right then and there to reproduce the plans for the clearing of Hanfield's forests. He had already done much of the research and identified the necessary loopholes to avoid breaking any regulations. Richard would stay up all night as he used to do when he first embarked on his career, putting in the work and the hours to get what he wanted. He would present it on Monday, knowing that really, he only needed to convince a handful of people, the Mayor being one of them, and the only thing he liked the sound of was money.

Getting the figures and data together to showcase the proposition in the best light wasn't the hard part, remaining focused was. When all Richard wanted to do was drive over to Rhompskis' and ask her to run away with him; to accompany him in his new life away from Hanfield. It wouldn't be wise to do that he thought, but then everyone else seemed to suit themselves. His remaining daughter Isabella had totally withdrawn from him, Dana had asked for a divorce, and his colleagues and friends would act awkwardly around him, sometimes even being overtly rude. Ms. Rhompski was all he had, the one good thing he seemed to have in his life now.

Looking bitterly ahead at the wall in front of him, his eyes were drawn to a framed photograph of his family taken last summer in their back garden during the annual street BBQ they held. Every time he looked at that photo recently, he could never quite believe how much had changed in a year. He downed his second whiskey while looking over at everyone's smiling faces. It had been a happy day and as he compared his life then to his life now, his bitterness turned to hope, hopeful that maybe this time next year again things might have changed for the better. He got up from his desk and poured a third glass of his favourite spirit and in an impulsive uncharacteristic move, he picked up his mobile and called Ms. Rhompski.

"Richard? What's happened?" Also aware that this was out of character for him, she answered assuming the worst.

"I'm getting a divorce my Apple. Finally, we can be together!" Feeling tipsy now, Richard hardly even whispered despite Dana being in the house.

"Does Dana know about us?" Ms. Rhompski sounded surprised.

"I don't know. I don't much care anymore Apple, there's nothing for me here, I'm leaving Hanfield. I don't know where I'm going yet but I'm packing my bags and getting out of here," Richard slurred slightly while he sipped his drink.

"What if Amy comes back? The people here care about you," she sounded concerned.

"Amy's mother will be expecting the house. Dana will die in Hanfield!" Richard almost let out a chuckle, "Anyway Apple, the reason I'm calling is because I'm sitting here working, and I would like nothing more than for you to tell me... you'll come with me."

"Oh Richard I..."

"We could start afresh like we always said we should. We'll go anywhere you like, a new start," Richard said enthusiastically.

"But my life is here. It's been such a long while, I don't think that-"

"You said you loved me. All those times you said you wanted to run away with me, they were lies?" Richard began to feel angry.

"It's, well to be quite honest with you, I don't know if it's since Amy went missing or what. I've been getting these dreadful nightmares about you Richard," Ms. Rhompski explained.

"Nightmares!" Richard repeated sarcastically.

"Dreadful ones Richard, I'm getting over one of the worst bouts of illness, I've never felt so sick lately. I've had memory loss and everything. A friend has been staying here to help me." She described experiences like those that Richard had gone through recently.

"A friend? So, you've moved on to the next guy, is that it?" Richard was raising his voice, he was furious, "You are an ungrateful creature!"

"I can't speak to you while you are like this. I'm sorry things are tough Richard. Goodbye!" Ms. Rhompski calmly hung up on Richard, ending their long-time affair with a single action.

Richard began pacing his office in frustration. He had treated her like a princess when they would go out, and he would promise that when the time was right, they would be together. She had played him, while he had been dealing with his missing daughter, unable to see that she had moved on.

"Argh!" Richard shouted into his hands. The glass of whiskey had been polished off before their sour conversation had even finished: "And now what? What else will life throw my way?" asking the room, rhetorically. He felt like he despised the town and everyone in it. Looking at the monitor, with the spreadsheet for his industrial plans half-completed, he spoke aloud again, "You commit your life to your community, you try to live your life right, treat people right, and give your family everything and this is where you end up!" he slurred loudly, his eyes darting between the photo on the wall and his computer screen.

It was probably the drink, but Richard felt he was being watched. He stopped talking out loud to himself and looked towards the window. He could see the streetlight outside and total darkness beyond. Going over to close the blinds, he thought he saw something crawl along the roof of the house opposite. Straining his drunken eyes to see clearly, it looked like a hunched-up alligator or demon running along the tiles, jumping from the roof and into a tree. He rubbed his eyes again. *I need to get more sleep.*

Before sitting back down at his desk he decided at that moment that he would now only look out for himself. He had tried for too long to hold everything together, but he could trust no one in this town. Richard grabbed the large aerial photograph of the area showing almost the entire forest. A quarter had been circled off, which would be the proposed expanse of the works, and in his rage, he redefined the circumference, doubling the size of the area to take up more of the forest.

Having worked almost through the night, Richard woke up. He was still sitting at his desk, his mouth dry with the thick aftertaste of a night's drinking, his desk lamp still on and the morning's sunshine filling the room through the gaps in the blinds. Richard's neck ached from his posture, but he couldn't remember falling asleep. He must have nodded off during his research. Determined to finish it in time for Monday's meeting he decided to grab breakfast, a change of clothes and freshen up to begin a full day of work again. He felt groggy and tired, but this was nothing a couple of cups of coffee couldn't fix. Climbing the stairs towards the bedroom he made eye contact with Dana. She stood at the top of the stairs, exactly where she stood a couple of nights previously, when she first told Richard she wanted a divorce. She stood there again just as stony faced, only this time, wearing a white linen knee-length dress with a thin navy cardigan over the top. Her sunglasses were perched on her head pulling her auburn hair back from her face.

"Where are you off to?" Richard asked, having noticed she had her car keys in her hand.

"Nowhere that should concern you," Dana stated, moving aside to let Richard pass "You stink of alcohol."

Sometimes Richard thought he knew Dana more than she knew herself, and right now he knew for sure she was trying to provoke him. The best thing he could do was to remain indifferent. He continued to walk through to the bedroom to try and restart his day somehow. He presumed that she would be going to see a divorce lawyer to get the ball rolling. Dana was too productive not to already have something in hand before bringing it up with him in the first place.

By the time Monday rolled around, and with Dana seemingly too preoccupied with her grand plans to divorce him, he had just about managed to prepare everything. It wasn't perfect and if he had his way, he would spend another week on the figures in order to get them looking as attractive as possible, but he didn't have the time. Richard did, however, have his natural charisma, and looking out across the boardroom onto the bemused Monday morning faces of his colleagues, he believed he would win them over.

"We need to start implementing measures to increase our capital as a town. We have all known for a long time now that Hanfield's orchards have not been as profitable and have continued to decline. Plus, we have all of this redundant forest space," Richard spoke to the room, noticing that the Mayor's eyebrows had raised noticeably.

"Hanfield's heritage is the woods, and you want to demolish them, I don't agree with this Mr. Ferhulse. It's irresponsible!" one of his red-faced colleagues blasted.

"With respect, we're sailing into a difficult position financially, and Mr. Mayor, don't forget that you employed me to avoid these difficult times. This would create a whole host of jobs and trading opportunities. Yes, a portion of the forest would need to be given up, but the risks are minimal compared to the opportunities," Richard explained confidently. Before long, he had the majority of the room eating out of his hand, which was all he needed to get things underway.

He felt rather pleased with himself. His plan was on track having laid the groundwork for a quick turnaround on this project. He had enough companies already lined up to take up tenancies when the development was finished, that he would make more than enough of a personal profit to enable him to vacate Hanfield for good. The Mayor liked his idea, and for once Richard was happy that the office was gossiping about his plans and not his personal life. Rather than having to hide in his office, avoiding every opportunity to converse with his colleagues, he now decided he would go to the canteen to get his lunch. Making sure his appearance was pristine, he strolled through the office, a self-satisfied expression on his face.

"...surely the police must think it is the same person who took Amy Ferhulse." Richard caught the very end of a sentence as he entered the canteen. A group of employees were huddled together, talking over each other in an earnest discussion.

"What's being said here?" Richard demanded; his ears having pricked up at the mention of Amy's name.

"With this second young girl having gone missing, have the police told you it could be the same person that took Amy?" one lady asked a perplexed Richard.

"Enlighten me please ladies. Who's missing now? The rumour mill is very productive these days!" Richard added, half intrigued but also scanning the canteen counter to see what was available for lunch.

"You must not have heard. The Briggs' daughter went missing on Saturday," another woman said, before taking a big gulp of her tea.

"She left her home on Saturday morning and never came home. The police will want to speak to you soon I'd imagine," said another, "Awful, just awful news again for this town."

"Hang on, why do you assume the police would want to speak to me? I had nothing to do with Amy going missing. I wish you idiots would stop with the speculation!" Richard's euphoria had quickly turned to frustration.

The crowd all stopped eating and looked at Richard, most with awkward or sympathetic looks on their faces.

"I meant to discuss any similarities in the cases, that was all," explained the woman, awkwardly.

Feeling like the suspect that protested too much, Richard decided against eating lunch with everyone as he had intended. He didn't let it completely ruin his day though. He was irked that he couldn't seem to do anything right when it came to his colleagues. He used to get it so right. It was almost like something had changed within him recently. Returning to his office with his takeaway sandwich and cola, he discovered an email from the Mayor approving the plans which cheered him up.

Not long after he had taken a bite from his sandwich, there was a knock at the door. The building had recently been refurbished, and much to Richard's annoyance, the entire wall separating his office from the rest of the floor was now opaque glass. Usually it reminded him of bathroom windows, but as he had a mouth full of sandwich, he was thankful for the glass this time. He knew exactly who it was standing behind the door due to his large, round frame. It was the Mayor.

He's just emailed me... this had better not be some sort of retraction. I can't deal with any more setbacks. He quickly hid his sandwich in his desk drawer.

"Come in!" Richard shouted and in walked the Mayor as predicted. He was a large man with a red face that huffed and puffed around the building whenever he was in, which usually was only Mondays and Wednesdays. He strolled into the office with the usual big grin on his face, still breathing heavily and with a clear collection of sweat on his forehead and chin. Summer was not his friend.

"Richard, Richard, Richard!" The mayor had a loud booming voice, and he would always greet people the same way, shouting their name three times, "Don't get up! Just wanted a quick word about this... this... new... innovative... project of yours," he waffled, gesturing with his arms towards the documents on Richard's desk. Richard did as he was told and sat there looking up while the Mayor began to pace the room. "I trust you received my email."

"I have indeed. It's great news, Sir. You won't regret it!" Richard said, enthusiastically.

"It's great you have brought this to us now, and if you've heard, you'll realise why," the Major said conspiratorially, his loud voice lowered to a normal tone. Richard had come to learn that this was his way of whispering. But Richard didn't know what he was talking about and couldn't fill in the blanks. "It's important that we get the community on board with this. With a second missing person, which you'll appreciate more than anyone, the public are more likely to see the forest as a dangerous place."

"Ah yes, Sir. I can speak to the Hanfield Post and have them run the story in that light." Richard knew now why the Mayor had visited his office, rather than putting it all in the email. It could be seen as public manipulation. Richard knew it probably was, but the Mayor was right. He was more qualified than anyone to make that judgment. He didn't know where Amy had gone to, but he knew the vast forest had certainly hindered their search.

With the Mayor's approval and support, he knew it was all downhill from here. He did, however, have a lump in his throat after hearing about Izzy Briggs' disappearance, despite his reaction in the canteen. Some would call it a coping mechanism, and others might call it downright cold, but Richard had always told himself Amy had left on her own accord. She was adventurous, self-assured, and above all, she was smart. Only now he wasn't so sure. *A second girl of Amy's age.* Someone could have abducted *his* girl.

When he arrived home, pulling into the driveway, he saw Bella sitting on the step outside the front door. She never really looked particularly happy to him, and she wasn't someone that expressed happy feelings outwardly, but he could immediately tell that something was wrong straight away. Assuming it would be due to her schoolmate's disappearance, he walked over to her, ready to hug her tightly and have a chat with her.

"Oh baby, I heard today... Are you alright? Did you know her well?" Richard sat down next to Bella and tried to put his arms around her, however, she suddenly appeared more furious than sad.

"No!" Bella shouted at her father, pushing his arms away and standing up to move away from him. Richard looked shocked but remained silent. "Is it true that Hannah Henry is my sister?"

He realised how Bella had found out about. Ms. Henry had been adamant that he was Hannah's father. Years ago, they'd had a fling, a short affair when he was first engaged to Dana. Her claims that

Hannah was his, coupled with her outlandish behaviour, made him assume she wasn't well, mentally. He denied it and paid her to be quiet. He never heard the claims again.

"Did Ms. Henry tell you that? She's crazy Bella," Richard reacted, trying not to show the anger he felt towards Ms. Henry, and avoid making things worse with his daughter.

"No Dad – I know she's my sister... you're a liar!" Bella shouted before getting on her bike and darting off quickly.

XXI
Dreams Come True

"What is wrong with you Hannah? You're an evil, jealous monster!" Monica hissed in front of all the other members of the dance team, who were now thoroughly entranced by the scene that was unfolding, watching with open mouths and wide eyes.

Hannah didn't even flinch, she simply looked up from her phone towards Monica with a look of disdain, before a quick smile darted across her face. The plan to upset Izzy had worked better than she could have imagined, and the satisfaction showed on her face.

"You've just *crushed* her world over something that might not even be true," Monica continued, "and all because she's a better dancer than you, and you know it!"

Hannah inhaled slightly as Monica's comment hit a nerve, but playing it off as nothing, she tilted her head to one side like a confused puppy.

"Oh please! Go run after your little sad case friend and stop ruining my lunch with your dramas!" Hannah spoke as if Monica had been the one causing trouble. She was very good at calmly

The Familiar Encounter

deflecting and manipulating situations to suit herself and her image, especially when she had an audience. As if by magic, the rest of the group were now looking at Monica like she was the one causing the disturbance.

Monica continued to look Hannah right in the eyes. She knew she was only jealous of Izzy's natural ability to dance, and now that she had said it out loud, she could see that behind Hannah's cold, nonchalant exterior, she was unhappy. Monica wanted to keep deriding Hannah, as it felt good to release her true opinion of her, but Monica knew it wouldn't change anything. The best thing she could do was to control the damage, and breaking the intense eye contact with Hannah, she left to go after Izzy.

"You young kids, I can't keep up!" a large, older lady, wearing the waitress uniform, shouted out playfully as Monica ran past her and out the door. She moved towards the kitchen to change the order accordingly.

Monica pushed open the heavy double doors to follow Izzy out of the diner. The warm air hit her as a welcome reminder that the colder days were not due to set in anytime, soon despite it being the end of summer. The gardenia bushes nearby filled her nose with beautiful floral scents, reminding her of fun weekends hanging out with friends all summer long, but unfortunately also a smell that was sure to set off her hay fever.

She ran in the direction of town on a whim, although she could only have been a few minutes behind Izzy she couldn't see her. The diner was situated on top of one of the higher hills in Hanfield, giving a great view of the streets, but there was no sign of her upset friend. She felt awful and wasn't even sure what she might say if she did catch up to her. Monica's legs were taking her to Scott's house, and she wasn't going to argue with that, as she didn't have his number. Maybe he would know where Izzy was. Plus, it wouldn't be a bad idea to ask him if anything was *actually* going on with Bella. She didn't quite know herself if she should hate Hannah *and* Scott right now.

As she jogged down to the bottom of the hill, surprised at how warm she had got in just a few moments, she started to call Izzy's phone repeatedly. No answer, no surprise there, but for the sake of trying every way to reach her, she kept at it. She had only been to Scott's house once when she and Rick were dropping Izzy off after one of Dana's early evening rehearsals. She couldn't quite remember where it was, but she knew it was somewhere near the street where all the small houses looked the same.

She stopped to look around and find her bearings, now feeling the effects of the pollen in her nostrils. Her eyes had become watery, her vision was slightly blurred, and her throat was scratchy. Her thick dark hair hung around her neck as she didn't have a hair band, making her sweat even more. *Urgh come on just answer your damn phone,* Monica thought looking down at the touch screen with Izzy's name illuminated, showing a photo taken at her recent birthday. She was, grinning from ear to ear, wearing a funky hairband, back when times were happier, and they had all laughed together, without a care.

Monica hung up and continued to walk along the street, looking at the identical houses. With a bit of luck, she saw Scott's mother in their front garden. She recognised her from some of the football games at Hanfield High.

"Hi there... Mrs. Bowers, you won't know me, but I'm Scott's friend from school. Is he home?" Monica came right out and asked regardless of the slight wheeze in her breath, and the beads of sweat running down her rather rosy face.

"Oh, hello Monica, no he must have gone out early this morning on his bike... I suppose it's a lovely day for it," Mrs. Bowers said, with a trowel in one hand and a bag of soil in the other.

"No worries, Mrs. Bowers. I'm sure I'll catch up with him later." Monica's luck had proved short lived.

"I'll tell him you came by," Mrs. Bowers assured Monica with a kind smile.

A failed plan and perhaps the proof she needed. Scott could well be with his friends, however she suspected he was not. Somewhere in her gut she knew he was with Bella Ferhulse today, and it made her feel sick to her stomach, or maybe that was the heat. *It's so warm,* she thought, licking her dry lips and closing her eyes in a prolonged blink to try and ease the burning sensation. With her eyes closed, Monica felt as though she was spinning, as if she were flying. Quickly opening them again, she felt the burning return to her eyes. Her eyelids were swelling, and her neck was becoming irritated and itchy. She needed her antihistamines and so, made the difficult decision to temporarily abort the hunt for Izzy, and return home to recover. She knew she would be no good at talking Izzy round if she found her mid heatstroke. Walking out onto the main street past the quaint little post office and small boutiques, unable to breathe properly and half-blind, Monica tried Izzy's number again, once more staring down at Izzy's Birthday photograph while the phone rang out.

To Monica's momentary disbelief after a couple of rings the phone's display changed from *'Ringing...'* to a timer counting upwards from zero. She lifted her phone to her ear quickly as she stood still in the middle of Hanfield's busy town square, full of Saturday shoppers.

"I'm so glad you answered! I've been trying to find you!" Monica spoke with relief.

Izzy didn't respond. Monica heard static at first, then rustling, and then footsteps. Loud footsteps as if someone were running on dried leaves. Weirdly, the steps became increasingly louder, and this drew Monica's focus further into the call making her forget about her breathing, her painful eyes, and her dizziness in the sunshine.

"Hello? Hello? ...Izzy?" Monica shouted. She had heard these noises many times before, and it frightened her like no other 'pocket dial' could, "Hello?" she shouted desperately trying for a real response. People were now staring at her as they walked by.

As she continued to listen, she heard someone breathing heavily. It didn't sound like Izzy, but it was familiar. Monica's chest felt tight with her heart beating quickly, her bloodshot eyes darting around the busy walkway looking at the different faces, searching for something familiar, seeking help.

"Tell me who's there!" Monica demanded, now shouting down her phone back at the loud commotion. She couldn't stand to listen. The shoppers around her were now moving well out of the way as she was making a scene, her hand shaking as it remained holding her phone to her ear. "Tell me now!" she shouted again. Everything stopped. No footsteps, no breathing, not even a hint anymore that someone was on the other end of the phone. Had it gone dead? Monica took the phone from her ear and checked, the timer was still rolling, the call was still connected. She brought the phone tight against her ear now to listen out for any clues at all as to where Izzy might be. Her tummy felt like it had flipped upside down. The line wasn't dead, and Monica realised she could hear something again, very soft whisperings, the feeling of déjà vu was overwhelming. It was a female voice, and Monica's ear ached as she held her phone tighter and tighter to her face, her head now bowed as she looked down at her feet in concentration. The voice was replaced by a hair-raising scream, loud enough to shock Monica into throwing her phone halfway across the road.

Pausing for a moment, she was sure someone was saying something to her from the street, but she couldn't focus enough on them. She ran into the road to quickly retrieve her phone before a car came by. The screen was shattered, but luckily the phone still worked. Disturbed, and noticing a few people around her had stopped to see if she was okay, Monica realised she must also have screamed aloud at the shock. She took a deep breath in a failed attempt to calm her racing heart rate and ran home, ignoring the concerned onlookers nearby.

Going straight into her room, she knew something terrible had happened, the memory of what she had just heard was sending shivers down her spine, and with her parents and brother now out for the day, the house had a silence she found eerie. She pulled her dream journal out from under her bed. Monica had recently told Dr. Banner about some of the nightmares she'd had and how they were now beginning to leak into her day to day life. However, after seeing the look on Banner's face, Monica had decided not to go into all the finer details. She avoided mentioning that she saw Amy around more often, as she knew it would sound crazy, and she was sure there was some teacher's rule that would involve her reporting it to a higher body. The dream journal had been a great suggestion by Banner, they'd had a lengthy chat about dreams and how your mind can forget about most of it, so now Monica would write each one down as soon as she woke up, even if it was the middle of the night. It had only been a few days, but it had made her feel better, like she was somehow getting the dreams off her chest by putting pen to paper. Monica flipped through the few pages of dreams already recorded to remind herself of the details.

I'm running through the forest again like before, not just running aimlessly, I'm running from something. It's dark and cold and I can only make out the trees at the last minute, so I'm dodging them quickly. I'm trying to catch my breath, but I'm scared and even grazing my shoulder against a branch and scraping my legs on some thick bushes doesn't bother me, I'm just trying to get away. I think it's working; I feel calmer with that thought, but just as I think I've got away, I run into something I can't avoid. It feels cold to the touch, freezing cold and so white it almost glows in the dark. It feels hard like stone, but I know it's a person, I scream continuously and helplessly before waking up.

Monica knew she had heard that call before; the sounds were in her dream. She didn't know what it meant. She took her phone out of her pocket, and it automatically unlocked, opening into her call log, but it didn't show the call at all, only a list of all the unanswered calls to Izzy. It was as if it had never even happened.

She stared down at her book of scribbled nightmares and felt disturbed. She told herself she would tell Dr. Banner everything on Monday because it probably wouldn't be such a bad idea after all if she did end up getting referred to some child therapist. She just wanted all of the visions and dreams to stop and putting her dream journal back under her bed she rubbed her itchy eyes, curled up and fell asleep on top of her bed, confused and upset.

Hours later, she woke up noticing her room was no longer as bright as before, as the clouds had set in for the night, and the sun was making its way down on another day. Her eyes were still burning, and although it was a bit late, she tried to think where her mother kept the antihistamines.

Getting up and going to look in the bathroom cabinet she heard something as she crossed the corridor, it sounded like a girl's laugh, and it was coming from downstairs. For a second, she thought it sounded like Amy's laugh. Monica felt so frustrated with her confused mind she could have cried, and having found no sign of the tablets anywhere in the bathroom cabinet, she headed downstairs to seek them out. Just as she was about to enter the kitchen, the giggling laugh filled the room again, and Monica paused for a moment. *No this isn't real, this just is not real*, she told herself before heading into the room.

"You think I'm a monster?" Hannah was standing in Monica's kitchen, a full glare in her blue eyes and a malicious kind of smile on her face.

"Hannah? So, you've followed me home?" Monica asked in surprise. She suspected Hannah was a psycho at school, but to now turn up *in* her house was another level of weird, that is unless she was seeing things again.

"You have no idea how much of a monster I can be, Monica, everyone underestimates me, and I'm sick of it!" Hannah sounded incensed, and her voice got deeper as she spoke. Monica looked on in horror as Hannah's eyes darkened, and her body started changing shape. She grew taller, her shoulders broadened, her soft tan skin transformed into a dark green colour with black scales, her teeth became sharp while her face became pointed and furrowed. "Izzy will be taken care of, but you... I'll take care of you myself!" Hannah growled.

Monica didn't know what was going on, but this felt really real to her, *but so had the phone call earlier, and the random sightings of Amy.* She was terrified as Hannah, who no longer looked like Hannah at all, advanced on her, with a big grin showing all of her horrid teeth, and her eyebrows pointed with the most grotesque expression.

This is not happening, it's not real, don't react, Monica told herself with her eyes closed as tightly as possible. She thought back to the nightmares of running away from something and all of a sudden, the whole dream played out from here, flashing through her mind. She would run away from Hannah right now and straight towards the forest behind her house, as she realised Hannah's true form had been revealed, and was very real. She ran and ran to get away from her, she could hear her gaining on her, careering into the sides of trees, she could barely see or make out where she was running to, and bumping into someone hard, cold and frightening just as she had done in all of her nightmares, she screamed as loudly as she could. Monica opened her eyes again, this was it, this moment was what her dreams had been warning her about, and as her skin tingled all over, she went to scream in Hannah's, now monstrous, face.

Monica sat up at the end of her bed, just as she had done moments ago, this time she was listening out for it... she knew to expect, the cold laugh, the giggle she had heard before which was only meant to lure her downstairs. It was crazy, but Monica knew inside, what was about to happen, and she needed to get out of there.

"Click!" Monica was listening out this time. *I could swear that was the back-door latch.* Monica knew Hannah was now in the house with her, it was as if she had just foreseen what was about to happen, or maybe it had happened, and she somehow did the impossible, going backwards in time. Monica carefully got up off the bed still listening. She grabbed her backpack and slowly shoved one of her jackets and her dream journal into it along with some other items she thought she might need.

Her ears pricked up at the sound of the giggle. Again, to Monica, it sounded like Amy's laugh, but she now knew Hannah wasn't even human, so she couldn't question how she was able to mimic Amy's voice like that. It was her ploy to get an unsuspecting Monica to run downstairs, but this time Monica would have the element of surprise, and although she didn't have much time, she wasn't going to squander it. The nightmares she had so disliked and cursed, were blessings. Monica had somehow been given a sight into the future.

As she grabbed her water bottle from her desk in a quiet rush, she accidentally knocked over the dolphin trinket her grandmother had got her from America. It fell on the ground and bounced off of the hardwood floors. *Damn it, damn damn damn it!* Hannah would now know Monica was in the house, the second giggle coming from the downstairs kitchen could now be heard, even more chilling now that Monica knew it was Hannah coming to get her.

She wasted no more time; she opened one of her windows as far as it could go, climbing out of her bedroom, and using all of her upper body strength, attempted to lower herself down off the ledge and onto the extended kitchen roof space below. Her father had always told her to do this if there was ever a fire in the house, so to Monica, this was permission enough from her parents.

Once she let go, the sound of her landing on the roof below wasn't too bad. She knew Hannah, ready to change into her true reptilian form was waiting just below her. Monica looked around to calculate her next move. She identified the only area on the roof avoiding the skylight to head to the ground floor was right next to the back door where Hannah had entered moments ago, Hannah could follow her straight out of that door if she suspected she was trying to run, so she had to be careful.

Monica's balance wasn't great as she waved and weaved about on the slippery moss carefully edging herself to the end of the roof. Passing the skylight, she could see that Hannah was standing right where she had been when Monica had seen her in her dream, only ten minutes ago. *Urgh horrible creature,* Monica had this thought about Hannah often when she would notice her being cruel to other classmates, but she didn't know how right she had been all along. Looking at what Hannah was doing through the skylight instead of concentrating on where she was putting her feet for a moment too long, caused Monica to lose her balance, sliding uncontrollably down towards the end of the roof space. She managed to grip the drainpipe on the way down to slow her enough to find her bearings and land on the ground, thankfully on her feet. She was sure she hadn't been too subtle about it though and without looking back began to run as fast as she could through her back garden and towards the forest.

In another moment of déjà vu, she remembered that had been the downfall of her nightmare, she realised she shouldn't run through the forest as it would most certainly not be to safety. With the image of the peculiar man in her mind she made a U-turn at the bottom of her garden and headed towards the lamp-lit street between her neighbour's house and her own. She could see Hannah had realised she was making her getaway and had begun to change into her terrifying alternative appearance while running towards her. Monica used all the force she could to propel herself forward and tapped into her sprint training, imaging she was in just another school race.

Monica made it out onto the street, and from there she ran towards the Ferhulse house. It was the only one she remembered from all those times practising with the Hanfield Heartbeats before Dana could face going back to work at the school. Rick lived outside of town and Izzy wasn't close enough either. She didn't know Isabella Ferhulse well, she probably hadn't ever had one conversation with her, but it was all she had. Concentrating on running away, she had no idea whether Hannah was close behind her or if she was managing to outrun her. Monica remembered that one of the essential rules in racing was to avoid looking back at your opponent at all costs, and as stressed as she was, she kept her focus forward, trying to get to Bella's front door. She ran up the driveway and banged on the door with what little energy she had left. She didn't stop knocking until she could see through the small patterned glass that someone was coming.

"Well what a nice surprise! I didn't know you and Bella were..." Dana greeted Monica in the usual happy, enthusiastic tone she always had in school before it trailed off into concern. "Is everything ok? Come in!" Monica knew that Dana was most likely reacting to the fact she was entirely out of breath and had a look of sheer distress on her face.

"Thank you, Dana, thank you!" Monica blurted out between deep breaths and walking into the safety of the house a little too quickly, she realised she was going to freak Dana out if she didn't have a good enough answer, "Yeah I'm ok thanks – decided to jog here!" Monica said, forcing a more chipper tone of voice and trying to conceal her body language, hiding her shaking hands behind her back.

"Is that all Monica? You were looking rather desperate a moment ago?" Dana looked dubious and who could blame her, Monica needed a better excuse than that.

"Well actually..." Monica needed to think up a lie and sharp, "...it's this Maths coursework I'm stuck on, it's kinda stressing me out, and I wondered if Bella was home to give me a bit of help?" Monica said as convincingly as possible with a remnant of a tear running down her cheek.

"We've all been there!" Dana seemed to buy the last-minute lie. "Go on up to Bella's room. I don't think she's doing much!"

Suddenly Monica realised she had no clue where Bella's room was, but following Dana's hand gesture to the stairs, she went ahead. Thankfully, she could tell Bella's bedroom door. Each one was a plain cream colour apart from one which was baby pink, and another which was dark purple. Although Monica had never spoken to Bella, she was seen to be a bit of a goth around school. This has got to be Bella's room. Trying not to dwell too much on how much of a creep she felt, turning up to a random girl's house, she knocked lightly on the door. Monica could hear rock music was being played inside the room, which further confirmed she was at the right door.

With no response she knocked louder but again was left with nothing. Now feeling totally awkward she opened the door, slowly.

"Hey, erm, Isabella? It's just Monica, you know, from school." Monica cringed as she said it, opening the door a bit more.

"Who?" Bella shouted, she watched as Monica opened the door fully to reveal herself as one of Amy's friends from school. "Ok? You know my sister's not here, right?" Bella joked, getting up from her desk and turning down the music. She looked puzzled to see her despite her quick wit.

"Yes... well it is you I'm here to see, well I mean I was erm..." Monica didn't quite know where to begin or what to say. She fidgeted with her hair and rubbed her face, suddenly feeling shy.

"What is it? I'm busy. I don't have all night!" Bella started to become frustrated and impatient.

"Well, I was sort of, chased here really... by erm Hannah... you know, also from school." Monica was now starting to see how crazy she was soon going to sound.

"Oh *Hannah Henry'* yeah I know her, I've just about had enough of her today... so why are you here again?" Bella was beginning to lose interest already and was starting to look over at the notebook on her desk.

"Yeah... she's not human. Hannah, that is. She's not er..." Feeling pressured, Monica confessed expecting to now be laughed out of the house entirely.

To her surprise, Bellas attention instantly moved back onto Monica, and she walked over to close the door behind her: "I'm looking into something similar right now. It might sound strange to other people, but not me. What else do you know?"

"No, I mean she is not human... I'm being genuine," Monica said with more confidence this time, as she wasn't sure if this was sarcasm she saw from Bella. She seemed like a dry humoured sort of person and how could anyone understand what Monica had just seen and been through.

"Me too... I'm pretty sure my sister's been abducted by aliens and Hannah is probably one of them. The more you tell me, the more I can help you!" Bella sat down with her pen and notepad ready to begin writing it all down. Monica wasn't sure at this point if maybe Bella was completely crazy, or if she had also been experiencing weird occurrences. Monica thought she probably couldn't be any more freaked out than she currently was. In contrast, Bella didn't seem shocked at all, almost like she was expecting her, and whatever it was, this was as good a reception as she could have hoped for, So, she did as she was told and explained everything, "It started with these dreams... well more like nightmares really..."

XXII
The True Capture

Bella had noticed Monica in her garden when the Hanfield Heartbeats would practise for hours. She would watch them out of her bedroom window sometimes, and she noticed Monica looked the quietest out of them all. She stood out to Bella more than the others as she hadn't ever seen someone as shy looking as her within the group. Usually, they would all be bursting with confidence. She was simply the new girl at the beginning of summer, trying to fit in. Now Bella sat in front of Monica, excited at the prospect of another lead. She felt at ease telling Monica everything in exchange for hearing the reason that had brought her running to her home that night, completely out of the blue.

Meeting Mrs. Samuels had blown the mystery wide open, and the moment she met her through the window at Cliff Edge she knew she was looking back at her future self. Her skin was wrinkled and aged, but she recognised herself in Mrs. Samuels. It was like she had been expecting Bella, she had hurried to take the chain from her wrist and had pushed it into her hands, as if she knew she was going to be needing it for something. From there, Bella got her next clue.

"Get to the orchard for 5 am," Mrs. Samuels whispered. Behind her a couple of care workers had noticed Bella in the window and were rushing over. At the time Bella didn't understand what Mrs.

Samuels meant, and she didn't know if she would ever see her again to ask her all the questions she longed to ask, but she trusted her gut and needed to get out of there, to avoid explaining to her parents why she was hanging around the old folk's home after dark.

"Are you still listening to me? You've stopped writing things down?" Monica asked, looking concerned. She was now sat on Bella's bed with her legs crossed, and had been explaining her story while playing with a loose thread on her sweater, she would wrap it around her finger and unwrap it repeatedly while discussing in detail the unusual visions she'd had. It was then that Bella noticed Monica didn't look as polished as she had at school, maybe the hallucinations were weighing on her mind so much she looked run down, or possibly without the hype of the Heartbeats surrounding her, she was just a normal girl.

Bella was still sleepy after napping all afternoon. She'd stayed up all night after speaking to Mrs. Samuels. She didn't want to chance sleeping through any alarms for her 5 am mission and felt as though she had loads of research to carry out now that she had another lead to go off.

"Sorry! Yes, I'm listening, I guess I'm still processing some news I heard earlier. Hannah is a bit of a touchy subject." Bella felt bad that she wasn't giving Monica her full attention. She had been talking about having seen Amy, which was massive news, even if Monica was calling them hallucinations, Bella thought otherwise.

"She looked so... devil-like, her entire appearance and body changed before my eyes. I thought I was seeing things again, and that's when it happened, it was like I pulled back in time and went back twenty minutes. I knew what was going to happen already, I could see into the future, and that's how I just about got away and ended up here," Monica revealed.

"That sounds frightening, the alien I saw looked different... maybe Hannah is something else altogether!" Bella began noting something down in her book.

"What has Hannah done to you? Have you had a similar run in?" Monica asked curiously, still twirling the thread around her index finger.

"I don't think Hannah has ever dared say two words to me, even in school she seems to avoid me, I guess 'cause she was such good friends with Amy." Bella stalled, unsure if she should tell the truth to

Monica, but she had told her everything else about the Crimpets and Mrs. Samuels. She hadn't been able to get a hold of Scott, yet again, and she needed someone on board. "When I was meditating this morning, it was as if I saw a vision from the past. I suppose it's similar to how you described your feelings of déjà vu. It was a strange feeling, I guess. I could see that Hannah was related to Amy and me. My half-sister. My lying father must have had an affair!" Bella couldn't hide her undertone of upset in a rare occurrence of showing genuine emotion.

"Wow, that's heavy! Have you asked your dad about it?" Monica asked, sympathetically.

"Urgh, I don't see the point," Bella sighed, ending the conversation abruptly.

They were both silent for that moment, having both got a lot off their minds. Bella's phone vibrated on the desk behind her, breaking the quiet and demonstrating how on edge they were as they both jumped up from their seats in surprise.

"It's Scott!" Bella said out loud as she entered her phone pin to reveal the message.

'Izzy is in danger. I'm in the forest near the old bus driver's house. Amy is with me! Meet us there.' Bella read the message twice to make sure what she was reading was correct... he was *with* Amy.

"What did he say?" Monica asked, having seen the look of total disbelief on Bella's face as her eyes read over the message.

"I need to go to the forest right now, and you're coming with me!" Bella commanded, getting up from her seat and grabbing Monica's bag from the floor. "You got a coat? Borrow one of mine... or freeze, whatever." Bella said, as she quickly put her grubby looking trainers on, the ones she had worn repeatedly to go walking around the forest late at night and headed out of her room.

"Wait for me!" Monica shouted after her, awkwardly, taking the first jacket off the back of her bedroom door, which happened to be a long black leather trench coat.

"Your parents didn't even ask where we were going!" Monica mentioned in shock, "I wish mine were that chilled out." Bella was power walking down the street.

"They used to be very involved, they have a lot going on." Bella responded, her voice trailed off while she thought of how they would react if she brought Amy back home with her tonight. She could picture their reactions quite clearly but could not imagine her own. She hadn't had the best relationship with Amy in recent years but the thought of seeing her again seemed too good to be true.

"What did Scott say?" Monica asked again, noticing Bella's mood had changed entirely. They were now arriving at the forest edge.

"He's got Amy!" As Bella responded, she turned her head slightly to watch Monica's reaction, as some curious way to get clarity on how she should feel.

"He's found Amy? She's alive?" Monica sounded more shocked than Bella could have imagined. Bella felt something but it wasn't shock, which confirmed that in her heart she had known her sister was out there alive, all along. She had known, deep down, that they would be reunited again, but it was only a question of when. Having been met with silence by Bella, Monica began to retract: "*Obviously* she was still alive... I just think after all this time, where has she been? This is an unbelievable story Bella. You surely must admit that?" Monica was too honest sometimes, and it was perhaps why Bella had trusted her right away. Monica couldn't be anything other than genuine.

"I told you, she was taken by aliens, we already knew this," Bella was even more honest and quick to tell things how they were. That was how she needed to be to keep herself from disbelieving everything she had worked to uncover.

When they finally arrived at the bus driver's old house, there was no sign of Amy, or Scott for that matter. Bella looked at her phone to find she had no messages and no signal.

"I had no idea this place was here. It's creepy right?" Monica made conversation while she looked around, it was night time, but their eyes were already well adjusted to the dark from their walk.

"I came here on my own last time. I didn't think many others knew about it, but I guess Scott does." Bella was starting to wonder given Monica's recent run-in with Hannah, if maybe this was a trap. Listening out for any noises, she found it to be eerily quiet. Even the night breeze was silent. The only weapon she had was her gut feeling, and it didn't feel right. Bella began walking closer to the small house, peering into the window using her phone light. She saw that it was just as empty and derelict as it had been on her last visit, too sinister and too stil. She began to walk around the back of the house. Bella could tell there had once been a garden, but it had been neglected and had become overgrown over time, and she was walking over weeds which had overpowered the flower beds that had once been there. Monica followed closely behind, both keeping parallel to the building's stone walls.

Bella peered around the first corner out into what would have been the back garden, a clearing in amongst the trees. She squinted her eyes while, asking them to adjust even further to the darkness. She scanned the dark landscape and noticed something strange in the distance. Narrowing her eyes further she peered into the night. She took a deep breath, *what am I looking at?* she asked herself, watching the colours flash against the darkness, it could have been anything.

"Is someone there?" Monica asked, and the question sent a chill down Bella's spine because she knew someone *was* there.

It could have been anything, but Bella wasn't patient. She liked to jump into action and so, she stepped out from behind the house, exposing herself to whatever the weird shapes in the night were.

"Are you crazy?" Monica shouted.

"Hello? Who's there?" Bella shouted out. She was determined to get to the bottom of this once and for all.

"Isabella?" It was a voice Bella knew better than anyone's, and she instinctively ran towards it and embraced her sister. Amy was about the only person their age that called her by her full name. Her frame felt no different to Bella, not underweight as one might think, but then they never really did hug. Bella was speechless; she closed her eyes and took it all in for a moment. She felt a completeness she hadn't felt for months. "It's good to see you." Amy said as she turned to look at Scott. Bella noticed she was just the same, her glowing skin, her bright red hair, that same energy.

"Can I bring him out yet? She won't freak out, Amy?" Bella could hear Scott's voice shouting out from beyond where the treeline began again. She still couldn't quite make him out.

"So what's the story?" Bella asked. This was always something their parents would say when the two of them were children, it was the only sentence that came to mind after so much time had passed, and Amy laughed for a moment.

"Okay Scott... Isabella, meet Frank!" Amy announced, her eyes widened expectedly, and she smiled her huge smile at both Amy and Monica.

At first, Bella could just about see Scott coming out of the woods, but someone was with him, although she couldn't tell who it was. But as they got closer, the creature was revealed. It walked towards them slowly by Scott's side, with Bella speechless the entire time. The thing she had spent so long sketching, reading and thinking about, was now in front of her. It existed and she really had met this creature once before when she was last here.

"I know you! I've seen you before!" Monica exclaimed. She had been standing back to let Bella and Amy have their much-anticipated reunion, but now she moved forwards, "I thought I had gone mad!" Disbelief sounded in her voice, but there was also relief.

"I'm glad to meet you!" Frank stood behind Amy, towering over her he held his right arm up and performed a waving motion, too erratic and robotic to seem natural.

"Don't overreact, he's my very good friend... be nice Bella," Amy said in her smooth, calming voice.

"How can I not? You must have Stockholm syndrome! ...Scott?" Bella encouraged Scott to back her up.

"He's pretty cool... they all are, they've been trying to help Amy with her new powers. It's awesome!" Scott shrugged. "He's our best bet for getting Izzy back from the real bad guys!" he said quietly, looking down at his feet.

"What *powers*?" Bella was outraged by this. She had spent all this time building a case against them.

"I can reach out to people with my mind. Just before I went missing, I thought there was something very wrong with me, but it turns out we're just the same Monica, you know that, don't you? I tried to reach out to you," Amy explained, "...you saw me a few times, but you didn't want to accept it."

"I did, it er, freaked me out, freaked my boyfriend out too," Monica tried to sound light-heartedly thinking back to when Amy seemingly ran in front of Rick's truck. "Why me though, Frank?" Monica wanted answers after all this time, after all the dreams and sightings at school, while Bella stood there taken aback that Monica was speaking to *Frank* like he was any other guy.

"You both, along with Hannah, consumed a Kryton, which I'm sure is a real pain for you humans to come to terms with." Frank tried to explain.

"The apple pie that Hannah's mum made us that time Monica, remember? It was special, and it affected us all differently... very differently." Amy added.

"You can say that again!" Monica laughed hesitantly.

"Hannah is some sort of monster and was trying to attack Monica tonight", Bella told Amy. She wondered if the same would eventually happen to Amy and Monica, that they would slowly morph and become something else entirely. Frank looked over at Bella as the thought entered her mind.

"The evil was always in Hannah's genetic makeup, Isabella, from birth. Many years ago, her father made a deal with the Fangrogs, the ones that have Izzy." Frank spoke factually and steadily, while looking at Scott with concern, like he knew Izzy was particularly important to him.

"Our father?" Bella asked Frank.

"In return for his success. She's your family but cursed nevertheless." Frank agreed.

"We need to head back and tell everyone, tell everyone she's dangerous, and that you're back Amy and you're safe!" Bella smiled, trying to remain positive that her sister had returned.

"I can't, not yet Isabella. We must get the Fangrogs. We have to get Izzy back." Amy had always done the right thing. She was kind and compassionate, yet, determined, and Bella knew she wouldn't be convinced to come back with her tonight. "Scott has agreed to stay with us this one night."

"We can help you Amy!" Monica volunteered enthusiastically.

"It's appreciated but Hannah will be looking for both of you at school tomorrow, you need to be there to keep up appearances." Amy seemed to have a kind of self-assuredness Bella had never seen before, "both of you; keep up appearances, she can't hurt you, I won't let her."

The darkness around them increased, as if a dark cloud had floated by and blocked out the small amount of light they were getting from the moon, darker and darker until Bella couldn't see anything.

Bella opened her eyes as her stomach flipped upside down, like she had gone over the highest road bump in the car, to find she was in her English class at school. She looked around confused at first, trying to calm herself. She looked down towards the schoolbook in front of her, the top of her worksheet stated it was Monday. She felt strangely refreshed, *have I just daydreamed that whole scenario?* Bella wondered. But as she looked around in class, she was comforted at the sight of Monica's backpack behind her chair. *Last night did happen.*

As soon as class finished, she wanted to seek Monica out, just as she was sure Monica would also want to talk to her about the night before. Bella had all these thoughts running through her mind; she felt like she needed answers from her father, she couldn't imagine what these evil creatures looked like and what would possess him to make a deal like that with them. The sense of relief she felt knowing Amy was alive, filled her with hope that things would be okay again soon.

Instead of heading to their next lesson, the school's staff asked everyone to go to the main hall, and as crowds of students filtered into the hallway, Bella's eyes darted around to try and catch sight of Monica.

Once the students were all seated in the large echoing hall, the headteacher stepped out onto the stage. The school wouldn't usually hold a service in the middle of the day like this and so there were whispers throughout the room amongst confused students. The whispers then doubled in volume once two men in smart suits stepped onto the stage to stand next to the headteacher.

"Some of you may know why we've gathered you here this afternoon. Unfortunately, Hanfield has had to deal with yet another missing person report, and it is, yet again, a treasured pupil from this school. I'm sure all of you know Izzy Briggs." The mention of Izzy's name stirred the room up into further gasps and whispers. "She was reported missing on Saturday evening, and so this needs to be taken extremely seriously. The two men standing next to me today are detectives. Throughout the week we will be calling you out of lessons to speak to them, however, if you have any information from this past weekend, my office is open to you at any time." By the time the headteacher had stopped speaking, the room was in silence. Izzy was loved by every person at the school, she was everyone's friend, and the concern in the air was palpable.

Getting up to leave the hall, Bella saw Monica and Scott had been sitting next to each other. She decided to wait outside for them as they all headed to their next lessons separately.

"So, no sign of Izzy last night then?" Bella whispered to Scott, as the three of them were reunited walking down the corridor together.

"No luck at all, and I suppose the police will want to speak to me today too." Scott sounded nervous.

"And me, I feel awful, she was upset, and she ran off... I don't know what I'll even tell the police!" Monica sounded as though she might burst into tears at any moment.

"Why was she upset?" Bella asked bluntly. Monica looked awkwardly down at her hands; she was playing with one of the rings around her middle finger as they walked along.

"Hey Monica!" Suddenly, from the crowds of students Hannah appeared in front of the three of them, stopping them in their path and smiling from ear to ear. "Bella and Scott, I guess you can both hang out all the time now there's no Izzy standing between you."

"What have you done?" Scott blasted, loud enough to catch the attention of some of the students walking by.

"Scott - not here!" Monica warned.

"And what's that smell on you, Scott? Is that Amy's scent?" Hannah laughed. "Do you three know where she's hiding? I hope it's not from me." Hannah laughed again before continuing to walk off and disappear back into the crowd.

"We should stay out of her way until we can figure out how to get Izzy back, one thing at a time!" Bella instructed.

"But I have a plan Bella! I had a dream last night that the Fangrogs took Izzy thinking she was me, at the very end of the orchard... I could see it in my dream. They want someone who's eaten the Kryton apple! If we can go back there tonight, they might be up for an exchange!" Monica said.

"But swapping you for Izzy isn't the answer, Mon!" Scott responded.

"No... but Hannah also ate the apple pie that time Amy said. If we can find a way to get her there too... " Bella suggested.

The Familiar Encounter

"They will, I saw it, they won't want Izzy... she's no use to them. Hannah is eager to see Amy, trust me on that - she'll follow us right to her!" Monica answered.

"Bella? We're all waiting for you!" Bella's Biology teacher called out to her from the classroom doorway. Monica and Scott moved along.

The atmosphere at school was strained since the announcement of Izzy's disappearance. Although Bella was satisfied with the team they now had, that they were sure to bring Izzy back, this atmosphere brought memories of when Amy had first gone missing. How awful school was to go to as usual, and all the unforgettable conversations with teachers and police officers that were filled with sympathy. Cycling home with so many questions still going through her mind from the weekend she'd had, and the uncomfortable feeling of what tonight would bring, the realisation of how quickly her entire life had changed in only a few weeks, hit her. Bella's whole outlook was adjusting, and she felt a shame fall upon her because she had never had much time for others in her life up until now.

When she arrived home, she sat on the concrete step next to the front door. She removed her headphones from her ears and took a few moments to think and take it all in. She noticed how today was probably the first real day the weather had an autumnal feel. The leaves on the large trees lining the pavement of the street were starting to show a hint of yellow. She sat there for a couple of hours while she told herself that even if things went back to how they were before Amy went missing, she wouldn't take her new friends for granted.

Earlier than usual, her father pulled up in front of the house returning home from work. He came straight over to her, and as he put his arm around her, she couldn't help but confront him about Hannah. Bella had envisioned the lies he would tell and how he would protest his innocence during her meditation with Ms. Henry, but it didn't make it any easier to watch him avoid admitting the truth. Putting her headphones back in and getting back on her bike to ride off, she noticed a message flash up on her phone from Scott again.

'Meet you at the orchard!' That was the confirmation she needed to know that the plan Monica had quickly mentioned earlier on that day, was still going ahead. Her solo investigation had started off the back of the tiniest hunch but had now grown arms and legs of its own.

Bella took a shortcut down one of the narrow pathways, taking her off the street and through some of the trees to arrive at the orchard. Upset about her father, she pedalled faster, riding over bumps and rocks along the uneven path. Flying around one of the sharper corners, she was surprised by someone walking out in front of her bike, far enough away that by squeezing the brakes as hard as she could and swerving heavily, she was able to avoid colliding with the individual. But it resulted in her coming off her bike on the muddy ground and sliding over sharp stones. Bella took a second to check her arms which were all bloodied from the crash, before looking around to find Hannah was standing in the middle of the pathway laughing.

"I'm *your* sister?" Hannah continued to laugh, making it clear to Bella she had been spying on her exchange with her father.

"You'll never be my sister Hannah!" Bella shouted back, getting up from the floor and attempting to dust herself off.

"I don't know, let's go and ask Amy!" Hannah said, moving towards Bella. As she got closer, her body began to change and get larger, and her skin became green and scaly as her face turned to look as monstrous as Monica had previously described. Bella had been fearless up until now, but the grotesque appearance of Hannah's pure form, made her scream as she left her bike behind to run away. But Bella didn't get very far down the quiet path before Hannah had her large arms around her.

"Amy come and get her!" Hannah shouted out. She was using Bella to try and tempt Amy out. Hannah wanted rid of any chance that Amy would return to Hanfield again.

"Don't hurt Bella!" Amy shouted, coming out from amongst the trees. Bella noticed she appeared to be on her own, with no Frank in sight, just as Scott appeared on his bike with Monica on the back.

"I'll try and move us backwards in time!" Monica shouted, her face crumpled up as she closed her eyes tight still on the back of Scott's bike.

"Drop Bella! Isn't it me you want?" Amy shouted out. As she did so, the trees began to move with the wind, and the wind grew louder until the forest floor began to move, paving the way for Amy to appear from beyond the trees.

"You need to disappear, or I'll kill her!" Hannah growled, her large scaly hands clutched around Bella's neck, who was now struggling to breathe, her legs squirming in the air.

Amy looked over at Scott with an expression of defeat in her eyes, and he looked back at her with sympathy, before his eyes widened, and he pointed towards her.

"Behind you, Amy, behind you!" Scott shouted as two giant rounded monsters, their jaws hanging beneath their gaping mouths, appeared from behind the trees and began manhandling Amy. A large bright light began opening up beside them between two solid oak trees. It got bigger and brighter, stealing Hannah's attention away from throttling Bella.

"Push her!" Monica screamed; her eyes were now wide open as she shouted towards the back of Scott's head. He ran, swinging his elbows out as he did so, scowling, he bypassed Bella and pushed Hannah's body as hard as he could towards the bright white light. Hannah still had hold of Bella's neck as she fell into the emanation, and as Amy screamed and fought off the Fangrogs, they both disappeared.

"I only saw Hannah get pushed into the light!" Monica cried while Amy stood, helpless.

"I thought she would have let go!" Scott declared.

The three of them stood around, looking at each other for ideas. Hannah had vanished, but so had Bella.

"Wait!" Monica said, still looking concerned, it seemed as if she knew something Scott and Amy didn't.

Only a few moments went by, but it felt like forever to the three of them. However, the same light began to glow again, it slowly increased in brilliance as it had done before. Scott stood back while Amy braced herself for Hannah's return.

"Bella!" Monica shouted, and as she did Bella flew through the air as if being flung from her bike all over again and landed next to Monica who helped her up. The light disappeared as quickly as it had appeared.

"It's just another part of the forest, it's like a clearing in the forest!" Bella said she had seen where the Fangrogs lived, before they threw her back into the portal.

"What about Izzy! Did you see her?!" Scott asked Bella anxiously.

"No... I didn't see her Scott, I'm sorry." Bella avoided his eyes.

"Scott... the change has effectively been carried out, they have Hannah, and we have Bella," Monica said regrettably.

"But what about Izzy?!" Scott shouted.

"This makes me think that maybe the stuff I see in my dreams doesn't always come true." Monica went on to say, sounding upset.

"We'll all find another way to get Izzy, I promise Scott." Amy came forward to join them.

XXIII
Some Time Later

It was the end of Amy Ferhulse's first week back at school since miraculously returning home after spending months living in the forest. Firstly, with the curious yet forceful Fangrogs, the ones that truly made her feel stolen away from home, before she found herself aided by Frank and the Crimpets. The Crimpets had taught her things about life she would never forget, and this was only the tip of the iceberg of her revelations.

Of course, Amy, Bella and her friends all agreed they wouldn't tell another soul what they had uncovered that summer, and following her return, it wasn't long before she adjusted back into her life, but still knowing that things would never really be normal or the same again.

Amy got off her bus from school that Friday and walked past the entrance to the pathway that was used so often by her peers to cut through the forest and into other parts of Hanfield. The path was now barricaded with police tape, and the street was littered with bright red official notices forbidding residents from entering the forest. Something that had come into force since Izzy and Hannah had gone missing. Regrettably for Amy, all over the bus shelter and streetlamps, were the new posters informing of the disappearance of one of her oldest friends.

Along with Monica, Amy still had much to learn. She had adjusted her outlook to start utilising her Kryton powers to help people, rather than involve herself in the ongoing popularity contest at school. Inspired by Izzy, she decided to begin volunteering at Cliff Edge. She had paid her first visit last Saturday and had been excited to meet Mrs. Samuels after listening to stories of discovery from Bella and Scott. So, intrigued to meet her, she asked the care home nurse where Mrs. Samuels was when she noticed she wasn't sitting by the window as Bella and Scott described.

"Mrs. Samuels passed on a couple of weeks ago, darling!" the nurse said to Amy, giving her a sympathetic smile, "she was very old and..."

"No that's fine... that's part of life." Amy reassured the nurse. Later she would wonder if handing Bella the Tentescope chain was what Mrs. Samuels had been waiting for, and maybe it was more significant than they had all first thought.

Each day after school, Amy had come straight home to her parents both waiting by the door for her. She had managed to convince them both she didn't need picking up from school, but she knew the least she could do for now was reassure them by coming straight home. They had been through a lot, and although she could tell they were not as close as before she disappeared, Amy had managed to convince Bella to hold off on shouting at their father for now.

"How was school?" Her mother had asked her each day: "not too much too soon is it? You can stay at home a bit longer; it must all be so overwhelming!" she would say while holding Amy tightly.

"No Mum! I love being back at school; today was great!" Amy reassured her parents as much as possible. She was happy to be back and couldn't wait to settle in further.

Bella could get away with staying on after school for a few extra hours to join in with the book club she'd recently joined. Amy loved how she now socialised with friends, rather than shut herself away in her room as she used to.

The police had brought in a curfew for Hanfield since Izzy and Hannah's disappearance, so Bella was always home in the evenings, and Amy would sit and watch TV with her mother on the sofa, something simple she had taken for granted before. Sometimes, her father would join them, but Amy could tell things were not going well for him despite the act he was showcasing. It made her think, if Richard always being home early from work had something to do with the way they had returned Hannah to the Fangrogs, maybe, just maybe the deal struck long ago, had been broken, and the success he had previously negotiated was no longer guaranteed.

Sometimes, when Bella had returned home, the two of them would wait for night to fall upon Hanfield and sneak out past curfew. Their mother would usually be asleep in bed while their father was always preoccupied in his office. They would sneak past and out the front door, listening to him shouting at someone over the phone.

Bella and Amy would head straight for the forest, avoiding any police patrol cars and jumping over a weak point in the fencing that had been put up. Heading towards the apple orchards, they would meet Scott, Monica and Frank. All would wrap up warm now as the nights were much colder. They would talk and plan how they would work together to get Izzy back, or sometimes they would look back and reminisce at fun memories they'd had with her. The more they all met up, the more often the conversation would flow into discussing their days at school and other things life threw at them. It was their escape into a different world that had brought them together outside Hanfield, all under the unspoken agreement that it would lead them to further adventures throughout the rest of their lives.

Jessica Strong

The Familiar Encounter

Printed in Great Britain
by Amazon

47531898R00124